CHILLING TALES

TALES

EVIL DID I DWELL; LEWD I DID LIVE

edited by Michael Kelly

EDGE SCIENCE FICTION AND FANTASY PUBLISHING
AN IMPRINT OF HADES PUBLICATIONS, INC.

CALGARY

Edge Science Fiction and Fantasy Publishing
An Imprint of Hades Publications Inc.
P.O. Box 1714, Calgary, Alberta, T2P 2L7, Canada

Edited by Michael Kelly
Interior design by Janice Blaine
Cover Illustration by Les Edwards
ISBN: 978-1-894036-52-4

EDGE Science Fiction and Fantasy Publishing and Hades Publications, Inc. acknowledges the ongoing support of the Alberta Foundation for the Arts and the Canada Council for the Arts for our publishing programme.

Library and Archives Canada Cataloguing in Publication

Chilling tales : evil did I dwell— lewd I did live / edited by Michael Kelly.
Also available in electronic format.
ISBN 978-1-894063-52-4

1. Horror tales, Canadian (English). 2. Fantasy fiction, Canadian (English). 3. Canadian fiction (English)—21st century. I. Kelly, Michael, 1963-
PS8323.H67C55 2011   C813'.087380806   C2010-907826-8

FIRST EDITION
(g-20110113)
Printed in Canada
www.edgewebsite.com

TABLE OF CONTENTS

A DISQUIETING SOLITUDE

Michael Kelly

There's been a renaissance in Canadian horror fiction.

The last few years have seen a steady increase in the amount of literature published in the horror genre. And the title of this volume, along with Les Edwards' gruesomely macabre artwork, brooks no argument—this *is* a horror anthology. One might argue that the proliferation of fiction dedicated to horror and dark fantasy is simply a by-product of the sagging world economies, of xenophobic governments, of worry generated from the on-going "War on Terror." Or it may be that Canadian writers are merely doing what comes naturally—in this vast, sprawling land of ice and prairies, of wind and rock and water, of major urban centres encroaching on the barrens with spreading tendrils—exploring the *other*, that *vastness*.

Is Canadian horror different from other horror fiction?

This land is certainly fertile ground for imaginative minds. What I've discovered is that Canadian writers explore the same themes as their contemporaries. Inside you'll find tales of horror in urban and rural settings alike. There are stories of corporate horror; side trips into surrealism and modern supernatural horror. Tales of loss. And the all-too-real horrors of everyday life, of existing in harsh climates, whether literal or psychological. Not unlike any good horror fiction, then. Except I sense a distinctly Canadian worldview, a disquieting solitude, perhaps, or a tangible loneliness, that permeates all these stories and makes them truly chilling tales.

This book is a rarity, though, in the horror genre, in that all the contributors are Canadian, whether citizens, permanent residents, or expatriates.

I may be wrong, but I know of only 2 other *horror* anthologies in which all the contributors were Canadian: Tesseracts Thirteen, edited by David Morrell & Nancy Kilpatrick, and EVOLVE, edited by Nancy Kilpatrick. Both those titles were published by EDGE Science Fiction and Fantasy Publishing, not coincidentally the very same publisher of this current volume. For that, they should be applauded.

For a fascinating overview of Canadian horror literature I urge you to seek out Robert Knowlton's essay "Out of the Barrens, " published in Tesseracts Thirteen (EDGE Science Fiction and Fantasy Publishing, 2009).

Indeed, there have been notable Canadian horror anthologies in the recent past: Northern Horror (Quarry Press, 1999), edited by Edo van Belkom, and the late, lamented Northern Frights series (Mosaic Press), which ran for five frightful volumes between 1992 and 1999, edited by the redoubtable Don Hutchison. Those anthologies, as good as they are, were not exclusively limited to only Canadian contributions. While the bulk of the tales included were penned by Canadians, writers of other nationalities did contribute. *Chilling Tales* is, then, a rarity. One of only a few horror anthologies devoted to truly *Canadian* horror writing.

But we don't want this to be a rarity, a curiosity. We want this to be the norm. Our hope is to make this an annual volume, highlighting the wonderfully diverse and talented Canadian writers penning horror fiction. We hope that you will enjoy this collection enough to make that a reality.

Bring on the brand new renaissance!

Michael Kelly
January, 2011

Tom Chesnutt's Midnight Blues

Robert J. Wiersema

What's the worst thing you can imagine? The worst punishment someone could wish on you? To forever be cut off from those pretty young girls, the ones who look at you like you're a god? To wander the world looking for peace, but never knowing a moment's rest? To have your finest song never be heard?

"Can I get the houselights up?" Tom Chesnutt muttered into the microphone as he fumbled with his guitar strap. He cleared his throat and tried again. "Hank, can you bring up the lights?"

Cheers washed over him as Hank brought up the bar's main lights. The crowd was on their feet—they had been for most of the night.

It took a moment for his eyes to adjust, for the figures on the other side of the spotlights to start to come into focus.

"This is an old song," he said into the mic, almost as an aside, as he tightened the E string. He made it sound off the cuff, but it was the way he introduced the song every time he played it. A couple of people cheered; they'd seen the show before, or recognized the words from the record.

"It's nice to finish a night like this with an old song," he continued, looking down the guitar's neck. "A song everybody can sing along." He ran his pick lightly over the strings, listening to the tuning in the monitor. It was fine, but he fumbled with the keys a little longer. For effect. Playing it out.

More of the crowd cheered—people were starting to figure out what was coming. The sound of the crowd had changed; it was darker now, lower than it had been when he first took the stage. Two hours of cheering and drinking and smoking had taken their toll.

"It's been a good night for me, Victoria." The crowd exploded with the mention of their city's name, same way they always did. "Hope y'all have had a good time too."

He shook the neck of his guitar decisively and straightened up in front of the mic.

"This song's called *Jolene*."

The crowd roared, and Frank started beating out the rhythm heavy, almost a Bo Diddley beat.

Tom let the guitar hang loose around his neck, curled his right hand around the microphone and leaned in, closing his eyes as he sang against the backbeat.

FROM WWW.THEWEBMUSICGUIDE.COM:

TOM CHESNUTT—SINGER, SONGWRITER, GUITARIST

Born in Santa Fe, N.M., but based for most of his career in Spokane, Wa., Chesnutt met with early success as a songwriter, penning tracks which included *Love and Smoke*, *Brokedown in Your Eyes*, *Right Child* and *Tell-All Eyes*, which charted briefly for Stanza in 1987. His early albums, though critically well received, sold poorly. After a brief hospitalization following the death of his fiancée Emily Grace in 1999, Chesnutt burst to national prominence with the album *Emily's Song*. Recorded in three days, the album is widely regarded as a dark masterpiece in the tradition of Bob Dylan's *Blood on the Tracks* and Neil Young's *Tonight's the Night*.

He'd got to the bar a couple of hours early, same as he always did. The place was a crappy little club right on the water that had once hosted bands, before they discovered that there was more money in techno and drunk university students. Now, the only time they cleared the DJ and his equipment off the stage was for a Very Special Event—namely someone the owner or promoter really wanted to see for themselves.

Tom didn't mind that: Very Special Event. Had a nice ring to it.

He had wandered around while the guys loaded in and set up, watching the pretty girls and the pretty buildings, the boats and the water. He had to stop to rest a couple of times; two nights without sleep and he was running on fumes. He got back to the club for a quick sound-check, then he sent the boys off to find some food while he bellied up to the bar.

The bartender, a kid with a shaved head and a pierced lip, was still setting up, but he was kind enough, thank you very much, to provide a bottle of Maker's Mark and a glass. Tom's needs were simple.

"Water water everywhere," he muttered as the bartender turned away. "Only whiskey's fit to drink."

He drank slowly but steadily, savoring the flavour and the burn of the whiskey, relying on it to cut through the last of the pills, bring him down a couple of notches to let him play.

When he poured the first glass, his hand was shaking so bad he thought he might actually spill. A couple of drinks later and his hand was perfectly still, the jangle gone from just behind his eyes.

"Better living through chemistry," he muttered.

The bartender glanced down at him and Tom shook his head. "Just talking to myself."

Emily smiled at him from the empty bar stool to his right. *"Is that what this is, you and I? You still think I'm some sort of projection?"*

"Or psychosis," he muttered. The words could have stung, but he offered them up with an easy familiarity. He and Emily had been having this conversation for a good five years now. Since the night after she had died.

"I can't say it's good to see you," he lied, glancing toward the bartender, who was shelving glasses and sniffing like he was fresh from Colombia. It was good to see her, everything considered. She was just as beautiful as she had ever been, just as funny. It made him miss her even more, her showing up every third day.

"You're such a sweet talker," she said, breaking into a grin. *"You knew I'd be here: that's why you started in with the whiskey rather than popping another handful of pills. Think you're getting some sleep tonight?"*

"God willin' and the creek don't rise," he said, taking another swallow. "She'll be here."

She made a production of looking around the empty bar. *"I dunno, Tom. The prospects for a Jolene here...they're not filling me with a whole lot of optimism."*

"She'll be here," he stressed. "There's always a Jolene."

"What?" The bartender asked from a few feet away.

"Nothin'." Tom waved it away. "Just goin' over the setlist in my mind."

"You gonna do *Jolene* tonight?" the kid asked, upping him considerably in Tom's esteem.

"God willing and the creek don't rise," he repeated, slinging his feet over the empty chair beside him, leaning back to take a hearty swallow of bourbon straight from the bottle.

Jolene.

She had come by the merchandise table after the show at the Creekside Tavern. She waited for most of the line to clear out before she approached him. Always a good sign.

"Mister Chesnutt." She was bubbling over, her hair damp from dancing and sticking to her pale, pretty face. Her body was swaying to some internal music as she spoke. "I just wanted to tell you how much I loved the show tonight." She pushed a CD across the table toward him, and he uncapped his marker.

"Well thank you for sayin' that," he responded, laying on the country charm extra thick. "And you can call me Tom." She smiled and he fumbled with the CD booklet. Usually he just scrawled his name on the hard plastic shell, but when he wanted to spend a little extra time, he went for the booklet.

He glanced up, did a quick surveil: Emily was at the bar across the room, keeping company with a couple of good ol' boys.

He paused with his pen over his picture on the CD sleeve. "And what shall I call you, darlin'?"

There was a beat, a moment's silence. "Call me Jolene," she said.

He raised his eyebrows. "Honey, that song was a hit before your mama was born," he said as he autographed her CD and slid it back across the table toward her.

"Almost," she said, with a twinkle and a smile he could feel in his stomach.

"Now, Jolene..." He glanced up at Emily, safe out of earshot, as he spoke. "What say you stick around for a bit? Maybe we can have a drink once this place clears out some."

She didn't answer, but the smile she gave as she turned away said more than enough.

FROM "THE WEARY WARRIOR OF THE ROAD", MONDAY MAGAZINE:
Chesnutt won't discuss the mental breakdown which resulted in his forced hospitalization following Grace's death. "I think I've said enough about that for a lifetime," he says with a chuckle.

The accident and the hospital stay resulted in *Emily's Song*, the legendary album that has kept Chesnutt on the road since its release more than four years ago. "I don't even know if I have a house anymore," he laughs. "The mortgage payments keep coming out of the bank, but the place could have blown away for all I know." The singer hasn't been to his Spokane-area home more than a few nights since Grace's death. "It's too hard," he says. "There's really nothing for me there. Not anymore."

No one really notices when he takes the stage. The room isn't full: lots of people outside smoking, hanging out, enjoying the cool summer evening breeze off the water. He's got no use for introductions, so when he picks up his Martin, people think he's a roadie or a guitar tech.

Without any sort of fanfare, with the houselights still up, he starts to tap the body of the guitar just above the strings. Tap tap. Tap tap. Two fingers, nice and soft.

People start to turn toward the stage as the sound carries out to them. The band is standing at the side of the stage, waiting.

He loves this part, the way the evening starts to take shape. It's one of the few things he still loves, these days.

Tap tap. Tap tap.

Over the speakers, over the monitors, the tapping sounds like a heartbeat.

Tap tap.

Somebody whoops. Nice to know somebody's buying the records.

Tap tap.

Eyes closed, he leans into the microphone, whispers the word "Jolene" and the place crackles with sudden electricity. People come to their feet, crowding to the stage. As he sings the first words of the song, just the name, over and over, in a whisper, the band files in behind him.

Tap tap.

And just as the first chorus comes around, he turns to Frank and nods. The drummer kicks into *Right Child* and the band is right with him, right on the money. Smooth as an old dollar. Smooth as a well-told lie.

FROM WWW.THEWEBMUSICGUIDE.COM:
TOM CHESNUTT—LIVE AT SLIM'S
This album does little more than capture another night on the road for wandering troubadour Chesnutt and his crack band. It is anything but perfunctory, however. From a haunting, a capella opener of Dolly Parton's *Jolene*, a harrowing set drawn largely

from *Emily's Song*, through an intense, full-band encore of *Jolene* again, this is a transfixing set. Chesnutt sounds like a man possessed. Despite his well-deserved reputation as a songwriter, Chesnutt gets good mileage from several well-chosen covers, including a countrified stomp through the Rolling Stones' *19th Nervous Breakdown* (which Chesnutt introduces with a meandering story about time spent in a mental institution, finishing "And when you're faced with a 250 pound orderly with a sixteen inch needle in his hand, the last thing you wanna say is "Yeah? And what are you gonna do about it?") Conspicuous by its absence is the title track from *Emily's Song*: Chesnutt, despite his near-constant touring, has never performed the song live.

He caught a couple of glimpses of her during the set.

His eye was drawn to her. He followed her as best he could through the night.

"You always liked that type," Emily whispered in his ear.

It wasn't until the encores, until the second run through *Jolene*, that he was sure.

It was almost a Bo Diddley beat, and he could feel it in his sternum as he took the microphone and started to sing. He poured all of himself into the words, and fed off the sound of the crowd singing along.

When he hit the first note on the guitar, the place exploded, and he rode the crowd like a wave. There was no longer any resemblance to the pretty song that Miss Parton sang. This was more like Crazy Horse, a shuffling stomp that they'd still be feeling in their ears come morning.

The crowd bounced in place, punched the air, their faces contorted as they struggled to hear their own singing over the band.

She worked her way to the front, dancing by herself, holding her hands over her head. She moved with an easy, slow grace, a movement of her body that let anyone watching know that she knew how to move it.

Tom was watching.

"She's just your type, isn't she?"

With a single motion of his hand he brought the band down for the bridge, Frank tapping lightly on the snare, Billy walking the bass.

He stepped toward the microphone and whispered her name into it.

The crowd roared back

The redhead in front looked at him.

"Jolene." A little louder.

He let his eyes close, focussing all his energy on the name, on the sound of it on his lips. He repeated it over and over like a prayer, building gradually from a whisper to a full-throated roar, the energy of the crowd buoying him up, all that energy, all that passion, focussed on a single name.

"Jolene!"

The band kicked back in as he opened his eyes. All he could see was her, the pretty redhead in the front row, the one who had been dancing by herself but now just stood, staring at him.

He met her eyes, and she smiled.

"There's always a Jolene," Emily Grace whispered.

FROM THE DAILY RECORD (TV TRANSCRIPT):

Interviewer: It's been five years since the tragic death of your fiancée Emily Grace. Has it been difficult to move on?

Chesnutt: I do nothin' but move on. Every night a different town.

Interviewer: But are you able to put that tragedy behind you?

Chesnutt: That's not how it works. I carry her with me. Everywhere I go, Emily Grace is right there with me.

After the show, the sound of the crowd still echoing, Tom stepped out the back door of the bar, wedging the fire exit open behind him.

His hands were shaking as he lit a cigarette with the Zippo Emily had given him, but it was pure adrenalin. Not the drugs, just the rush of the show.

"Those things are gonna kill you," Emily said.

She was standing in the alley, looking up at him on the stoop.

He shrugged and took a heavy drag. "Lots of things that might kill me first."

"Most of them self-inflicted."

"Funny thing about that. Not a whole lot of things are self-inflicted if you look back far enough."

"Very profound, Tom. Are you trying to impress me, or just warming up for that pretty girl waiting for you inside?"

"Just feelin' good. It was a good show tonight."

She took the steps up to the stoop, laid her hand gently on his cheek. He wished he could feel it. Wished he could touch her again, even just once.

One more for the road.

"Don't sell yourself short, Tom. You always put on a good show."

He took another drag off his cigarette, listening to the crackling of the paper as it burned. "I can't tell if that was a compliment or just you bein' mean."

"Oh, Tom. I think we both know the answer to that question."

He chuckled.

"You tired, Tom?"

He hadn't noticed it. In the rush after the show, he felt light, almost weightless, vibrating like a plucked string. As soon as she asked, though, the weight of his exhaustion crashed in on him. His knees almost buckled under the weight.

He nodded. "It's been a couple of nights."

"I know it has, lover. How're you holding out?"

He took a last drag, ground out the butt under his boot-heel. "I'm all right." Thinking about the pretty redhead, about what would happen later, the mix of guilt and anticipation turning in his stomach.

"That's funny. 'Cause from here, you look like ten pounds of shit in a five pound sack."

They both laughed at that.

"Tonight might be your night, though. That girl had nothin' but you in her eyes."

He nodded, his head heavy, spilling over with regret for things he hadn't done. Yet.

"You'd better get back in, Tom. Don't want to keep your public waiting."

FROM WWWWEBMUSICGUIDE.COM (EXCERPT):

TOM CHESNUTT—EMILY'S SONG (SPOKE CANE RECORDS)

Fittingly, the emotional centerpiece of the album is the title track. As achingly personal and immediate as Neil Young's *Borrowed Tune* or Tori Amos' *Me and A Gun*, *Emily's Song* is six minutes of unalloyed pain and loss, set to a forlorn acoustic guitar. This is the sound of a heart breaking, the midnight blues of Tom Chesnutt's dark night of the soul.

"Thanks for comin' out," he said as he passed the signed CD back to the middle-aged man across the table.

"Do you say the same thing to everyone?" the pretty redhead asked, picking a CD off the table and pretending to look at the track list.

She had waited over by the bar, keeping her eye on the line, gliding over when there were just a couple of people left.

"That wouldn't be very much fun, would it?"

"I suppose not."

"*Jolene*," Emily whispered.

She was pretty, but not the kind of pretty that would necessarily catch most men's eyes. Her curly red hair was short above her shoulders, framing a roundish face. She wasn't tall, but she was curvy in all the right places, wearing a green sundress. Tom could see the straps of a red bra at her shoulders.

She nodded slowly as she pretended to read, the sparkle in her eye a dead giveaway that she knew he was looking.

"I'll take this one."

"Good choice."

"I bet you say that to all the girls."

"You'd win that bet." He fumbled with the booklet. "And who's this for?"

"Me," she said.

He leaned back in his chair and raised his eyebrows.

"Collette," she added, blushing a little. "I'm Collette."

Jolene.

That blush was the prettiest thing Tom had seen in days.

When he looked up again, she was fumbling with her wallet. He shook his head, waved away the twenty she held out to him. "Nah. Let's not worry about that." He handed the CD to her, making sure their fingers touched. "This is my gift to you. Because you waited so long in line, and I hate to keep a pretty lady waiting."

There was that blush again. He could feel it down to his toes.

"Well thank you, Mr. Chesnutt," she said, genuinely surprised.

"Just don't call me Mr. Chesnutt," he said. "That's all I ask."

"All right, Tom." She stressed his name, drawing it out a little, finishing with a little giggle that made him feel like he might just spontaneously combust.

"That's better."

"Listen, Tom—" She leaned into the table. "—Can I make you a drink?"

He looked away from the low neckline of her dress, down to his nearly empty glass of bourbon. "Well, they're taking pretty good care of me..."

"No." She shook her head. "I was thinking I could make you a drink at my place."

Tom waited a beat before he even acknowledged having heard her. In that moment, he could see what asking had cost her. She wasn't the sort that came to every show to hit town, notches in her bedpost or whatever. When she made the offer, she had put herself out there. And here he was, letting her dangle.

"That'd be very kind," he said slowly, looking up at her. "Fella works up a hell of a thirst doing what I do."

As she smiled, she seemed to sag a little. Relief, he thought. She'd been holding herself tight, waiting for him to answer. "I've got a car, if..."

He nodded. "Sure. Listen—" He leaned across the table, and she leaned in to meet him and he could smell the shampoo, and sweet sweat boozy smell of her and it made his head swim.

He waited another beat, until she said, "Yeah?" This time, her voice was playful, flirtatious, and her lips seemed to linger on the single word.

"Do you mind if I bring my guitar?"

From KWAS Television, The News at Five:

Voice-over: Investigators now believe the car was driven by Spokane resident Emily Grace, who apparently was en route to Moses Lake early this morning when her vehicle left the road and plunged down the embankment. Investigators aren't confirming, but alcohol is believed to have been a factor...

"I thought I'd take a longer route home," Collette said, a little nervously. "Show you a bit of the city."

"That sounds fine." His guitar case was in the back, Emily sitting beside it. Tom was slumped in the passenger seat, watching the lights passing by in blurry streaks of gold, watching her drive. If he kept his head angled just right, he didn't have to see Emily at all.

"Is there anything you want to listen to?" she asked, flipping down the visor to reveal a CD holder.

"Nope. Anything's good. So long as it's not me." He chuckled.

"You like Nina Simone?"

"Sure."

There were a few moments of small club applause before the music started.

She mouthed some of the words as Nina sang; it made Tom smile.

"Just your type, isn't she?"

"So are you from here?" he asked.

"Nah. Nobody's *from* Victoria. Everybody just ends up here."

"So where did you start out?"

"A little town you've probably never heard of. Henderson? On the mainland. You don't have to pretend like you know where it is; most people have never heard of it."

"Small town girl."

"Farm girl," she corrected him. "My family grew corn, raised beef cattle."

"Sounds like where I grew up."

She nodded. "A lot smaller, though."

He got lost in the way the streetlights fell across her pale skin, the regular flashes of beauty, of softness. He realized that he was drunk, in that comfortable place where you're warm, where the world is filled with beauty, where every word has meaning.

"You're feeling pretty good right now, aren't you?" Emily asked.

"I was actually in Spokane for a little while."

He pulled himself together enough to respond. "What brought a girl like you to a place like Spokane?"

"I came for the waters," she said, glancing at him to see if he caught the reference.

"You were misinformed," he said, playing along.

"That I was," she said, shaking her head.

"So it was a man?"

"Isn't it always?"

He shook his head ruefully. "The things we do..."

"I was supposed to marry him."

"Really?"

She nodded. "I was young. Dumb. In love. I met this cowboy and he swept me off my feet."

"They do that."

"Yeah. Anyways, this was almost six years ago now, I guess. I fell madly in love. Would have followed my cowboy anywhere. Ended up following him to Spokane."

"That'll learn 'ya."

"Yeah."

She drove in silence for a few moments.

"So did you marry your cowboy?"

"No, I got wise. He introduced me to some of his friends. And their wives. And they were all sweet men, and their wives were lovely. Beautiful and kind. But they all had this look in their eyes, this caged, sort of desperate look. Trapped and they knew they could never admit it."

"Sounds familiar."

"That was enough for me. I broke that cowboy's heart, ended up here."

As she said the words, she turned the car into the driveway of a rambling three storey house, killed the engine.

"This place yours?"

"The second floor is. My landlady has the main floor, and a friend has the attic. You'd like the place. Full of artists." She started to open her door.

He shook his head. "I don't know. I don't hold much truck with artists." He waited a beat. "What do you do?"

She leaned back into the car. "I'm a waitress."

He smiled and opened his door. "I get along with waitresses just fine."

FROM KWAS TELEVISION THE NEWS AT FIVE:

Voiceover: Spokane Police are reporting that this afternoon's standoff at a downtown bar ended peacefully when country singer Tom Chesnutt surrendered himself to police a few minutes ago. Chesnutt reportedly entered the Creekside Tavern at shortly after one this afternoon with a loaded firearm. A police spokesman says they are not regarding this incident as a hostage-taking.

Interview: Mister Chesnutt made no threats to the staff or clientele of the business. According to eyewitnesses, he was visibly upset, and threatened to take his own life.

Voiceover: Speculation is that this afternoon's incident is related to the death of Mr. Chesnutt's fiancée Emily Grace in a car accident earlier this week. Mr. Chesnutt has been taken to a mental health facility for observation...

"Can I get you that drink?" Collette asked as she pushed the door closed behind them.

"No matter how many times you hear them, those words are like music."

She dropped her purse on the couch, looked back at him over her shoulder in a way that made his stomach drop. "Bourbon, right? Maker's Mark okay?"

"That'll do just fine." He leaned his guitar case against a battered armchair, covered with an old quilt.

"You want anything fancy?"

"An ice cube?"

"I think I can manage that."

As she went into the kitchen he looked around the room.

She had done her best to keep the place homey, with tapestries and batiks on the walls, a couple of small tables with vintage lamps, a battered couch to match the battered chair. The air smelled faintly of incense and pot smoke. He didn't see a TV anywhere, but her stereo...

He had to get up to get a closer look.

"This is a nice rig," he said when he heard her feet padding across the floor. She had taken off her shoes: the sound of bare feet on hardwood...

She pressed the drink into his hand. "Did I get it right?"

He took a swallow as if to test it out. "That tastes just fine." He clinked his glass against hers.

She turned to the stereo. "It was my father's," she explained.

"And he left it to you?"

She choked back a chuckle. "No, he upgraded. He likes his toys and he likes them new." She shrugged. "It works out well for me."

He picked up the record sleeve that had been leaning against the amplifier, looked at the picture of himself in full flight at Slim's. "So you're the one."

She looked at him quizzically.

"The one who keeps buying vinyl."

"Nothing else like it."

He sat in the chair, and she settled on the couch across the coffee table from him, next to Emily Grace, who just stared at him without blinking.

"You're in fine form tonight," Emily said.

Collette took another sip from her drink.

"So which guitar did you bring?"

He glanced at the case beside the chair. "My old J-45. Best guitar ever made. I bought it to celebrate my first record deal."

She nodded appreciatively. "Nice." Another sip. "Does it play?"

"Not by itself." He laid the case on his lap, lifted out the Gibson. "Time to sing for my supper, I guess." He played his fingers across the strings, tightened a couple of the keys so little he might not have done anything at all—he could hear the difference, though.

"Any requests?" he joked.

"Freebird?" she asked, not missing a beat.

He chuckled, plucked out the first couple of notes.

"Should I get my lighter?" she asked, with a playful grin. Her lips glistened, thick and wet in the dim light.

He smiled, nodded at the joke, then asked, "Now that you mention it, though: do you mind if I smoke?"

She shook her head. "I'll just..." She bustled around, cracking open a window, bringing him an ashtray. He watched every movement, every breath.

"You like this one, don't you?"

He sighed, dug his pack of Lucky Strikes out of his pocket.

"But you like all of them, don't you, Tom? That's the problem."

"That should do," she said, returning to the couch.

"Thanks. I 'preciate that." He lit the cigarette and took a deep, hot drag.

"I'm gonna play you a song—" She had a smile that could light up the darkest of hearts. "—that I don't...I've never played this for anyone. It's got a story that goes with it, though. I'll tell you the story first, then you can let me know if you still want to hear the song."

He rested the smoke in the ashtray, took a long swallow and set his drink down next to it.

Collette leaned forward on the couch; Emily leaned back. They both stared at him.

What's the worst thing you can imagine, Tom? The worst punishment someone could wish on you?

"I've been doing this a long time," he started, not looking at either of them, staring into the wood grain of the guitar's face as the well-practiced patter started to come out of him. "I've travelled a lot of miles, sung a lot of songs, met a lot of women." He smiled, let his eyes connect with Collette's, then looked away.

"But there's only one woman I've ever loved. Only one woman I'm ever likely to love."

"Emily Grace," Collette whispered, and hearing her name in the girl's voice gave him a chill right to the heart.

"I loved her. Not well. And I lost her."

"I was there," Collette said quietly.

"What?" He wasn't used to being interrupted, not at that part of the story. It threw him.

"I was there. In Spokane. When Emily died. When you..." Her voice trailed off. "That was when I was in Spokane, not getting married to my cowboy."

"Seems you've got yourself a ringer," Emily said, smiling.

"I watched it all on the news. I always wondered—"

"There's a lot you don't hear on the news. A lot of half-told stories. This is...This is the whole truth—"

"Oh, honey."

" —The only way I can tell it."

She nodded, her eyes wide.

"I loved her. And I lost her. And it was all my fault."

He took a long drink from the tumbler. His hand was shaking again.

"I met Emily Grace when I was 27 or 28. I say we met then, but she'd always been around. One of those people you see around, but you never really notice."

"Thanks."

"But we met. She was 20, I guess. We fell in love, got a place together, this shitty little walk-up. I made my music. She waited tables."

Collette bowed her head.

"We were happy. We had no money, not a pot to piss in, but we had each other. We were happy."

"We were."

"But I was a road dog. I was on tour a lot in those days. Not as much as I am now," he barked out a laugh. "But a lot. Away from home. Away from her. In the path of vice and degradation. Opportunity, I liked to call it."

"Dogging, I used to call it."

"See, I love women. I love all women. Always have. I love the way they look, they way they smell, the way they feel." He looked at Collette, then shook his head, trying to clear off the reverie.

"I was in love with Emily, but..." He shrugged.

"You were incorrigible."

"Incorrigible. That's a good word."

"That's a good word for it. The road's a hard place if you're trying to stay true. And I didn't even try. I slept with a lot of women, but, I don't know how, in my heart I stayed true."

"Did she know?"

"Yes."

"Maybe. It was something we joked about: me and my groupies. But we didn't ever really talk about it."

"What happens on the road stays on the road."

"Something like that, yeah."

She nodded slowly, like she was trying to figure out her place in all of this.

"I carved up a lot of road in my younger days."

"A lot of notches in your guitar strap."

He grinned. "Yeah."

The bourbon went down just fine, thank you very much.

"When I was first together with Emily, I managed to stop, though."

"For a while."

"For a while. But a pretty girl is hard to resist."

She blushed again, and Tom had to look away.

"We were happy. When I wasn't on the road, we spent all our time together. We got engaged. Bought a house. Started talking about how it might work to have a family. We were together for more than ten years."

"And then she died."

He shook his head. "Don't get ahead of me now, darling."

"Sorry."

"Round about six years ago now—"

"You know exactly how long it's been."

"—I was doing some local shows. Road-testing some songs I was working on. I played one night at the Creekside Tavern. That's where I met her."

"Jolene."

"She called herself Jolene."

"That's not your real name, is it?" he had asked her, after, his arm around her shoulders, her head nestled on his chest.

"You'll never know," she whispered, still playing.

He smoothed the hair away from her face.

"Like the song."

"Yeah. She came up to me after the show. Waited until she was the last person at the merch table."

Collette looked down at the floor.

"I asked her if she wanted to stay around for a while. Maybe have a drink. She did."

"Of course she did," Emily said.

"Of course she did," Collette said quietly, staring a hole into the hardwood.

"I had her wait for me at the bar. The other end of the bar from where Emily was sitting."

"Emily was there?"

"I'm always there."

He nodded. "She'd been there all night. Listening to the new songs. Standin' by her man. When she asked if I was all done, if I was ready to go home. I told her—" He took a deep breath. "—I told her that I was headed out for Moses Lake with the band.

We had a show there the next night. I made it sound like this had always been the plan, that she and I had talked about it, that she'd forgotten..."

"*Bastard.*"

"And the whole time I was spinnin' her this line, I could see Jolene at the far end of the bar, looking at me over Emily's shoulder, this little smile on her face as I was lying to the woman I loved, trying to get rid of her."

He lit another cigarette, hands shaking something fierce now.

"Emily was confused, I guess. A little drunk. She had no idea what I was talking about, but she ordered us another couple of drinks—"

"*One for the road.*"

"—And we drank and she gave me a kiss goodbye and told me to behave myself. Told me she loved me. And the moment she was gone, Jolene up and took her place at the bar."

"I expected Emily to go home. It never occurred to me that she'd head out to Moses Lake as well. But she talked to Frank as she was leaving, found out what hotel they were staying at without letting on that she thought I was coming with them. And then she went home, packed a toothbrush and whatnot, and headed out to surprise me."

"Jesus," Collette whispered.

"Yeah. I figure it must have been about the same time I was, well, I figure it was about the same time I was back at Jolene's that she lost control of the car—"

"*One more for the road, baby.*"

"—And went over that embankment. Police said it looked like maybe she fell asleep. That she probably didn't feel anything."

He looked at Emily for some comment, some sign that the police were right, that she hadn't suffered, but she just stared him cold.

"I killed her," he said, plain and true. "I killed her as sure as if I put a bullet in her. I killed her because I couldn't resist a pretty girl." He shook his head, waiting for Collette to contradict him. Waited in vain. "If it wasn't for me, she wouldn't have been out there on the road that night. If it wasn't for me—"

"She'd still be alive."

"*Smart girl.*"

He took a deep drag off the cigarette then balanced it on the ashtray, folding his arms around his guitar and hugging it to himself.

"But that's only part of it."

Collette's eyes were wide, and Emily leaned forward on the couch, watching him watching her.

"I spent the night with that girl. Let her make me breakfast. And then I went home to pick up some clothes and such for the night in Moses Lake. She was supposed to be at work. The car wasn't in the driveway. But when I got inside, Emily Grace was waiting for me."

She was wearing the same thing she had been wearing in the bar, sitting on the couch in a slant of sunshine. She looked at him as he came through the door, but she didn't make any move to get up. Just looked at him.

"Did you have a good time, lover?" she asked, and his heart dropped between his boots. Busted. "Did you have a good time? I hope she was worth it."

He started to argue, tried to make excuses, come up with some story, but she just shook her head. Then she asked, "Tom, what's your worst nightmare? What's the worst thing you can imagine?"

The question came out of nowhere, and as he tried to answer, there was a knocking at the door.

"You're gonna wanna get that," she said.

"It was Highway Patrol, come to tell me that Emily Grace had died. I tried to tell them they were wrong, but when I looked back, she was gone."

Collette was no longer even trying to meet his eye.

"I thought I was going crazy. I *did* go crazy. You were there, you remember how hot it was that week: I couldn't sleep, I couldn't eat, I couldn't cry. The police, they showed me pictures of the wreck, pictures of her. I couldn't hold it together. That first day I must have drunk my way through two bottles of bourbon trying to ignore the phone, trying to put her out of my mind. It didn't work. I was wide awake, sober as a judge, when she walked into our room that night."

The red numbers on the clock radio read 3:11. He didn't hear anything, but he could feel her there, knew she was with him.

"Emily?" he said.

She sat down next to him, but there was no weight to shift the balance of the bed. She leaned over him, close to his ear. He was hoping for words of comfort, something to let him sleep.

Instead, she sang in a whisper, words from an old Leadbelly song. *"My boy, my boy, don't you lie to me, tell me where did you sleep last night?"*

She disappeared before he could answer.

"The next day was the same. More booze. People coming to the house, but I pretended I wasn't home. That night, though—" He nodded heavily. "That night I cried. I bawled like a baby, for everything I had done, for everything I had lost. I cried like a child, and when she came to me, she took one look, shook her head, and disappeared. The next day...Have you ever gone three days without sleep?"

Collette thought for a moment, then shook her head.

"It's rough at the best of times. Your mind starts to play tricks on you, talking nonsense, but making it sound like wisdom. So it made perfect sense to me to take my daddy's gun and head back to the Creekside. Scene of the crime. I thought... I figured I'd end it all. Put myself out of my misery. People thought I wanted to kill myself so I could be with her. Truth is, I wanted to kill myself so I wouldn't have to see her, ever again."

"Funny how things work out," Emily said.

"It's funny how things work out. She was there, sitting at the bar like she was the last time I saw her. And I pulled out that gun and I put the barrel in my mouth, I had my finger on the trigger, and she leaned in, she leaned in real close, and she said, 'You can't do it, can you? All your big hat, big balls posturing, and you can't even muster up the guts to take the cowardly way out.' And then she asked me again, 'What's your worst nightmare, Tom?' but this time, she had the answer."

He had lowered the gun as she stepped toward him, letting it dangle at his hip.

"I'm gonna tell you what your life is gonna look like, Tom," she said, in the same reedy voice she had once used to say she loved him. "You're not gonna sleep. You'll barely eat. You'll be so close to snapping all the time, you'll feel like a rubber band." The words didn't sound like a threat or a curse, just a description of the way things were gonna be. "And the only thing that'll help you, the only way you'll have to find some peace, to find some rest, is gonna be to tell your story. To find someone, and tell them what you've done."

"Rime of the Ancient Mariner," Collette whispered.

"She's brighter than most."

Tom nodded. "Yeah."

"So that's...Why me? Why'd you pick me?" He could see the distaste forming on her face, the blossoming sense of betrayal. That's what it looks like when you realize you've been used.

Tom had to look away. "Because you wanted to listen. Because it's been three nights since I last told anyone. Three days since I slept. Because I get so tired..."

"Tell her. You have to tell her."

"Because you're Jolene," he said, and the words felt like they might break him, same as they always did.

The look of horror on her face was the same, too. How many times had he seen that? Too many.

"There's one in every crowd: the girl who waits till the end of the line. The girl with the secret smile. The girl who I can feel right down to my toes."

He shook his head.

"The sort of girl I'd do it all for again, if the circumstances were the same."

Collette gasped, and Emily smiled, and Tom just went on talking. "The girl who helped me kill her, and didn't even know. That's what she wants—she wants you to know. Emily wants you to know what you've done. She wants you to know what it's in you to do."

She looked at him for a long moment, tears streaming down her cheeks, betrayal working hard in her eyes, and then she crumpled, her back jumping as she cried. Emily looked at her for a moment, looked at Tom, then vanished, as if she'd never been there at all.

He thought, for a passing moment, that he might go over to Collette, rub her back, try to comfort her. He liked this girl; he didn't like to see her in pain. In pain that he had caused.

But that was the point, wasn't it?

Instead, he put his guitar back in its case, unplayed and forlorn, his song unheard for another night. His cigarette had burned itself out, leaving a white column of ash.

He didn't say anything as he left—there was nothing he could say—but he looked back at her, thinking wishes and might-have-beens.

He closed the door behind himself. Heard it lock.

The sound of his boot-heels on the sidewalk echoed in the empty night. Behind him, the road stretched on forever, disappearing into the sea and the dark sky beyond. Ahead, just ahead, a hotel. A bed. A night of broken sleep, from which he would wake sadder but no wiser.

And tomorrow...

The weight of his guitar case was almost too much to bear. He wondered, as he walked in line with the journeying moon, when, if ever, he might have the guts to put it down, once and for all.

KING HIM

Richard Gavin

Joelle Russell felt a deepening pressure on her arm, which had been dangling over the mattress edge like a stray vine cadging to be cut. The squeezing sensation had been strong enough to wake her, and it quickly became vice-like, painful. Joelle flinched, opened her eyes to the dimness.

The casement window sat open, resembling a book with glass covers. March night winds took advantage of the aperture, gusting in to refrigerate the bedroom. Barbs of panic passed through Joelle as she gazed at this evidence of a home invasion.

Something shook her. She jerked her head down and saw that the figure clutching her arm was, "Theo?"

He was crouched down at the bedside. The hand on her arm appeared grubby, stained. Joelle could hear him snivelling. "I need to tell you something," he said. "I can't believe this is really happening..."

His voice was a strangled whimper. His body trembled as though there were live wires beneath the skin. Lengths of glistening secretions hung from his nostrils, his mouth.

"What happened?" Joelle pleaded. "Tell me!"

Theo pressed a finger to his lips, hushing her. He quickly looked to the parted window, peering into the black yard beyond it.

"Theo," she said, quietly this time, "you're scaring me."

He turned back to face her briefly before flinging his arms around her blanketed legs. He pressed his head against her and began to sob. It was the first time she had ever seen him cry.

"Christ, Joelle...I killed your baby."

Her stomach flipped, her throat and tongue became desiccated. The shadows that surrounded her all seemed to be swaying.

"Oh, God! I wanna die!" he howled.

"You...you had a bad dream, Theo, that's all. Maybe you walked in your sleep. But you *know* I don't have a baby, right? That proves it was a dream. Now...now stop this. Please."

Theo's eyes appeared lidless as he stared at the hook rug at the foot of the bed, studying it as though he were a yogi and it an ornate mandala.

"You were pregnant." His voice was as flat-line as his stare, as cold as the perennial gusts from the still-open window. "You've been pregnant for weeks. I couldn't tell you. I didn't know how. I thought I was okay with it. I really thought I could let Him go through with it. But when He told me what the baby would be like, I couldn't allow it to be born. I tore it out of you!"

She watched him flinch, double over, then vomit onto the floorboards.

"How could I do that, Jo? How? What kind of man can just rip out an unborn child like he's cleaning a turkey?"

"Stop!" Joelle's reach for the lamp chain was fumbling, but she eventually found and yanked it.

The burst of light made her squint, and when she ultimately looked down at the quilt she noticed stains, ugly dark blotches. Some of these spots evaporated once her eyes grew accustomed to the lamp-glow, but those that remained became even blacker and uglier. She poked one. It was wet, and some of it came off to stain her flesh.

She flung back the covers, stood, gave her body a frantic inspection.

There were no visible injuries, no telltale reddish stains on her nightgown.

"It's not your blood," Theo explained, "it's mine." He turned his arms over to expose red-weeping divots in his flesh.

Joelle quickly yanked two T-shirts from the stack of laundry on her dresser and wound them over Theo's forearms. She told him to get up, but Theo didn't want to. He rose only after she forced her arm beneath his and attempted to yank him to his feet. She slapped the casement window shut before leading Theo out of the room.

Once inside the bathroom Joelle uncapped the peroxide bottle and began to clean his wounds; nearly a dozen jagged, angry-looking rings marred his forearms, palms, left wrist. The nail of his right thumb was dangling by its root, exposing the delicate pulp beneath.

"Jesus, Theo, what did you *do* to yourself?" she managed before the lump in her throat stopped her voice.

"The baby did this, not me," he said. "I didn't think it'd be that strong or that big. And I didn't expect it to have teeth. But once I managed to fight back with my silver hammer, the thing came apart so easily. It just crumbled in my hands...like it was made of wet newspaper." Theo rested his head against the tile wall.

"Your silver hammer?" Joelle asked thinly.

Theo nodded once. "Sleepy," he whispered.

"That better?" she asked Theo as she lowered the quilt onto his trembling form.

"Yes."

She'd transformed the sofa into a makeshift bed for him after he'd refused to leave the living room, claiming it was the only place he felt safe.

Theo's mouth widened with a yawn. Joelle hoped he'd fall asleep. He needed it, but before he drifted she needed something too.

"I have to ask you something," she said.

"Okay."

"You know you were just having a bad dream, right? I mean, now that you've seen that I'm fine, you know I wasn't really pregnant."

"If you say so."

"I'm serious! I need to hear you acknowledge that you were just confused; that you know you didn't really hurt me. You were sleepwalking or hallucinating. You hurt yourself in your sleep. But I was never pregnant and you never aborted my baby with your hammer, right?"

"It wasn't *your* baby. It was King Him's"

A frigid winter passed through Joelle's insides. "What?"

"King Him."

"I thought all that was settled a long time ago, Theo."

"*We* did settle it, King Him didn't."

"But you said you banished King Him after...that you banished King Him the last time."

"I did. King Him came back."

"Enough!" Joelle turned away. She was shaking, uncertain of what to do or say next.

"So tired..." Theo mumbled, "I'm so..."

Joelle lit a cigarette and went to the kitchen to fix a cup of mint tea while Theo dozed. Mint tea had long been a nightly ritual, though Theo had always prepared it. His special brew had never failed to make her deliciously sleepy.

She sipped her own blend, surprised at the clarity and mildness of its flavour. It had none of the bitter aftertaste of Theo's.

She settled into the armchair and clicked on the plasma screen; infomercials, a Bollywood musical, cartoons in French. The all-weather channel was, sadly, the most interesting of the lot.

She poked at the soft flesh of her belly; compulsively, absent-mindedly. Now and again she would check her fingers for any telltale globs of red, would study her torso in search of some occult wound. She lit another cigarette.

Theo's delusion had been upsetting enough, but another fact was equally disturbing; her cycle, which had run with Swiss watch precision since she was thirteen, was off by a few weeks. She hadn't mentioned it to Theo or anyone else, assuming that it would resume at any time. She wasn't one for immaculate conceptions. Nevertheless, Joelle found herself unable to dismiss Theo's delusion as just that. Had he sensed something?

The awfulness of their long ago seemed to be reviving itself in their here and now.

Theo stirred and grumbled something in his sleep. Joelle switched off the TV. The room fell silent for a beat before Theo jerked upright and bellowed. The ceramic mug jumped from Joelle's hand and burst upon the hardwood floor.

"You're all right!" she cried. "You must've had another nightmare. Just go back to sleep. You're all right, Theo."

He lifted his knees to cradle his head.

"Sleep," she repeated.

Eventually Theo heeded. When she was sure he was out, Joelle began picking up the glass shards from the floor.

"Intheshed..."

She whirled around at the sound of the murmured words.

"Theo?" she whispered with reticence.

"In the shed...I left it in the shed, in an old rucksack."

"What's out in the shed?" she asked, not truly wanting the answer.

"The baby. We have to get rid of it. King Him can't know about this."

"Lay back down. I'll take care of it."

Her initial walk to the rear of the house and the unlocking of the patio door was done as a pantomime; a ruse to trick Theo into thinking she was making good on her promise to take care of whatever he believed was in the shed.

Had he really gone outside earlier tonight, crept through her bedroom window like a prowler? Were his superstitions becoming dangerously elaborate again after all these years?

The answer came in the form of a backyard shed...its door wide open.

Joelle slid the glass door open as noiselessly as possible. She heard a persistent thudding outside, like an irregular pulse. She stepped out onto the deck and watched as the winds pushed the shed door back and forth, pounding it against the jamb. The soot-dark interior beyond the flapping door made Joelle feel ill. She forced herself to descend the deck steps.

An old rucksack drooped over the shed's edge, its frayed hem rising and falling, lung-like, with each gust of wind. Her pace slowed as she neared the shed. The door swung back again but Joelle caught it before it slammed.

Theo's ball peen hammer was lying on top of the rucksack. Its silvery head coated in something dark, thick.

"No," Joelle whimpered, "no..."

The fibres of the sack looked to be soaked with the same reddish-black sludge. An acrid stench hung heavy inside the shed's hull. Bile climbed up Joelle's throat. She quickly swallowed it back.

'You're dreaming. I'm fine. Stop this.' Joelle heard her words echoing through her head, only this time she was using them in an attempt to calm herself.

She snagged the rucksack, pulled it out into the fledgling daylight. It was heavy and leaking foul liquid onto the snow. She held the sack closed and stood questioning whether she could even bring herself to glimpse inside.

She hurled the sack to the ground, repulsed by the possibilities of its contents. She turned, sure to keep her eyes off the dropped bundle, and tore up the deck stairs.

Theo was sitting up when she re-entered the living room. He was balancing a stack of junk mail upon his bent knees and appeared to be scribbling on one of the envelopes.

"What are you doing?"

"I'm trying to jot something down before I forget it again. It came back to me just as I was falling asleep."

She neared him, looked over his shoulder and read:

KING HIM'S CARDINAL RULES

1. KING HIM MAY ALWAYS VISIT, BUT KING HIM MAY NEVER STAY.
2. KING HIM MOVES IN ANGLES BECAUSE PEOPLE THINK IN ANGULAR WAYS.
3. KING HIM COMES AND GOES THROUGH "THE MATHEMATICS OF MAKE-BELIEVE"
4. THINGS ARE WHAT THEY ARE, BUT NOTHING IS REAL UNTIL KING HIM UTTERS ITS NAME. WE KNOW A CHAIR IS A CHAIR BECAUSE EVERYTIME WE SEE ONE, KING HIM SAYS THE WORD "CHAIR" IN OUR EAR.
5. IF KING HIM NO LONGER SPEAKS OF SOMETHING, THAT THING IS IMMEDIATELY BANISHED TO THE BELOW.
6. WHAT MOST PEOPLE CALL THOUGHTS ARE REALLY KING HIM'S INSTRUCTIONS. KING HIM IS ALWAYS TALKING. HIS NEVERENDING LECTURE IS WHAT PEOPLE CALL "KNOWLEDGE."
7. —

"I think I've figured out how we can get through this, Joelle. King Him broke his first rule, see? King Him tried to get a foothold here by having a baby with you. When King Him told me that he wanted you...in *that* way...I assumed it was because King Him was attracted to you. Now I think it's because King Him was trying to keep a physical foothold in this world at all times. But that's against His rules."

"Theo..."

"It's okay. Things might work out because even though I crossed King Him by getting rid of the baby, King Him probably can't punish me because *He* broke one of the cardinal rules, get it?"

"I found what you left in the shed."

Theo swallowed. After a time he said, "It's okay. We can just put it in the Below."

"But you told me that the Below was forbidden." She hoped her tone did not betray her terror, or what Theo might perceive as her lack of faith.

"C'mon, Jo, we made it there and back once, we can do it again. It's been long enough. I doubt the Below is even being watched anymore."

Joelle shut her eyes, feeling their lashes growing dewy with tears. "Theo, the ground is still frozen. We can't send him there, not completely, not like we did when you...I mean when *King Him* took mom and dad. All we can do is hide it under the porch until the ground thaws."

"Okay, that should be enough." He was child-like in his exuberance. "It's springtime now, so we should be able to send him to the Below soon."

"Real soon, yes."

"Okay."

The siblings made their way to the backyard. They found the section of loose latticework around the deck's perimeter. Joelle pulled the gate to the Below free. Theo crawled in, dripping sack in tow.

"How did you do it?"

"Do what?"

"You know," she pointed to her belly. "How did you...get it out?"

Theo dropped his jam-slathered toast, lifted his hands demonstratively. "With these."

"You didn't need any surgical tools or anything?" She was almost toying with him.

"It wasn't that kind of procedure. I just did what King Him told me to do. I reached in and took care of the problem."

A pregnant silence grew between them as they chewed their breakfast.

"When did King Him come back?"

Her brother was visibly reluctant to answer, but eventually admitted he'd been lying. "King Him never really left," he said. "You remember how He used to come through the Kingdom in the Corner in my bedroom? Well, He's been hiding there ever since."

"How come mom and dad never saw Him, how come *I've* never seen King Him?"

"You have," said Theo, "or you've *heard* Him at least. Everyone has. King Him says that whenever people think they're just talking to themselves they never pay attention to the fact that there is a *second voice* that answers them. People hear it and they just think it's their imagination, the 'voice inside their head.' But if they weren't so stupid they'd understand how the Mathematics of Make-Believe works. They'd know they were really chatting with King Him."

"Is that why mom and dad had to be banished to the Below, because they didn't understand?"

"Sort of. But mainly because King Him said He couldn't let them take me from Him."

"How did King Him get me pregnant, Theo?" Joelle asked, not truly wanting his response.

"The same way he does anything, I guess," he said sheepishly, more to his tea than to her. "He talked someone into making it happen."

Joelle spent several minutes pacing the house, beginning chores but straying from them half-finished. Her nerves grew tauter, more tangled.

Once the stores were open she informed her brother that she was going to get some groceries for dinner. Theo suggested they have a roast and Joelle agreed.

Her departure was accompanied by a soundtrack of her brother's persistent whispering from beyond his bedroom door.

She remembered little of the trip to the supermarket. Once there she bought a roast, white potatoes, club soda, a lemon chiffon cake. And a small box from the pharmacy department. This final item she stashed discreetly in her purse.

Joelle saw the police cruisers as soon as she'd turned back onto her street. They were parked four doors down from their home, at the Irwin house. Joelle knew the Irwin's to see them, but was hardly friends with the couple.

Or rather the *family*.

Joelle remembered that the Irwin's had been in the local paper, it must have been over a year ago now, announcing the birth of their son.

Her mind quickly cobbled together a horrific explanation as to why the police were parked at the Irwin home, as to what exactly she'd helped Theo hide beneath the porch in lieu of burying it in the Below.

Once home, Joelle handed the grocery bags to Theo, who immediately offered to begin peeling the potatoes.

She went to the bathroom, extracted the small box from her purse. Her hands were shaking to the point of being near useless.

The test delivered the final cut in the unspeakable assault that seemed to be claiming her minute by minute.

"Do you want me to make you a mint tea, Jo?" Theo called. Joelle slipped back inside. Theo hadn't heard her escape into the yard, or her sneaking into the shed.

"What have you done?" she hissed as she stood in the kitchen entryway.

Theo whirled around. He tried to secret the small pill bottle in his trouser pocket. "You scared me," he said. "I thought you were in the living room."

"What did you do to me?"

Theo's eyes went saucer-wide. "Please don't tell King Him," he blubbered, tears streaking down his cheeks. "I thought I could trick Him."

Joelle marched to the counter, tipped the teacup, spotted the white powder piled along its bottom. Her palate conjured memories of the bitter tea that Theo brought her nightly. She now knew why the cup she'd prepared for herself that morning had tasted so clean. She also understood why Theo's special tea never failed to make her drowsy, to usher her into a deathlike slumber.

"How long, Theo?" she screamed. *"How long has King Him been telling you to do this to me?"*

He slumped down onto the floor, unable or unwilling to answer her. Down there, through a haze of tears, Theo saw what his sister was clutching.

"I'm being banished..." His voice was soft with resignation.

"Yes," Joelle managed, raising the silver hammer.

"I'm sorry! Please, Joelle! Please tell King Him that Theo's sorry."

She sat cross-legged on the kitchen floor, mindlessly chewing her lower lip, whimpering, crying, occasionally unleashing a helpless furious howl.

Her shoulders still ached from dragging Theo outside and underneath the porch. The weather channel this morning had said a thaw was near. She could banish both bundles to the Below very soon. She might just be okay.

She touched her belly, imagining that she could already feel the foetus kicking, squirming, growing into the grotesque it would enter this world as.

'Help me,' Joelle thought. 'Please, God, help me. What am I going to do?'

'*You can do this. You're strong. You've made it through things that would've destroyed other people.*'

'It's wrong. This whole thing is so wrong...ugly.'

'*Could you love this child, YOUR child?*'

'I don't know.'

'*You loved Theo. Couldn't you love this baby too?*'

"Help me!" she cried.

'*You're not alone, Joelle,*' buzzed the voice in her head. '*I'll help you. I'll tell you exactly what to do.*'

"Theo said you always knew what to do."

'*As long as people listen I do. Will you listen?*'

"I'll listen. I will."

'*Good. And if the child happens to come out different than we wanted, we can just banish it, can't we, Joelle?*'

"Yes," Joelle said back to the vacant house. She fingered the handle of the silver hammer, still lying in a blackish puddle on the tile floor. "Yes, we can, King Him."

404

Barbara Roden

"Any idea what happened to Dwight?"

"Christ, don't sneak up on a person like that," Wilson snapped.

"Sorry." Armstrong didn't look sorry as he stepped into Wilson's office; worried, wary, but not sorry. "Just wondered if you knew where he'd gone."

"Didn't know he'd gone anywhere."

"Well, he has. I went by his office earlier and it was empty."

"Maybe he's sick."

"No, I mean empty. Nothing in it except a desk and a chair."

"No idea." Wilson gazed at the pile of folders perched on the corner of his desk. They had appeared overnight, with no note on them. "Explains these, though."

"What are they?"

Wilson shrugged. "I haven't really had a chance to look. Some sort of demographic study. That was Dwight's area, wasn't it?"

"Yeah." Both men stared at the files. "Wonder why you got them?" asked Armstrong finally.

"Don't know. I don't need the extra work right now, though. I've been working twelve hour days as it is."

Wilson hoped that Armstrong would take the hint, but the other man moved closer to the desk, flipped open the topmost folder, and began leafing through the sheets of paper, which contained charts and lists of names. He nodded.

"Yep, this is Dwight's. Told me he was working on this. Said he didn't know how *he'd* cope, since Jenkins left."

"Jenkins? Tall guy, glasses, corner office?" Armstrong nodded. "Where's he gone?"

Armstrong shrugged. "Didn't say. Hey, d'you think they've heard something we haven't?"

"Like what?"

"I don't know. Maybe we should..."

"Staff meeting, gentlemen? Very remiss of you not to tell the rest of us."

Both men jumped as Mr. Edwards' voice sounded from the doorway, and Armstrong brushed against the pile of folders, which slid to the ground. He scrabbled around on the floor and gathered them into an untidy heap, which he piled haphazardly on the corner of the desk.

"I'm sorry, gentlemen, but *is* there a staff meeting in progress? Or am I interrupting something else entirely?"

"You're not interrupting anything, Mr. Edwards," said Wilson. "Armstrong was just going; weren't you, Armstrong?"

"Yes, yes, of course. Er, thanks for the help, Wilson. Appreciate it. Uh, excuse me, Mr. Edwards...." Their supervisor made no move to get out of the way, causing Armstrong to sidle awkwardly past him. When he got through the doorway he turned back to Wilson, mouthed "Sorry", and disappeared.

There was silence for a moment. Wilson tidied the pile of folders into a neater stack, then pushed them well back from the edge of the desk. When there was no more avoiding it, he turned to the doorway.

"Is there something I can do for you, Mr. Edwards?"

"I was coming to speak with you about those files. I see you've already found them."

"Yes. I was, uh, wondering about them. They don't really appear to be in my field."

"You have, then, had an opportunity to peruse them?"

"Well, no, not really." Seeing his supervisor's raised eyebrow, Wilson added, "I was...I mean, I took a quick look at...Armstrong said Dwight wasn't here, and they look like the sort of thing he did, and that isn't my field, so I just..." Wilson trailed off.

"That explains your colleague's presence in your office. What else did Mr. Armstrong have to say?"

"That was all, really, just that Dwight wasn't here."

"And did Mr. Armstrong offer any opinions as to the cause of this absence?"

"No."

"I am glad to hear that. Idle speculation has no place in this office, Mr. Wilson. We carry out very sensitive work, as you are aware, and it would not do for employees to begin speculating in the absence of any facts. Speculation turns to gossip, which becomes rumor, which then takes on a life of its own to become fact, and the rot sets in. Demoralization! Depression! Disintegration! I suggest, in future, that you do everything within your power to discourage this."

"Yes, Mr. Edwards. I understand."

"Do you? I am very glad to hear that. Carry on, Mr. Wilson."

"Mr. Edwards?" The other man halted in the act of leaving the office. "Er, about these files. You still haven't told me what I'm supposed to do with them."

"Ah, of course. The question of the hour. Was there no note with them?"

"Nothing that I've found."

"I see."

"Maybe there's something in Dwight's office that will help. I could go look."

"No, Mr. Wilson, a visit to that office will not, I fear, prove edifying. I am positive, however, that upon closer inspection all will become clear."

"I could wait until he comes back...."

"The truth of the matter, Mr. Wilson, is that your colleague will not, alas, be returning to the bosom of this office."

"I see."

"Do you really? I wonder." Mr. Edwards gazed at him thoughtfully for a moment, then sighed. "No, he will not be returning. A shame; his grasp of the minutiae of his employment was second to none. These days, however, one cannot be too careful, particularly in our line of work. I am sure you understand."

"Yes, I suppose I do."

"Suppose?" said Mr. Edwards. "There can be no 'suppose' about it, Mr. Wilson. Security and vigilance must be our watchwords."

"I'm not sure I know what you mean, sir. Did Dwight...I mean, did he do something?"

"No, he did not 'do' anything. Suffice it to say that there were certain...irregularities surrounding your colleague, certain questions which he could not answer to our satisfaction. There is nothing more to say, except that no one currently employed here need fear anything; unless, of course, discrepancies come to light which cannot be explained. I am sure you have no such discrepancies in your own past, Mr. Wilson?"

"Not that I know of."

"Excellent. Then you will have no difficulty, I am sure, in satisfying our enquiries."

"What enquiries?"

Mr. Edwards waved his hand. "Merely routine, I assure you. A directive which has come down to us. We will be asking employees to provide us with various documents, so we may verify certain facts about those currently employed here; all of whom, you will agree, work with very sensitive information, which certain persons might be anxious to obtain."

"What sort of persons?" asked Wilson.

Mr. Edwards clucked his tongue. "Really, Mr. Wilson, I took you for an intelligent man. You cannot have failed to notice that there are people who would, for reasons best known to themselves, seek to undermine all that we hold dear. Against these people we cannot be too vigilant. Hence these routine checks."

"And you think that Dwight was..."

"*I* do not think that he 'was' anything, Mr. Wilson. It was determined, after a thorough check, that he was *not* a person who could, in these uncertain times, continue in our employ. Regrettable, but there it is." There was not a trace of regret in his voice. "Still," he continued, "you have assured me that all is well as regards yourself, which I am glad to hear."

"Does that mean that you won't have to check on me?"

"Ah, Mr. Wilson; such a sense of humour. I do appreciate that. Well, enjoyable as this interlude has undoubtedly been, I must let you get on with your work." He nodded towards the stack of files. "You do, after all, have a great deal to be getting on with."

All day the files sat on the corner of Wilson's desk, reproaching him by their presence, annoying him with their lack of explanation. He tried to send an e-mail to Dwight's inter-departmental address, but it promptly bounced back to him with a curt "Recipient not found". When he tried to pull up Dwight's profile on the company website, he found only a blank white screen with the words "404: File Not Found".

That evening, on impulse, Wilson drove to the apartment building where Dwight lived. He buzzed the security bell, but there was no response. Dwight's apartment faced the front of the building, but when he looked up at the window he could see no light. The curtains did not appear to be closed.

Wilson tried the buzzer again. A short, grey-haired man came up the steps behind him, a key clasped in his outstretched hand. "Looking for someone?"

"Yes. A friend of mine lives here; Robert Dwight. He doesn't seem to be in."

The other man shook his head. "Hasn't been in for a few days. Don't think he'll be in again, either. Moved out last week."

"Moved?"

The man shrugged. "Well, there were some men moving his furniture out and putting it in a truck. Looked to me as if he was moving out."

"Did you see Dwight? Did he say he was moving?"

"Nope, didn't see him, so he didn't say. If you'll excuse me...." The man unlocked the door, entered the building, and pulled the door shut quickly behind him, as if to prevent Wilson from following. Wilson, for his part, looked up once more at the dark window of Dwight's apartment, shivered, and headed towards his car.

Next day Armstrong seemed to be avoiding him; in the canteen at lunchtime he left the moment Wilson entered, even though his lunch was only half finished. Wilson finally managed to buttonhole him an hour later, when Armstrong went to get a cup of coffee from the vending machine.

"I need to talk to you," he said urgently.

Armstrong glanced left and right, then hissed, "You have some nerve, after what you did yesterday."

"What do you mean? What did I do?"

"You know. Edwards was sniffing around all afternoon. 'What were you talking to Mr. Wilson about?' 'Why so interested in your colleagues' whereabouts, Mr. Armstrong?' 'Do you have anything you want to discuss, Mr. Armstrong?' Then he told me he wanted to see my papers this afternoon. 'Routine enquiry,' he said. Bullshit! What did you say to him?"

"Nothing!" Armstrong made an inarticulate noise of disbelief. "Honest! We were just talking about Dwight, and those files on my desk, and he said the department was carrying out routine enquiries on everyone. It's nothing to worry about."

"Nothing to worry about!" Armstrong stared at him in disbelief. "And you believe that? Just ask Dwight, or Jenkins. Bet they weren't worried, either."

"But all they want to do is look at our papers. What harm can there be? As long as everything's in order..."

"Yeah, well, whose definition of 'in order' are we going by? Look, just stay away from me, okay?" Armstrong snatched his coffee from the machine and stomped off in the direction of his office.

Wilson shook his head. Armstrong clearly didn't want to talk, and Dwight was gone. Who else was there?

Jenkins. Had he really left? There was only one way to find out.

Wilson set off down the corridor. All the doors were firmly shut, and he could hear no noise from any of the offices. *Good soundproofing*, he thought. He rounded a corner, and there was Jenkins's door in front of him, shut tight like all the others. He walked up to it and gave a timid knock. There was no reply from the other side, and he knocked again, a little harder, surprised at how loud the sound was in the otherwise silent hallway.

Still no answer. Wilson hesitated a moment, then reached for the handle, turned it, and pushed open the unresisting door.

The office was bare of everything save a desk, a chair, and a battered filing cabinet in one corner. Wilson hesitated, then entered the office, closing the door behind him. He crossed to the desk and pulled open the topmost drawer, which was empty apart from two paper clips. The next drawer was similarly bare, and the bottom drawer contained only a few empty hanging files.

Wilson flicked through them idly, and a scrap of paper caught his eye at the bottom of the drawer. He reached in, pulled it out, and looked at it. It was a claim stub from a dry-cleaner's on the west side. The name "Jenkins" was scrawled on it, and underneath was "Thurs. April 17". A week ago.

Wilson gazed at the paper for a moment, then tucked it into his pocket. He glanced round the office again, shivered, and crossed to the door. It swung open to reveal Mr. Edwards on the other side, arms folded across his chest.

"Mr. Wilson. We meet in somewhat unexpected circumstances. You have an explanation, I take it?"

Wilson swallowed hard, willing his heart to stop thudding.

"I'm waiting, Mr. Wilson."

"Yes."

"Is that 'yes' as in 'Yes I have an explanation'?"

"Yes...I mean no...I mean...I was coming to ask Jenkins something—about those files, the ones from Dwight—because I remembered they were working on them together. I thought he might be able to help. But he's—well, he's not here."

"Obviously not." They both gazed round the office, taking in the non-presence of Jenkins. "That having been settled, Mr. Wilson, I suggest you return to your office. Much as I might like to chat, I have an appointment to see Mr. Armstrong in"—he glanced at his watch—"precisely five minutes. I dislike tardiness. So very unprofessional."

"Yes, Mr. Edwards. Back to my office. Good idea." He was several paces down the hallway and just starting to breathe normally again when his supervisor called, "One more thing, Mr. Wilson."

"Yes?"

"Perhaps you would be so good as to bring your papers in tomorrow. Merely a routine enquiry, as I mentioned yesterday, but I think in light of recent events sooner would be better than later."

"Yes, Mr. Edwards. What should I bring in?"

The supervisor waved his hand. "Oh, passport, birth certificate, driver's licence, anything from an institute of higher learning; those should be sufficient. Please be in my office at 3.00."

When he returned to his own office, Wilson picked up the files from Dwight. Page after page of names and addresses greeted him. The papers in the topmost files contained no notations, but as Wilson made his way through the stack he saw that other pages were covered with handwritten notations and abbreviations. Some of the names had marks beside them; others had been thickly crossed through with a red pen.

On impulse, he pulled up the company directory and clicked on Jenkins's profile. The message "404: File Not Found" came up on the screen. Wilson closed the folders, pushed them as far away from him as he could, and turned back to his own work.

When he left the office Wilson was reluctant to go home. He stuffed his hands into his trouser pockets, and was surprised to feel a piece of paper in one of them. Pulling it out, he saw it was the laundry ticket he had found in Jenkins's drawer. He knew where the dry-cleaner's was, and a few minutes later was pulling up outside it. No one was in evidence through the front window, but when he entered the shop a bell sounded in the back. Moments later a woman whose dark hair owed more to a bottle than to nature emerged through a door behind the desk.

"Help you?" she asked, and Wilson pulled the ticket stub out of his pocket.

"Yes. I'm here to pick this up." He handed the woman the ticket, which she merely glanced at before turning to the rack of neatly-bagged clothes beside her. Within seconds she found what she was looking for and handed Wilson a bag containing a suit and two shirts. Wilson fumbled in his pocket for the payment, thanked the woman, and went out to his car. Once there, he looked more closely at the bag. The other, larger, part of the laundry ticket was stapled to it, and on it was Jenkins's name, along with a telephone number.

Wilson drove home, where he sat looking at the ticket from the dry-cleaning bag for some minutes. Finally he picked up his phone and dialled Jenkins's number, which rang three times before being picked up. Wilson started to breathe a sigh of relief.

"The number you have dialled is not in service," said a recorded message. "Please check the number and dial again."

Wilson looked at the number on the paper and dialled again, more carefully. The phone rang three times; then the recorded message played once more.

He put down the phone. After a moment he picked it up again and dialled Armstrong's number. There was no delay there; the phone was picked up before the first ring finished, and an agitated female voice said, "What happened? Why did you hang up? Where are you?"

"Um, hello? Is that"—what was her name; Alice, right—"Alice?"

The voice on the other end of the line sounded wary, and slightly panicked. "Who is this? What's going on?"

"It's Ted Wilson, Alice. I just wanted to speak with Bill for a minute."

"You can't. He's not here. He phoned a minute ago, and then the line went dead. What's going on?"

"I don't know. Look, Alice, I..."

"Get off the phone. Bill could be calling back any minute."

"Alice, what did he..."

"Just hang up!" There was definite panic in her voice. "Get off the phone!" She heard the receiver on the other end bang down.

Wilson's hands were trembling. He got up and turned on a few lights, made himself some supper, and left most of it on the plate; then, remembering his meeting with Mr. Edwards the next day, he spent some minutes getting his papers together. They all looked neat, tidy, in complete order, and made a satisfying heap on the counter. He tried Armstrong's number again before going to bed, but the phone rang and rang, and no one picked it up.

There seemed to be few people about next day, and hardly anyone was in the canteen at lunch time. Armstrong, he noticed, was nowhere to be seen. At five to three he gathered together his papers, and at 3.00 knocked at Mr. Edwards's door. A voice called "Come in," and he entered. His supervisor looked at his watch and nodded approvingly.

"Precisely on time, Mr. Wilson. Admirable. Please take a seat. You have everything there? Excellent! As I said, purely routine. I am sure you have nothing to fear."

Was it Wilson's imagination, or had his supervisor put a slight emphasis on the word "you"? He sat down in an uncomfortable chair with minimal padding, and watched as the other man looked through one document after another. He made no sound, other than an occasional "Hmm"; once he nodded his head, and at another point, more worryingly, shook it, a faint frown creasing his face. Wilson did not want to check his own watch, so had no idea how long he had sat there before Mr. Edwards placed the last document carefully on top of the others, leaned back in his chair, and cleared his throat.

"Have you ever considered, Mr. Wilson, how very fragile one's identity is? All these items which 'prove' who you are, for instance: think of what these are made. Paper. Ink. Words. A name of an issuing country, or agency, or institution; an official stamp here, a signature there, and *voila*, one has a piece of paper which, on cursory inspection, appears to be in order. Words, however, can have a multitude of meanings; countries, agencies, institutions come and go; an official stamp may be stolen, a signature may be forged. At the end of the day, all of these"—Mr. Edwards waved a hand towards the pile of documents on the desk—"add up to little more than the probability that you are who you say you are. They do not 'prove' anything."

Wilson tried to speak, could not, swallowed, and tried again. "I'm, uh, not sure that I follow you, Mr. Edwards. Are you saying there's something wrong with my papers?"

"Nooo..." said Mr. Edwards, "I am not saying that. Neither am I saying that everything is necessarily in perfect order. You will agree, Mr. Wilson, that I have only taken a very superficial look at your papers. I will need to examine them more closely before I can give you a definitive answer. For example"—he shuffled through the documents in front of him, plucked out a large piece of paper, and held it out—"this diploma indicates that you obtained a degree from University College of the Caribou. I am unfamiliar with that institution."

"Well, it doesn't exist anymore," said Wilson. Mr. Edwards eyed him keenly. "I mean, it does, it's just not called University College of the Caribou now. It became Thompson Rivers University a few years ago."

"My point exactly, Mr. Wilson. You have shown me a piece of paper which indicates you have a degree; issued, however, by an institute which does not exist. It might, therefore, be fair to say that it is not—if you will excuse my little jest—worth the paper on which it is printed. A somewhat similar situation arose with Mr. Jenkins, whose birth certificate stated that he was born in Southern Rhodesia. Do you know where Southern Rhodesia is, Mr. Wilson?"

"Um, no...not off the top of my head...."

"Hardly surprising. And if I were to show you a current atlas, or map of the world, you would be no further forward. Southern Rhodesia, Mr. Wilson, does not exist. Oh, it undoubtedly *did* exist, for a certain period of time, but the fact remains that it no longer does, and hence a piece of paper, however official looking, issued by that country cannot now be verified with any degree of certainty. And Mr. Dwight: there were certain anomalies regarding his birth certificate, which was *not* issued with a last name of 'Dwight'. Something to do with his mother remarrying, or so he claimed."

"And what—what about Armstrong?" asked Wilson. "Surely his papers were fine?"

"Ah, Mr. Armstrong. You appreciate I cannot comment on investigations which are still ongoing, Mr. Wilson. Suffice it to say that his name—his full name—is similar to one which appears on a certain official list which has been circulated to all departments. The matter is...under review."

"I see."

"I am glad that you do, Mr. Wilson. You are free to go. Ah, no"—this said as Wilson reached across to pick up his documents—"these will remain with me, Mr. Wilson. You recall what I said about examining them more closely. I am sure that the... discrepancy regarding your degree, and any other discrepancies which arise, will be quickly and easily resolved. Tomorrow, in my office, at 3.00? Very good. Oh, and Mr. Wilson"—this said as Wilson's hand was on the doorknob—"I would appreciate it if you would be so good as to ensure that all the files you are working on are in order. It might be an idea to put a note inside the topmost one, with a brief précis of what has been done, and what remains to be done, with them. Thank you."

Back in his office, it took several tries before his hands stopped shaking enough to allow him to type Armstrong's name. He was not surprised by the message which appeared. He debated typing in his own name; then, after a moment, he pulled a blank piece of paper towards him and, one eye on the files, began writing.

STAY

Leah Bobet

She felt the storm come in her kneecaps, then her thighs. By eight o'clock, it blew from the north into Sunrise, January-hard and fine like sand, and Cora's hip was aching.

She asked Johnny Red for a smoke break and limped out back to the storeroom, kneading the hip with her right hand while her left cupped the cigarette. The storeroom was cold and cluttered, a tiny junkyard of boxes and broken chairs, but normally it was quiet; the rattle of pots in Johnny Red's kitchen didn't quite reach through the door. Tonight, though, the back door banged like an angry drunk; the snow hissed and ground at metal, brick, bone. Cora lit a second thin-rolled smoke off the first and listened to the rattle of the heartbroke wind.

When she came back through the storeroom door, half her tables had up and left.

"Better service across the street?" she asked. The plates were half-full, still steaming. There was nothing across the street. There was nowhere else to eat in the whole town: just the service stations, the Tutchos' grocery, and the snow.

"Transport truck's gone off the road," Johnny said behind the counter, and crimped a new coffee filter into the brew basket. A few hairs pulled loose from his straight black ponytail and drifted into his face; he brushed them back with a callused brown hand. "The boys went to haul it to Fiddler's."

Georgie Fiddler ran one of the two service stations in town. Mike Blondin, who ran the other, was still at his table, hands wrapped thin around a chipped blue pottery mug. He held it up and Cora grabbed the stained coffeepot.

"I want the fresh stuff," he complained; she didn't answer, just filled the mug with sour, black coffee. He waved her off before it hit the brim and flipped open the dented metal sugar tin.

"You didn't go out with them," she said. Not a question.

Mike Blondin's fingers moved like a stonecarver's, measured sugar with chisel precision: one pinch, two. He had big hands. "Wouldn't want to just abandon you," he grinned. There'd been a time, not too many years past, when Mikey Blondin's grin had got him whatsoever he desired anywhere from Sunrise to the Alberta border.

"Thoughtful," she said, dry, just as Johnny Red hit the percolator button and called out, "What'm I, chopped liver?" Gertie Myers, back at the corner table, rolled her eyes. Cora ignored it all and covered the cooling plates.

An hour passed before the menfolk trickled back in, red-faced and damp with winter-sweat. "Hey," Johnny Red said, and ladled out eight bowls of steaming chicken soup. "What's the news?"

"Went hard into the ditch," Fred Tutcho replied, and sucked back soup straight from the bowl. The steam set the ice in his eyelashes to melting. "Georgie got the tow and we managed to fish it out, but the front axle's pretty busted."

"The driver?" Cora asked.

"Got him up at Jane's." Jane Hooker ran the Treeline Motel, which was ten rooms and a Dene crafts shop, old-style porcupine quill-and-hair work, out by Blondin's. In the deep wintertime most of her rooms were closed; the only visitors to Sunrise in January were family and the odd long-haul trucker. "She'n Georgie are checking him out."

"I'll bring them something, then," Cora said, and ducked into the kitchen. She filled three thermoses and screwed the lids on tight, shrugged on her long, thick, battered coat. She wound three scarves and a hat about her head before stepping out into the storm.

It wasn't enough. The storm cut. It had blown in from the north, where there weren't no buildings or shrubs—whitebark pines or larches—to beat down the wind. Even breathing through thick wool, Cora's nostrils froze together at the first sucked-in breath, and her jeans were stiff by the time she reached the Treeline Motel. There was only one light on. Cora hunkered deeper into her scarves and scooted, knees-bent against the slippery gravel, down the battered row of doors with fingers clamped around her canvas bag.

Room six had been converted into a warm and stuffy sickroom. Jane Hooker leaned over the bed, obscuring her patient from the knees on up, and Georgie Fiddler tinkered with the steam radiator, coaxing out a whining, clanking heat. The warm air made Cora sneeze, and two heads turned sharp around the double bed. She waggled the canvas bag and groped with her free hand for a tissue.

Her fingers were still stiff when she unscrewed the thermos caps and set them on the nightstand. Jane shifted over to make room, and she finally got a look at the driver.

He had soft, sweaty, messy hair. It fell dark across a white man's flattened cheekbones and was tamped down in a line where his cap would sit. The cap was on the dresser: white and faded red, damp from the roadside snow. The brim was bent almost double, into a fist.

Jane had the man's jackets off—one for winter and a checked old lumber jacket—and her broad hand felt the shape of his ribs. "Good enough," she said to Georgie with a nod, and he let out a little sigh; probably happy he didn't have to call to Hay River for the doctor.

Cora poured them half-chilled chicken soup and passed the mugs into reddened hands. "From Johnny," she said. Jane took hers with a nod, distracted; Georgie caught his up and resumed his regular pacing. She cupped her hands around a third mug, stealing what heat it had left, and leaned back against the wall to watch.

"Enough left for our boy here?" Jane asked, and Cora nodded. She'd ladled Johnny's soup pot dry. "Good," Jane replied, and stood with a long, loose breath. The lines around her eyes were windburned and deep. "I get the feeling he'll wake up hungry. Got a pretty good crack on the head."

"Lucky he didn't break those ribs too," Georgie said.

"Speaking of." Jane paused. "You find his seatbelt on?"

"He was clear across the cab." Georgie looked up at her, at Jane, and his brow creased into three fine canyons over his greying eyebrows. "I'll look over the truck tomorrow."

Jane nodded. "You're a good man, George Fiddler."

She didn't need to say it. But Georgie pinkened anyways over the rim of his mug, and those terrible fissures came out of his face.

"Hey," he said sudden, and both Jane and Cora looked up. "I think he's waking up."

Cora leaned in soon enough to see his eyes flicker. They were folded, turned a touch at the corners. Métis then, not white, but whatever blood he had, it wasn't Dene or Inuit. The nose was too narrow, the face too thin. Too thin for his own cheekbones, she realized. The man looked gaunt. Hungry.

"Hello?" she asked softly, then: "Wotziye?"

The creased eyelids opened.

The eyes behind them were bright and black, bone-sharp. They darted right and left like a trapped hunting bird's, taking in ceiling, walls, triple-paned window with the air of something captive. Cora jerked back and they tracked her movement. The gaze stung like wind-whipped ice on the edge of her cheek.

Cora had once, before she moved to Sunrise, seen a polar bear hunt. It crouched by a seal's breathing hole silent, waiting, waiting for a seal to draw breath, and then reached in and crushed its skull.

Those black winter eyes rested upon her, and she didn't breathe.

"Hey there," Jane said beside her, terribly far away. "How you feeling?"

That terrible watching, January-cold and fine like sand, *moved*.

Nothing happened. Jane Hooker, solid and dependable, didn't lean back or recoil. "Thought we'd lost you there," she said, all good cheer and good sense.

Cora exhaled, and for a brief second, her breath steamed in the air.

She felt a hand on her elbow and jumped; Georgie Fiddler, standing an arm's-length back. "You all right there?"

No. "Yeah," she said. Her jaw was numb, and it ached. Those wicked eyes looked at Jane Hooker and they were just brown: too-bright and confused, flicking back and forth between faces and the pitted white ceiling. The pupils were overlarge, crowding the skin-brown iris, dark and deep but normal.

It wasn't the pupil, Cora thought distinctly, and rubbed her palm against her cheek. The man's mouth shaped a question, and it was not at all the same.

Georgie quirked an eyebrow. "Go on, Cor. Johnny probably needs you back."

"Thanks," she said. There was gooseflesh on her hands. She stuffed them in her coat pockets and went.

She was ten steps into the crunching, wailing snow, her second scarf only half-wrapped around her ears, when she heard the bird cry.

There was a raven perched on the Treeline Motel's roof, still as an animal killed five miles from home and frozen rictus. The storm beat against it, passed around it, let it through. It cocked its head—a beak-shadow, a change in the darkness—and laughed at her once more, biting.

Oh hell, she thought.

And then it blurred against the snowfall, its wings black against white against bottomless black, and she ran.

"I saw a raven on the Treeline's roof last night," Cora said, no preamble, when she came into the diner the next morning.

Johnny Red was in the kitchen, fumbling for something that clattered and bumped and made him swear. "It's minus thirty," he said when he surfaced.

"Yeah," Cora said.

She felt his eyes on her as she hung up her coat and tied on her soft, worn-down apron. It was just the two of them here this time of day, but he still kept his voice low. "Think it's something?"

She pulled the knot tight, tugged at each of the loops to make sure they wouldn't give. The sun was brilliant outside, halfway through the sky and already falling: subarctic noontime. It turned the snow to pure light and slanted anti-shadow across the pale blue tabletops. "I don't know medicine, Johnny."

"Sometimes you don't have to," he replied, ducking back onto his haunches behind the counter and clattering some more. She had all the table settings in place and he'd started the soup before she said, "Yeah. I think it's something."

His mouth pulled down, grimmer. He didn't reply.

Georgie Fiddler came in right at the lunchtime open, pink with cold and puffy-eyed. He nodded to Cora and bellied up to the old-fashioned lunch counter. "Thanks for the soup last night," he said, and set the bag of empty thermoses on the counter.

Johnny waved it off, ladle in hand. "How's damages?"

"Bent front axle," he said, and tugged off his gloves. "Be a day or two before I can run up to Hay River for the new axle brackets. They haven't cleared the highways yet."

Cora looked out the restaurant's triple-paned windows at the glittering snow: knee-high if it was an inch. Terrible driving weather. "How's our trucker?"

"Awake," he said; the glance he cast her was only a little concerned. "Jane said he's just staring." He didn't need to say more; there was only one kind of stare in a town like this. Cora'd first seen it young, in an uncle home after a turn in Grande Cache who'd stayed only a week before drifting off one night to freeze. After that it showed up on mothers, friends, the boys who sniffed gasoline in tool sheds on long winter nights; it blurred.

"You reach his people yet?" Johnny Red asked.

"Jane don't think he's got any people. The only number in his wallet was the trucking company."

"That's a shame," Johnny Red said evenly, in a way someone else might have thought idle.

Cora lifted an eyebrow. He put his long chef's knife against the curve of a withered onion and said nothing.

Georgie Fiddler did. "Everything all right there, John?"

Johnny's knife paused. "Cora saw a raven on the motel roof last night."

"Johnny—" she said, sharp enough to surprise herself. His jaw twitched a little below the curve of his ear; the look he cast her said *sorry*, and *no*. She let out a breath and noticed her hand at her own jaw, rubbing it like a feeding baby's back. She put it in her apron pocket. She needed a smoke.

"It's thirty below," Georgie said.

Johnny Red nodded and snipped the shoot end off his onion.

Georgie Fiddler frowned. "So what's that mean?" He was one of the few fully white men in Sunrise, come up from north Saskatchewan twelve and a half years back. Nobody begrudged him for it—he paid better wages and kept better hours than Mike Blondin, after all—but it meant sometimes he needed a thing explained that should never need explaining.

"The problem with Raven," Johnny Red said delicately, "is that you're never sure *what* you're going to get."

"Oh," Georgie Fiddler said, in a way that meant he hadn't grasped the half of it. Cora couldn't blame him. *She'd* barely grasped the half of it.

"Anyways," Johnny said, brushing onion from his cutting board, "it'll go better when he's gone."

The silence puddled a little, chilly, on the tiled black and white floor.

"Well," Georgie said, stiff, "it'll be a good while for that. The other driver on the route went missing last week, just up and vanished from the depot, and they can't send another until next week. *If* they clear the highway tomorrow. So try to keep it under your hat, man."

Johnny's expression didn't change. "So that truck's gonna sit in your garage for a week?" he said as if he'd not heard Georgie at all.

Cora shot Georgie a *look*. He took the hint. "Looks like," he said, and ran a hand through his thin hair. "Northbest'll be pretty pissed. It's a perishable load, and boy is it gonna perish."

"What's so perishable?" she asked.

Georgie Fiddler smiled dryly. "Fruit. Veg. Stuff I've never even seen before. Don't know how good it'll be after another night in this weather."

Johnny put his knife down. "So you've got the phone number for this Northbest man."

Georgie set a torn slip of paper down on the Formica counter. "That's what I came to bring you," he said, still a little cool. "And to ask if you could run lunch for two down to Jane's."

"For him," Johnny said.

"And Daisy."

"I'll go," Cora said.

"Cor—" Johnny started.

"Not even Raven lives on thin air just yet." Her voice stayed level. The color rose behind his windburned brown cheeks, but he tipped her a nod.

"I can do sandwiches," he said, and disappeared into his kitchen.

"You sure you're all right?" Georgie Fiddler asked, and she wasn't sure if he meant Johnny Red or last night or Raven on the Treeline's roof, laughing bitter dark.

Cora untied her apron and let out a long breath. "If I don't come back," she said, "break all the eggs."

Inside the kitchen, Johnny Red snorted.

Daisy Blondin was in with the trucker when Cora tapped on the door. "Lunch," Cora said, stomping snow off her boots.

The trucker was propped up in Jane Hooker's clean white bed, tee-shirt thin and rumpled, bruise-dark shadows underneath his eyes. Light brown stubble was coming in on his cheek; someone would have to find a razor. Too far away to see his eyes, but Georgie was right: staring.

"Lunch!" Daisy said, and put aside a creased copy of *Canadian Technician*. Her feet were on the bed; two brown toes peeked out of a hole in her red-and-white striped socks. "No chance you could take over? Jane's sleeping and my brother's gonna kill me."

Cora unbuttoned her coat, but didn't take it off. Tough words in the presence of Johnny Red or not, she wasn't staying a minute farther than she had to. "I can't. It's lunch rush."

Daisy sighed. "All right. Let me go to the can." She wandered around the foot of the bed to the bathroom, and there was silence for a moment after the bathroom door slammed. Cora heard the click of the toilet lid hitting the tank, and another sound: the steady thud of an axe against a whitebark pine. Her forehead wrinkled. It was cold for cutting trees this afternoon, and as far as she knew, the gas for the furnaces wasn't anywhere near that precarious yet.

The heater pinged and muttered. It was cold in here, too. Her hip ached. The man on the bed pushed himself up to sitting, and she forced herself to stay still. "Lunch?" she asked, and it fell into the silence like a stone.

He was a big man; she hadn't noticed that last night. Tall and rangy enough that his feet stuck out over the edge of the double bed, his forearms pale but ropy and strong. It made the hollows under his cheekbones stand out even sharper. His shoulders hunched around his chin as if he wished himself disappeared. His nod was a ghost.

"So what do I call you?" she asked, trying to keep her voice normal.

"Aidan," he said. He sounded hoarse, quiet; like someone half out of the habit of talking.

"I'm Cora." She forced herself to hand him the waxed-paper package. He stared at it for a second, cupped in his two hands, before picking it open with a dirty fingernail.

"You were here last night," he said suddenly, and Cora realized he was watching her from behind that fall of mussed-up hair. She rubbed her jaw, little circles like Johnny Red cleaning his counter.

"I was," she said careful.

He rolled bread into a tiny ball between thumb and forefinger. He wasn't eating.

The sound of wood chopping was closer now, in the room, and heater or not, her breath steamed. She stepped backwards once, twice.

"You feeling better, then?" she asked to cover it, and he looked up at her full for the first time. He talked like a shut-in, but he stared like a resting lynx.

"Yeah," he said, soft and creaking, and the chill sound of trees falling, wood splintering in rhythm—*heartbeat rhythm*—almost drowned it out.

Her ears were ringing. Her tongue didn't want to move, and his eyes were so big, nighttime-big, dark as raven's-feather and sharp as a polar bear's, waiting. Waiting. "Well, we'll take good care of you," she blurted.

He stopped. Everything stopped.

The dizzying cold shattered.

"I...pardon?" he choked out. His face was dirty pale, hands shaking. The sandwich was squashed flat between his fingers.

What did I say?

Cora sucked in a breath. Her hip was burning with cold, wedged hard against the motel's plaster wall. She was shivering. She couldn't get warm. "They ain't coming to get you for a week. I just didn't want you to worry, that we wouldn't take good care of you—"

She was babbling. She was panicking.

She hadn't thought he could look any sicker.

"A week?" he asked, and there were funerals in his brown, big, human eyes.

The toilet flushed, and Daisy banged out of the washroom, Jane's bathroom towel trailing from her hand. "Thanks, Cor. Tell Mikey I'm here if you see him?"

"Yeah," she said unsteady, and Daisy Blondin, only six years younger than her but about twenty more invincible, flicked up an eyebrow and looked each to each.

"Everything all right?" she asked.

"Yeah," Cora said, automatic, regretting it a split-second after. "I gotta run." She had three smokes left in the pack. She'd counted them last night.

The skies were clear on the walk from the Treeline Motel to the Sunrise Restaurant. She scanned the skies and rooflines as she walked, and smoked them all.

There were things in the back of the produce truck that Cora had never seen: mangoes, persimmons, fine nubbly oranges, not to mention the vegetables she couldn't name. She and Johnny loaded a good third of the Northbest crates onto service station wagons after the lunch crowd trickled away, and then helped Magda Tutcho wrestle the rest into the General Store. It wouldn't last long—a week and a half at most, Magda said—but there was always Gertie's canning apparatus, and besides, it'd be a hell of a week.

Cora hand-lettered a sign for the Sunrise Restaurant's door —*Tropical Party 7pm Tonite: $15 Full Meal*—and tacked it firmly down by all four corners. Sunrise was a small town. Word would get around.

They sorted the oddest fruits on the countertop, next to the spine-cracked chef school cookbook left behind, mouldering, by the last owner of the Sunrise Restaurant. "What's this one?" she asked, balancing a red, round weight in one hand.

"Pomegranate," Johnny Red said. He'd worked as a cook down in Calgary for three years before he took over the Sunrise Restaurant. By the second year up north he'd mostly stopped complaining about how everything came in tins, but when he took the pomegranate from her hand, the look on his face was like the first day of spring. "All the rage out in BC. White ladies in workout pants beat down your door for them."

He waggled his eyebrows, and she laughed. It came out bad; forced. There was something cold stuck inside her. The sound of a chopped-down tree, creaking, falling.

"Cor?" he asked, and his eyebrows drew down. She shook her head. "It's the trucker, isn't it?"

"Johnny—" she started.

"You didn't have to go out there."

"Pomegranate," she said, firm, and crossed her arms.

He split it with his chef's knife, and a dribble of red juice wandered across the counter. The seeds were packed in tight, nestled together for warmth or love or safekeeping. They didn't part easy: Johnny had to dig in with two fingers and pry a cluster out. They were translucent when alone, and bruised easily. She held them to the light before popping them in her mouth.

"Sour," she said when she could speak again. Her mouth felt washed-out, astringent. They burned warm all the way down.

"That," Johnny Red said, "is the fruit that trapped a white girl down in Hell at the beginning of the world."

She ran her tongue over her lips. "Now you tell me."

He smiled, lopsided. "White people medicine only works on white people, dontcha know."

"I'm half that," she replied, mild.

Johnny Red sized her up for a moment, a stare that echoed like Aidan the trucker man's but much, much warmer. "Well," he said. "That means half of you is going to be bound three whole

months to me and this town. So better decide if it's the top half
or the bottom."

This time she really did laugh. "Oh, you'd like *that.*"

He waggled his eyebrows again—Groucho Marx had never
had a Dene man's sharp eyebrows, but it worked out—and
leaned over the counter at her. She leaned back a little, shook her
head smiling. "Nuh-uh."

He sighed, overtheatrical, and dusted his palms on his jeans.
They left smears and smudges of red. "What's a guy have to do?"

"Give me a raise," Cora replied, but her lungs had stopped
aching. *Thank you, Johnny Red.* She rolled a green-red oval at him
across the counter. "Next?"

People started showing up come half past seven: fashion-
ably late for a party in Sunrise. Johnny Red took their cash at
the counter and Cora steered them to their tables, each stacked
with the three-course menu they'd done in two shades of blocky
handwriting. It was fresh veg and mangoes, orange juice not
from a can; wedges of pineapple cut and perched on scratched
plastic glasses. There wasn't no pomegranate on it; either Johnny
Red hadn't found a use for it in time or he just didn't plan on
sending the whole town to white-man Hell.

Nate Okpik brought his fiddle, and Daisy Blondin her drum,
and by eight the whole place was hopping, Johnny slinging
plates as fast as he could. Cora dodged the odd dancer, coffeepot
and empty soup bowls balanced, rock-certain she wasn't getting
no smoke break tonight.

People streamed in and out, took seats, moved chairs, left
them for other tables; nobody sat alone. Nobody was *quiet.* She
noticed, then, the little puddle of silence at the corner table; the
little draft of cold air.

Aidan the bird-eyed trucker was hunched alone over a menu.

He was pale, even for a sick man—a sick half-white man with
a crack on the head the size of a trailer. He looked up, hunting-
hawk quick, and saw her. Two spots of red bloomed in his face:
frozen, helpless embarrassment. She reached out to steady herself
and caught the handle of the coffeepot, waitress's self-defence.
There was no pretending she hadn't seen him. No turning away.

She approached the table, holding the pot out like a shield.
"Coffee?"

"Sure," he mumbled, tilting his head away.

She poured. The stream of coffee arced into the cup: it only
trembled a little, only spilled a drop. "Sugar's on the table," she
said, unnecessary. "You take milk?"

He shook his head. He still wouldn't look at her. It made the back of her neck prickle in a way that Mike Blondin's too-big smiles never had. "No milk," he said, and fingered the edge of the menu. "This is from my truck?"

Nate Okpik, next table over, turned and grinned broadly over the booth's back. "That's right. You're drinking free tonight."

Aidan's shoulders folded in like a deflated accordion. "Let him be," Cora snapped. *Leave him alone. He's dangerous.*

"Fine, fine," Nate said, big and rumbling and good-natured, and turned back to his wife and boys.

Aidan had retreated even farther into himself, fingers plaited together as if groping for something to hold on to and finding only each other. "Sorry 'bout that," she said, and he flashed a wan, anxious smile. He looked like hell. Who was supposed to be watching him—Magda? Gertie? The man shouldn't have been out of bed.

It'll be better when he's gone, Johnny Red's voice echoed, and she shook her head. *Come off it. Do your job.*

She swallowed, tried to force up a smile. "Get you the special?"

He nodded, lifting his gaze from her knees to her belly, the apron tied snug about it. A whisper of chill wind wandered across her hip.

"Cor?" Johnny Red's voice rose sharp and tense across the floor. She looked up and he was right behind the lunch counter, ladle clenched in his hand like a weapon. "Need you over here, please."

Cora shivered with relief and steered back across the restaurant. The muscles of Johnny's face eased like she'd just walked back off a highway median. Behind him, over at table thirteen, Georgie Fiddler watched them and frowned.

Grandma Okpik had said Johnny had a bit of the medicine once, back when he'd rolled into town on the Tuesday Greyhound with nothing but a few changes of clothes and a set of knives that'd make your hair stand up until you found out they were for the kitchen. It wasn't the kind of thing she'd got around to asking about, and this was, unfortunately, not the time for a hearty and extended chat about what it was Johnny Red saw.

"What d'you want to do?" she asked.

Johnny looked over her shoulder; watching him. "I don't know yet," he said, and went to whisper in Mike Blondin's ear.

Aidan No-Last-Name picked at his food; the violent green vegetable soup Johnny Red had fixed for starter was barely below the rim when she came back to refill the coffee. His spoon leaned unused on his napkin. "He your boyfriend?" Aidan asked through a fall of brown hair.

"No," Cora said, though Johnny Red had managed to kiss her in the storeroom once or twice, and she'd not turned away. "He just likes having people to boss around. Everything all right here?"

His hands stilled. He looked up at her. Opened his mouth and shut it again. *He knows*, she realized, sharply. Everything was not at all right.

He's scared.

"Something I can do?" she asked carefully.

His hands were still on the table. He was staring, and she realized, not at her; past her, out the big windows of the Sunrise Restaurant, into the snow. She turned, and on the featureless white there was a splotch of black; low to the ground, ruffled, feathered.

The raven hopped one step, two, in the soft-packed January snow. It twisted its head near backwards, like birds do, and cawed a wicked laugh at the both of them.

Something dropped from its sharp little beak and landed in the snow: long, and thin, and red.

Aidan scrambled up against the back of the booth and *howled*, all the voice of wolves and snuffling bears and winter, eyes big and black and wide, and the cold spiralled out of him. The cold rushed in.

The raven fluttered into the night laughing, its wings snapping like falling trees. The coffeepot slid out of Cora's hand and rang on the black and white tile. Coffee splashed her trousers, her shoes. She flinched back from the window, the raven, the boiling hot liquid on the floor. The fiddle had stopped, and the drum. Every head in Sunrise turned to stare out into the dark.

He took one step towards her. Two.

And ran.

Aidan jostled past her, between tables and chairs, out the oak front doors. "Hey!" she called, slipping in coffee, limping after him. The cold air hit like a knife to the throat. "Wait!" she managed, before she doubled over coughing.

He didn't wait. Coatless, hatless, Aidan ran across the path and to the highway, head down and legs working like all the wickedness in the world was right behind him. His breath misted, a little plume to follow, and then her hip tightened sharp and he was disappearing, farther away. Going, smaller and smaller. Gone.

"Shit!" she said, and the footsteps behind her caught up: Johnny Red and Georgie Fiddler, one after the other, Johnny still with his fat blue oven mitts on.

"Cora," he said, and threw an arm full around her to keep her from falling, or maybe just running any further. "What the hell?"

"He got away. The raven," she said, and burst out again coughing. "It was out here. It dropped something—"

"I felt it," he said. *Felt, not saw.*

"He's scared," she said. "It scared him."

"We need coats," Georgie called, and they picked their way back over the broken snow. Their feet had churned up the bird-tracks.

"It wasn't too far." Her teeth were chattering. She curled out of Johnny's bracing arm and picked her way back to the parking lot: back under the edges of the sodium lights. Nothing. Nothing—

And then the wind rose and ruffled the snow, stirred it up and out and away, and Cora looked down at the smooth brown finger, slowly turning blue in the January snow.

The search party came back cold and empty-handed, and Johnny Red had nothing left over for soup.

"We found Gertie," Jane Hooker said, staring at the specials board and the remains of Tropical Party Night. Her right mitten dangled from a string on her coat sleeve. "She's..."

Mike Blondin swallowed. "We're gonna need to call her nephew."

Bile nudged into Cora's throat. She forced it back. "Oh," Daisy said, and it sounded like all the air had left her lungs forever. Johnny held his coffee filter between thumb and finger for one long moment, turned it around, and crumpled it in his fist.

"I went by Jane's. We got an APB 'bout an hour ago," Georgie Fiddler said, his face sallow and sick. Smudged fax paper fluttered from his left hand, limp as a dead child. "From the Mounties over in High Level."

Cora took the paper. She read it briefly, like a dry goods manifest or a power bill. "Suspicion of murder and—" her voice failed. Johnny Red took the page from her. "Desecration of a corpse?" he finished, both eyebrows up high.

Jane's cheeks were red: bright and hot and burning. The tears in her eyes were probably scalding. "Her fingers were missing," she said, out from somewhere far away. "And her stomach—"

"Hey," Georgie said, and held up one hand. Big Mike Blondin looked like he planned to be sick.

"Wendigo," Johnny Red said quiet, and it cut every voice in the restaurant dead.

Cora felt for her pack, dipped into it with chilly fingers: empty. "Bum a smoke?" she asked Mike Blondin quietly, and he didn't even try to make her give him a smile for it. She rolled it between her fingers like a raven's trophy, held onto it like there was nothing else to hold.

"What do you mean?" Georgie Fiddler said. He was sweating. "Wendigo's a monster. They're made up."

She shook her head. She couldn't explain wendigo to Georgie Fiddler, not now. Jane stepped in smoothly, taking his arm. "Wendigo aren't made up," she said softly. "My grandpa knew one."

"What happened?" Georgie asked.

Jane hesitated. "They found him at the river and shot him down."

"We can't—that's murder. He's a person."

"Not anymore," Fred Tutcho said softly.

Poor Georgie Fiddler looked around the circle for backup; found none. "Maybe he won't come back," he said weakly.

Johnny Red shook his head. "He'll come back." There was no food or shelter for two hundred miles in any direction, and he had no jacket, and he was unarmed. Cora didn't know a whole lot about wendigo, but there were ways in which they were just like people: they wanted above everything to live through the night.

"So what do we do?" Georgie asked.

"We get the shotguns," Jane said, and shoved the restaurant door open, letting in the night.

"He's still a person," Georgie muttered, and the cigarette between Cora's fingers bent and tore.

There were seven shotguns in the town of Sunrise. Six of them worked. The six shotguns and their owners gathered close in the Sunrise Restaurant with the other eighty-three townsfolk crammed in around them. They locked the doors and turned the outside lights on full. Whatever came, if it threw a shadow, they'd see it coming.

Jane and Georgie and Nate and Daisy and Fred Tutcho and Johnny Red stood behind the counter, lining up ammunition.

It was most of it deershot: there weren't no licences to carry for much else in this small a town. "They're hard to kill," Johnny Red said softly; loud enough for Cora to hear where she was pouring hot cocoa into salvaged and washed-up mugs. "You got to shoot and shoot again. Don't stop, even if he's got his hands up. Don't stop 'til he stops moving."

Cora popped one more marshmallow into the cocoa mug and drifted back to the counter, to the always-filling coffeepot. "Have a minute, Johnny?"

He looked down at her with a frown she hadn't seen before; tense, old. Tired. "What's up?"

She glanced around at her people, her family: the Okpiks and Tutchos and Blondins and Hookers and Fiddlers and Johnny Red Antoine from down south in the plains. "Georgie's right," she said. "He's still a person."

"You didn't see what he did to Gertie," Nate said, and she held up a hand, but gently.

"I looked into his eyes," she said, swallowing back the thought of fingers snapped at the bottommost joint, of intestines looped and gnawed, teeth marks like wolves'. "The real ones. And...that's still a person. He's scared." She hesitated, gathered her breath. "This isn't old times, where you could just hunt someone down by the river. The Mounties'll come. They'll have an inquest. And you know what that means."

It'd change Sunrise. Knowing everyone by name, knowing their children. Leaving your door unlocked at night. The way a man like Mikey Blondin was bad, but roll-your-eyes bad, and how people didn't get run out of town or live on welfare or huff rubber cement or sneak liquor before noontime.

It'd change everything.

"He knows something's wrong," she finished, weakly. "He's terrified."

"We could deal with an inquest later," Fred Tutcho said, but his heart wasn't all in. "He's out there, and the kids—"

"You don't want to do this," Cora said, soft. "I will not let no wendigo or man or Raven make me someone I'm ashamed to be."

A moment passed. Fred Tutcho let out a breath. He shook his head.

Johnny Red squinted at her. "So what then?" A real question, not a challenge.

"We heal him up," she said, faltering now. She didn't know what then. She'd never expected them to say yes. "We find a way to drive it out, or keep him tucked away until the Mounties get here. He was raised a white man. It's like as he doesn't know what's happened to him."

Georgie made a little noise of protest. "C'mon, Cor."

She patted his hand, absently. "There's knowing and there's knowing, George."

Johnny Red's shoulders were tight-wound. "Cor," he said. "You don't do medicine."

She didn't, and *Sometimes you don't have to* wouldn't cut no ice with Johnny. Grandma Okpik had been the first and last in Sunrise and she hadn't taught it; this wasn't an old community, where people could say *This is where my father's house sat,* or *Here's a spot cleared by ancestors.* Nobody here passed down traditions. Sunrise had been built, deliberate and slow like a snow dune: people washed up from the highway between north Alberta and the city, smelling the bad coffee, the music, something. The right ones stayed.

"We'll put the word out. Ask for help," she said. "We've gotta try."

Johnny Red looked at her for a long moment, then nodded once, slow.

"All right," Mike Blondin said. "We'll try not to shoot."

"Thank you," Cora said, and went back to washing dishes.

Johnny Red came into the kitchen a few minutes later. He bellied up to the sink beside her and dipped his arms in to the sleeve line. "You thinking something?"

"Yeah," she said. "A bit."

He didn't say anything. He didn't have to.

"You trust me?" she said anyways.

He rinsed a plate. Set it in the rack. "Yeah."

She nodded. "Okay." Behind them was the hum of worried voices; the clink of cutlery both in the sink and outside. Her elbow brushed his as they passed plates and bowls from the battered aluminum sink to the draining board. Water splashed and rustled, and outside, the wind.

Behind it all a sound, faint and creaking, like the chopping of a whitebark pine.

Cora slid her hands out of the water, dusted them gently on the front of her apron. "Going for a smoke," she said to Johnny Red, and walked slow and straight down the little hall past the kitchen that led to the storeroom door.

"She didn't have any left. Wait—" she heard behind her, but she didn't turn around.

When she passed the kitchen counter, she picked up a drying wedge of pomegranate and tucked it into her pocket.

She felt it right away in her kneecaps, her thighs: cramp and twist. The burn of cold so hard it wrapped your body like heat. Storm coming.

She closed the storeroom door behind her cautiously, sharp for any unfamiliar sound. The wind scuttled 'round the corners, wearing the heart out of the buildings inch by creeping inch. She stumbled into her milk crates, swore, and righted the top one before it fell. Plastic scraped plastic, terrifically loud. She let it go with shaking hands.

"Aidan," she said soft. Shifted her weight to her good leg, trying not to feel the burn. "C'mon, I know you're back here."

Something rustled behind the old stacked-up chairs. Silence.

"I can hear your heart," she whispered.

The blow blacked out her vision for two long, falling seconds, and then he was on top of her.

Aidan was sobbing. He wept like an animal, his hips pinning hers, his hands groping for her flailing wrists to hold them down. She tried to push with her leg, but her leg wouldn't work; the hurt turned to paralysis, muscles shutting down, giving up, playing dead. The back of her head felt bitter, bitter cold, and then it was nothing but pain; he must have hit her with something. He slammed her left wrist to the floor, and she gasped. It had only been his bare hands after all.

Too strong.

Oh, hell.

She screamed, and it was tiny; his chest was on hers too, pushing the air out, sinking the chill of every January night she'd ever known down through her ribcage, her bones. She couldn't scream. She couldn't get enough air.

"Why did you say that?" he said, and it took a second before she could make out the words through his shuddering, terrified tears. "Why'd you say it?"

"Say what?" she gasped, and his teeth glinted in the thin light. Man's teeth, not a predator's: dull and blunt and slow. It wouldn't be quick or clean, this. It would hurt like five thousand years of Hell.

"Why'd you say you'd take care of me!" he burst, and his hands were moving wildfire, moving without will; they spread her own hand out, palm up, on the floor. The specks cleared from her vision, and his eyes were black, all pupil, black as a raven's wing. "Nobody can take care of *this*—"

His voice failed. The hands grew steadier, firmer, and she hadn't realized that they were shaking until they weren't; that the look on his face had been the same that Jane Hooker'd worn when she talked about Gertie cut down. Broken in two, like a little child.

And now it was fading into something monstrous. Something not a person anymore.

"Aidan, stay—" she managed, and the smell of wind, the winter-mask that used to be a person's face faltered.

"What?" he whispered, pupils shrinking abrupt and small.

Oh please. A plan. A bit of a plan.

Cora rolled herself hard right and jammed a knee up against his thigh. Those brown man's eyes went wide—wide and betrayed—and his grip broke: just a man's again, weak and changeable, not a monster's anymore. Cora fumbled in her pocket, grabbed, slid out her weapon before the hand came down and smashed her skull against the concrete once, twice, three times.

She held on like it was the only thing left in the world.

There was a raven in the roof, shuffling its feathers, watching the wendigo in Aidan's flesh pry open that hand, lean down close, bare his teeth. Its eyes were bright and staring. It was curiously silent.

The monster growled through Aidan's throat. It flung itself down and bit.

Pain spiked through her fingers: second, middle, ring. They unclenched, unwilling, and then willing, and then she jammed a full wedge of pomegranate into his open mouth.

The seeds crunched between his teeth like bones, like something living. He choked.

She twitched out from under him, wheezing; she couldn't roll anymore, couldn't move right. Her leg was a dead weight, and her head wouldn't lift. There was winter in her lungs, and she couldn't cough it out.

"Once upon a time when the world was young," she forced out, rattle-quick and low, because white-people medicine needed invocations, needed words, "a white girl ate six pomegranate seeds and was trapped down six months in Hell."

His eyes went big. He knew this story, knew it to the bone. He spat, reflexive, and she let slip a grin through the tears. Too late.

"Now you're bound to us," she said. Her vision was blurring. She couldn't see half of him, couldn't see the dark that was from the dark that wasn't. "See all those seeds? Each one's a month. That's how long you're bound to me and this town." His mouth was stained red. Some of it was thin and some thick, drying. Some of it was hers: her hand stung, burned on three flat points on the ridge of each long finger. It'd all stain.

"Stay with me," she said, and cradled her bleeding hand; tried to say it like Grandma Okpik, like medicine, like somebody who loved you. "Stay people."

He opened his mouth, and the moan that came out was terrible, terrible, but not animal. Only the sound of a human being, pushed horrible miles too far.

"Good boy," she whispered, and leaned back against the hard, freezing floor. There were footsteps somewhere outside, footsteps in the hallway she could hear now that the sound of trees falling, wood breaking, living things dying was gone. The raven's eyes regarded her, black on black on black, and then one blink to the next, they were gone.

They broke down the door.

Shadows flicked across her vision: friends and neighbors, friends with guns. "Down!" Jane Hooker was shouting. "Stay *down!*"

"I'm done now," Aidan sobbed, rocking, hands clasped over his ears, mouth torn and bleeding fruit and flesh and saliva. "I'm all done. I want to go *home—*"

"Don't shoot," Cora whispered.

And then Johnny was beside her, gathering her up and calling for Jane, for Georgie, for the doctor from Hay River. She blinked slow and long and his face was above hers, lined with stark terror. "He won't be no trouble," she managed, and Johnny Red looked like he was about to be sick.

"*That* was your plan?" he said.

"He needs a bowl of soup," she told him, cradled lopsided in his arms, and the world went black as wings departing.

She came to in room five of the Treeline Motel, the last set of buildings standing before the end of roots and leaves and life and hope. Sunlight speckled across the ceiling, ice-light, winter-light, and the trees outside swayed quiet, and she was still alive.

She let out a sigh, long and shuddering.

Johnny Red was at her bedside in an instant. "You okay?" he said. His voice was snow-brush soft. He looked like he hadn't slept for at least a day or three.

She licked her lips. Dry. "Who's got the restaurant?" she croaked, and he went for a glass of water. He wet her lips, her bruised throat.

"Nobody," he said, and there was a rawness in it now. "Talk to me."

She stretched, cautiously; nothing broken. Jane Hooker's careful hands would have made sure of it. Her eyes wouldn't quite focus, but that was all right. There were three tidy, thick bandages wrapped about the fingers of her right hand. "I've had worse," she said.

Johnny Red flinched. "Don't tell me that."

His hand slipped down to her good one. Held on. She didn't shake it off.

"He's outside." Johnny's mouth twisted with something: fear, anger, distaste. The edges of a terrible hatred. "Has been all day, and all yesterday too. Crying like a dog."

"How much does he remember?" she asked after a second.

Johnny Red opened his mouth, shut it with a snap. "All of it."

"Did Jane call the Mounties?"

Johnny's expression went even flatter. "Not yet."

Cora leaned back against the soft pillows; heard a half-wendigo voice sobbing, burning, asking *Why did you say that to me? Why'd you say you'd take care—*

"It's gone now," she said. Then hesitated, turned her head to him half an inch. "It is, right?"

Johnny Red's lips pressed together. "Hard to tell. This could just be—" he paused with distaste "—a stronger claim. How long do we have?"

There were a lot of seeds in that pomegranate, nestled together like lovers, like houses perched on the edge of the highway to Hay River. It was past too late to find out how many he'd spit, how many he'd swallowed down. "I don't know," she said. "I guess we'll find out."

He didn't answer. He didn't answer for long enough that she turned her head another agonizing space, and saw him sitting in a chair beside her, elbows on his knees, head buried in his hands.

"The raven left," he said muffled. "Maybe that means something."

It means, she thought, *we're on our own now.*

"How much medicine d'you have?" she asked.

He looked up. There were tears in his eyes: sheer frustration, pain. Relief. "Not enough," he said. "Not half enough to make this safe."

"We'll be fine," she said, faintly.

Johnny Red stood up, all six feet of him, and leaned over her slowly, bracing himself with a hand on the yielding mattress. The kiss he left on her mouth wasn't hard—she was bandaged up too much for hard right now—but it didn't brook no questions.

"You," he said, "are bound to me three months, and next time you *talk* to me about the plan."

She didn't talk back to that.

Johnny Red went to the door, swung the hinges wide. She felt the cold air blow in, cold but not terrible bitter, and heard voices exchanged low, terse, cautious. One set of footsteps faded, and another stepped inside. Shut the door. Moved, soft and tremulous, along the faded carpet runner to the bedside.

The light was so much better now. It had to be past three. Spring coming, eventually.

"Hey," Aidan said, standing two feet away, hands clasped in front of him like they were the only thing in the world to hold; eyes big and brown and human and terrified and whole.

"Hey," she said. "You stayed."

BLACKLIGHT

Michael R. Colangelo

Jacob waits quietly for Atticus to give the signal.

All the details that led to this moment start to come back into focus.

It's a roadmap of regret. A path of bad decisions spurred into reality by worse intentions.

It's a few months ago.

They move into a new apartment well away from the university tenements that crowd the city. He wants to ensure they're far enough away from influences that Sarah could run afoul of prior to finishing her degree. Far enough, but still close enough to all the hangouts so she'll never be bored enough to leave him. It's selfish to contain her so, but he's a first year dropout and there isn't a whole lot waiting for him back home.

He doesn't want to run back that way with his tail between his legs. He doesn't want to lose his girlfriend to a better marriage prospect.

Despite his best efforts though, he puts in too many hours waiting tables to keep tabs on her every movement.

Soon, she's taking a night class in medieval pantomime. She says it's so she can add something smart to the 'Hobbies/Interests' section of her resume. 'Fucking' and 'Smoking' don't qualify at most employment centers.

One night he goes with her. He wants to see exactly what goes on at Medieval Pantomime 101.

That's where they find Shelly.

Shelly eventually leads them to Atticus.

The building where they hold classes is one of the older campus buildings. It's from before they added the east library wing and the newer housing tenements. It's composed of ornate stonework and crumbling gargoyles. It's crawling ivy and ancient Greek pillars. Inside, it's dingy and cavernous. The ivory walls are stained yellow with age. The elevator rattles fearsomely and crawls from floor-to-floor at a terrible, ice-layered pace.

Classes are held on the fifth floor inside an old office room. It's cold and drafty, with rattling windows and a thin, worn carpet covering the floor.

There are a few plastic chairs, a vending machine, and racks upon racks of costumes.

The costumes are nightmarish parodies of humans, animals, vegetables, and all hybrids in between. All are grossly exaggerated in bright felt, sewn buttons, and frozen papier-mâché faces. They sit forever in the stasis of whatever emotion their creator has seen fit to shape them into.

Jacob sits in class and listens half-heartedly to a thin woman in a cat suit. She reviews the finer points of blocking and emote techniques. He yawns. She stresses the importance of unwritten improvisation. Everybody else is taking studious notes.

Some of them ask questions. Most want to know when they'll be allowed to don the ghastly costumes that surround them.

At the end of the night, they're paired up and given an assignment. They are to return to class the following week with five emotions that a pair of actors can relay to the audience without sound.

Sarah chooses Shelly out of her pool of classmates.

Rather, she gravitates to her, and Jacob can see why.

Shelly is thin and quiet, and pale. She lurks at the social perimeters of the group, but not quite beyond them enough to draw her peers' ire by her detachment. She acts like she stands apart by choice rather than natural selection or mandatory exclusion. She's very Breakfast Club, and it's exactly where Sarah would like to be.

Later in the week, he's at the apartment when Shelly comes over. He stretches out on the couch and watches the baseball game with the sound turned low.

Sarah and Shelly sit on the other length of the couch at a ninety-degree angle to him with notepad and pen. They talk quietly between one another, trying to think of five emotions for next week's class.

All three of them drink copious amounts of wine, stolen from the bar where Jacob works.

They come up with four emotions – anger, greed, pride, and love. Then they argue over the finer points of green in the emotional sense.

They badger Jacob for a fifth emotion.

"You covered three of the deadly sins," he says. "I'm trying to remember the other four ... sloth and avarice?"

"Avarice is the same as greed," Shelly tells him.

"Sloth then. Laziness."

"How are two people supposed to act that out?"

There's annoyance in her tone. He's letting her down in front of her new friend. Again.

Jacob shrugs.

"I have one," Shelly says. "Lust."

He's unsure of how to respond. From the look on Sarah's face, she's unsure too.

Moments later though, Sarah drops the question with a tense mix of unease and amusement in her voice. "What does that look like?"

Shelly shows her.

She forces her legs open with a grin.

When she's finished showing her, she shows her again.

This time though, it's Jacob gripping Sarah's thighs with sweaty and trembling hands.

They practice first with their fingers, then with their tongues, and finally with the empty wine bottles strewn about the carpet.

When it's over, Shelly goes home.

The pair sit on the couch and Jacob feels a slight tug in his mind. It's like it has been hooked on a fishing line and it's being pulled somewhere.

The feeling is strong enough that he won't engage Sarah in small talk.

She must feel the same way. She says nothing and watches the silent television. Her eyes are glassy and ringed with dark circles.

He doesn't see Shelly again for a few weeks. Sarah is reluctant to talk about her or pantomime class. She changes the subject when he inquires.

She does mention that they did well on the assignment. They netted a score of eighty out of one hundred. Twenty points deducted for only having four of five emotions presented, instead of the required five.

When he gets another night off work, he goes down to the building to sit in on class. They're in the process of learning the four primary outfits of the original school of Greek pantomime. He barely pays attention to the class, or Sarah, for that matter. Instead, he steals glances at Shelly.

In turn, she pretends not to notice him.

After class, they get together in the hallway, and Shelly tells them both she has someone she wants them to meet.

They take the elevator up instead of down, to the sixth floor. Here, the electricity has been cut off and the floor is empty and abandoned.

In a dusty classroom stacked with pillars of old chairs and school desks, Shelly introduces them to Atticus for the first time.

He sits in a corner, positioned in a square of dirty streetlight that filters through the window. He's 40 pounds of white pancake-colored plastic. Cross-legged, stoned, and grinning into the void.

He reminds Jacob of a very precious doll. It's a mistake that Sarah has already made.

He can smell the adoration on her. It burns beneath the perfume and makeup and heaves between her breasts.

Shelly presents Atticus with a smile and they perform before him. She's forceful and rough with them both. Jacob gets angry and replies with a forcefulness of his own. It leaves bruises on their thighs and welt marks across their backs.

Afterwards, they sit beaten and quiet inside a coffee shop across the street. The big picture window beside their table is spattered in rain. The city outside distorts through the rain as it drizzles down the glass.

When they're ready to leave, Shelly winks at them with a black eye. "He likes you, I think. I really think he does."

A wave of ice washes over Jacob.

Sarah, on the other hand, seems ecstatic and impressed.

In hindsight, it's a pinpoint moment. It's right before reality completely melts away and everything slides furiously downhill.

The three speak little, and Atticus doesn't speak at all.

They spend the next few weeks meeting at the back room on the sixth floor of the university building and performing before Atticus.

Once their routine is set, they sit in the coffee shop afterwards and listen to the tinny radio music that plays behind the counter.

One night, Shelly makes a suggestion. Or rather, she relays Atticus's first command to them. "He wants a fifth."

"Where are we going to find a fifth, Shelly?"

She shrugs and smiles. Her face is thin and narrow. Her mouth is wide. Jacob doesn't like the way her teeth take up so much of her features. She looks odd and distorted. She looks grotesque.

"There are lots of bars. Lots of students."

"We're going to get caught. Or he's not going to like who we bring him."

Shelly shrugs and returns to her coffee.

Jacob takes the day off work and rents a van. They remove its license plates and go barhopping all night until they find someone they agree on. Jacob can't remember his name, but he's thin and slender and wears a beret. More importantly, he's pretty drunk when they find him, and alone.

Sarah and Shelly lure him with laughter and brushes of their tits along his arms. They get him down the street and into the rental van.

They take him to Atticus.

Everything makes Jacob sick.

All the beer sloshing in his stomach makes him sick.

The flickering overhead lamps make him sick.

The pounding music that blares through the thinly insulated walls makes him sick.

And moments ago, he has gotten blood on his hands. It's splattered across his bare chest.

Sarah and Shelly huddle naked in the corner.

That's when Atticus laughs. His short staccato notes echo through the damp air and drop the temperature in the room by a whole degree. The room seems to tilt with spinning vertigo.

Shelly vomits and Sarah screams. Both girls look terrified.

He isn't sure if it's Atticus's voice permeating his subconscious, or just the looks on Sarah and Shelly's faces, but he feels exhilarated and relived.

Found.

He's ecstatic that Atticus has found something too. His voice.

So ecstatic, in fact, that he doesn't even hesitate when Atticus orders him to kill both girls.

He begins.

Atticus continues to stare off into the room's darkened corners.

His face is a mask of frozen static.

He isn't even watching them.

THE DEAFENING SOUND OF SLUMBER

Simon Strantzas

"People are no longer sleeping well," Doctor Wy opined late one Thursday night during his regular telephone call to the sleep lab. Fisher yawned as he listened. "As a rule, they like things that are neither difficult nor bad and right now the state of the world couldn't be worse. The stock market, wars, crime; it all adds up to an existence that seems increasingly horrible and without end. What follows is worry, and with more worry comes less sleep. It's provable, and it's the basis for all my research."

But research was not Fisher's concern; he was just happy to be employed in such a downward economy. Doctor Wy spent little time at the lab, preferring to continue his work back at the university where he could see patients and evaluate their continuing candidacy for the program. Fisher had not seen the doctor in weeks — which was a relief. Though he found the end-goal fascinating, and was thrilled to play a small part in its hoped-for success, Fisher knew that without Doctor Wy's watchful presence he would be free to slip his headphones on and enjoy the sound of white noise rustling in his ears. It was the only sound he found soothing, and it helped block out those that he didn't.

Fisher had been lucky to find a lab located in a quiet part of the city, but he'd always been lucky at finding new jobs or places to stay, even when far from home. He didn't know why it came so easily for him. He imagined it was because he refused to worry about things he couldn't change. What was the point? Rather, he preferred to hope for the best, and more often than not the best found him...though not always right away. The sleep lab, for instance, despite being far from the hubbub and the noise of the major thoroughfares, was in a rundown district full of boarded-over buildings. Across the street, an urban renewal project promised changes in the near future, but until then it was merely another construction site from which emanated the grating noise of work—noise that Fisher, due to his condition, could not tolerate. Why, he wondered, did the work have to be done so late in the day, every day, and why had it been going on for so long? At times, the progress seemed so slow as to be nonexistent. Perhaps it was a manpower issue. After all, he never saw more than two people on the site at any time, though they made enough noise for twenty. It did nothing but add to Fisher's anxieties. At least Doctor Wy's lab was soundproofed, and the din of the outside world did not carry through its brick walls. The promised quiet was the biggest motivation to accept Doctor Wy's offer. As the doctor said, "Though your level of auditory anxiety is low, what better place is there to work than with the sleeping, overnight when the world is at its quietest? The night shift requires someone with a positive attitude, and from what I've seen you should not have any problems adapting." There was no arguing with that logic, Fisher thought, and willingly signed on. A position that kept the noise he encountered to a minimum was ideal, though he found it strange that he was asked to keep the door locked at all times. "It's a private laboratory, after all," Doctor Wy said. "The patients are at their most vulnerable."

Fisher was ostensibly in charge of the sleep lab, but recognized he was little more than another technician, hardly different from his partner Rose. She was younger than he by at least a decade, not to mention fifty pounds heavier, yet she was also the parent of a daughter already in that netherworld between child and teenager. She showed him photographs one after the other the first time they'd met, all the while telling stories of her daughter's exploits. He did his best to listen and appreciate them if only because of the joy it obviously brought her.

The lab was devoted to research, more specifically Doctor Wy's research, and as such was smaller than most buildings of its kind. Doctor Wy's lab consisted of three rooms, and even then he wanted no more than one occupied at a time. His testing had entered a new phase and he feared the reactions patients might experience were they introduced to one another. "Once a patient is exposed to information, even erroneous information, about his or her treatment, it's inevitable that the patient will suddenly believe they too are experiencing similar results. Again, this behavior is well-documented." Doctor Wy thus normally ran his tests with only three patients on a regular basis, and each was given a different day to come in. Great pains were taken to schedule them in such a way that no trace of one remained before the next arrived.

"I have to admit, it's a bit sad; we speak to them only long enough to put them to sleep, then stare at them all night long. At the end of it all, they wake up puffy-faced and then disappear without a word. I'm not even sure sometimes Doctor Wy's treatment is helping."

"Does it look like it's helping to you?" Rose asked. Fisher crossed his arms and leaned back from the console.

"I don't know. He assures me everything is normal and that the tests are producing the expected results, but I can't deny that no one *seems* any better. At least, not to me."

"If anything," Rose said," they're *worse*. We've already lost one of the sleepers, and the rest don't look like they'll make it much longer. Especially Sanderson."

Eric Sanderson was the first patient included in Doctor Wy's trials. He suffered from a form of central apnea that kept him from sleeping more than a few hours at a time. Since Fisher and Rose had met him, his appearance had deteriorated considerably. His once ruddy skin had turned grey, his complexion sallow. He was thinner, yet softer, so much so that Fisher had trouble keeping him in focus.

"What's Wy hoping to find?" Rose asked. "Sanderson is a walking corpse. Though, I suppose they *all* are, aren't they?"

"Apparently, the doctor is closer than ever to a breakthrough. He expects it at any time."

Rose snorted.

"Do you wonder sometimes if it's worth it? Look at everything that's going on. Recessions, Depressions... What's the point in dealing with people who can't sleep when all of *that* is happening?"

"You know what Doctor Wy would say: it's specifically *because* that's going on that they're being kept awake. He dreams of finding some way to ease people's minds about it."

Air hissed through Rose's teeth.

"Let me tell you a story about the way things are," she said. "My daughter is a good girl. Quiet, maybe a bit too shy, but she goes to school every day and works hard. There are two girls in her class who want to make her life hell. They push her around and taunt her and the teachers turn a blind eye. It's like they don't care. So you tell me, Fish: how much sleep *does* everyone need before that sort of thing goes away? How much, because I'd like to know."

"Please, not so loud." Fisher could feel his heart racing, pounding to get out of his chest. "Can't we talk about something else?" Rose though didn't seem sympathetic to his plight.

"Sometimes I wonder if you *can't* hear this stuff or you *won't*."

Fisher wasn't sure what she meant; he suspected it was the blood rushing to his head that made things so cloudy.

Before leaving for home the next morning, Fisher bid goodbye to the patient from Room Three. Martin Breem had been coming to the lab for a few weeks, but he already looked as though he'd been there longer. His thin beard had become patchy, and he complained about ulcers since taking his medication. The polysomnograph reported an increased level of brain activity, something that Doctor Wy was quite interested in. "The patient reports night terrors, yet I see no mention of them on your reports, Fisher."

"The polysomnograph is still a bit glitchy, Doctor Wy, and I wasn't sure about the results. I did a visual inspection at the time to confirm things but he looked fine. He was sleeping soundly and barely moved. Is that odd?"

"Nothing is odd in a trial, only statistically relevant or not. We'll know soon enough, I hope."

Yet Rose remained concerned.

"I don't think he'll make it to the end of the experiment, Fish. Have you taken a look at him? Those bruises don't look like the result of Wy's testing."

"I'm sure it will be all right. He's still getting used to things. They can't all be like Sanderson, can they?"

"No, thankfully. Still, he looks like he's falling apart right in front of us. I've tried to ask him about it but he won't say a word, and I'm pretty sure he wasn't entirely sober when he came in last week. Seriously, I don't have a clue where Wy picked him up."

Fisher looked at his watch. If he didn't go, he'd be stuck in the morning rush hour. The *noisy* morning rush hour.

"I wouldn't worry about it," he said.

"No, you wouldn't, would you?"

Two evenings later, while Fisher was running a repair sequence on the polysomnograph, looking for the glitch he knew was there, he heard Rose unlock the front door. He looked up to see Eric Sanderson wander into the lab with a pained look on his face. His eyes were blank and wide, as though he was unfamiliar with the surroundings. Fisher stood, brushed off his hands, and approached the older man, but Sanderson shrank away. Rose shrugged her shoulders in bafflement.

"Mister Sanderson, are you all right?"

It was as though Fisher's voice had blown the cobwebs from Sanderson's mind; the older man turned and Fisher saw recognition flicker in those bloodshot eyes.

"I'm sorry. I don't know where my head was. I haven't been feeling myself."

"It's possible it's a reaction to the dose. Have you mentioned it yet to Doctor Wy?"

Sanderson smiled sheepishly. "I figured it would sort itself out."

"These are drug trials, Mister Sanderson. Things *don't* sort themselves out. I'm going to have Rose make a note on your report, but you should talk to Doctor Wy during your next session."

He smiled again and nodded and Rose's words started to replay in his mind: when would Doctor Wy's trials be over? His subjects were looking exponentially worse each passing day. It was true Sanderson was sleeping longer, but the graphs were reporting more unusual activity than a simple glitch could account for, and Sanderson's appearance had taken an impossible turn for the worse. Fisher knew intellectually that the trials needed to be completed, and he had every faith Doctor Wy's research would prove beneficial, but Rose continued to question it. He wished there were some way to stop her, but the only thing he could think to do was put on his headphones and pipe more white noise into his skull. At least it quieted the repairs that had resumed across the street.

Rose led Sanderson away to Room One for prep while Fisher finished the maintenance on the polysomnograph. It had never functioned properly and he had yet to determine why. He'd reinstalled the software numerous times without effect, and at one point the system was crashing so often that an entire week's worth of data was lost. Yet Doctor Wy was strangely unconcerned when Fisher reported it. "There's nothing to worry about," the doctor said; "It's early enough that we can sacrifice some data. Still, let me send someone to have a look." A few days later, Fisher was surprised to find two thuggish men with shrill East European accents at the lab's door claiming Doctor Wy had sent them. The men remained in the office for hours while

Fisher and Rose prepared Room Three for Martin Breem's next session. Fisher began to feel concerned as the time for Breem's session drew closer and he still had no access to the control room. It wasn't until the patient arrived that he and Rose discovered the men had already gone without saying a word. "I'm sure there was a good reason," Fisher found himself trying to explain to a disbelieving Rose, but he too had difficulty with it, especially once the polysomnograph began to spit lines of black code across the console. A reboot of the entire network restored functionality, but only temporarily. Still, that time, Fisher would rather have dealt with the code than the crashing. At least with the former they could continue to work in some fashion.

After attaching the sensor wires to Sanderson's head and body, Rose closed the door to the room and then looked through its tiny window to make sure everything was in place. She then returned to the control room to join Fisher.

"He's ready to go," she said. "How are things on this end?"

Fisher entered data into the central console and tested the microphone. He walked Sanderson through a short series of exercises to test and calibrate the sensors. Then Fisher called up Room One's video camera. It had been outfitted with a light-gathering lens to boost the signal and give them a better understanding of how well the patient slept and what he or she did during surges in the graphed activity. It showed Sanderson lying on the bed covered in circular sensors, his sagging arms behind the back of his neck. He was looking straight up, his mouth stretched wide in mid-yawn. The lens gave the black and white image an otherworldly look, overly-heightened and enhanced, but when Fisher looked closer he saw a dark cloud over Sanderson's head, obscuring it like some dark halo.

"Is there dirt on the camera?" Rose asked, squinting at the obstruction. It was as though her words caused it to wriggle across the screen. Fisher hoped Rose had not noticed how startled he'd been by the movement.

"It's probably a fly trapped in the room."

"Should we do something?"

Fisher considered for a moment.

"Doctor Wy says we shouldn't stress the patients out once they've taken their medication. If it's still there once he falls asleep, you can go in and shoo it off the lens."

Rose nodded and looked back at the monitor.

"Hey," she said. "It's gone already."

Fisher wondered though how long it would take to return. They *always* returned eventually.

Sleep labs are funny things, Fisher mused, sitting behind the console filling out his daily reports. One would imagine no place quieter, and yet it still was not enough. Needles scratched across paper, computer consoles beeped when processes were complete, telephones rang to ensure the work was progressing normally; each cast a ripple of noise that barely registered on its own, but *en masse* they caused tempestuous waves in his calm. If he could, Fisher would have worn his noise-cancelling headphones throughout his shift to block out all but the direst sounds and communications, but it was impossible. Instead, he had to suffer the tumult and recognized that as far as jobs went it was the one most suited to him. He'd grown used to most of the noises, and he had managed to suppress the amount of anxiety they inflicted on him to a background level that, if not ideal, was at least manageable. Rose, on the other hand, was far more disruptive, and there was little he could do to quiet her. He *liked* Rose as much as he could, and he kept hoping she'd eventually come to understand his affliction, but nothing stopped her from taking any opportunity to speak to him. Her words were like flying insects that buzzed in his ear until he paid them attention.

"Did I ever tell you what I did?" she asked him. The sentence seemed to have started much sooner in her head.

"What do you mean?"

"About my daughter? About those bullies? I don't think you'd approve," she said, impishly. "Normally, I wouldn't have done anything in case I caused more problems for her, you understand, but it was clear that none of the teachers cared that those bullying girls were stepping up their attacks. Something needed to be done. So I did it."

"You confronted them?" Fisher tried to picture Rose on the school grounds, threatening two children. "I suppose they were terrified?"

Here, Rose's proud smile faltered and she turned back to the medical histories she had been sorting for Doctor Wy. "No, they weren't. They weren't frightened at all."

"What were they then?"

"Nothing. They were nothing. Their eyes were cold and black and empty. And the noises those girls made—"

A rapid banging interrupted her. The noise was so loud and sharp it drove cold sparks along Fisher's body like an electrical current. His tongue was bleeding from where he bit it but his teeth would not stop chattering. Rose however looked unfazed.

"There's someone at the door," she said.

Through squinted lids Fisher saw a pair of shadows move across the windows at the front of the lab.

"Find out who it is," he said, hands across his ears, "and get them to stop."

Rose sighed and picked up something Fisher didn't see from the desk. She looked back at him, holding up her keys, before shaking her head again. He looked over his shoulder at the camera footage of Sanderson's test. The display showed the patient lying motionless, the graph lines on the console barely moving. Thankfully he had not awakened.

At the door Rose spoke to someone who stood just out of sight. Fisher hazarded uncovering his ears, but though the banging had ceased it had been replaced by the drowning noise of construction that the open door permitted. The mere sight of the unlocked door unnerved Fisher; he felt the dread of a half-forgotten nightmare squeezing his chest, and took a step forward to see who stood there hidden. The sight of Martin Breem jittering into view was not a relief.

"You shouldn't be here," Rose said, following Breem inside. "Wednesdays are your day. You have to leave or you'll ruin—" Rose's voice faltered as she saw the dark bruises running down Breem's arms. It was clear the man had been crying; his whole demeanor radiated weakness and hopelessness. He looked at Fisher as the words tumbled out.

"My ulcers are back, and I haven't slept in weeks. There's something really wrong. I can *feel* it."

"Mister Breem, you know we can't have you in here."

"Why?"

"Because the experiment will be compromised," said Fisher, "and that compromises everyone."

Breem began to claw at his face. "Don't you get it? Don't you see what he's doing? Oh, God, I thought maybe you'd be different, but *you're all the same*." He dropped to his knees and started sobbing. Fisher looked at Rose who quickly mimicked downing a drink.

Fisher checked his watch. What were they going to do with Breem? The night was barely at its halfway point and the Sanderson trial could not be interrupted.

"Help me get him to Room Three, Rose; at least until he sobers up."

"But didn't Wy say—"

"I know what he said, but what choice do we have? We can't put him back on the streets like this. Look at him."

The two of them carried the weeping Breem to the empty room furthest from Sanderson. From that room Fisher knew it was impossible to hear anything in the next. Fisher himself had taken refuge there when the noise in the lab became too much for him, and yet once he and Rose carried Breem in, the drunken man stopped crying and looked dazed-eyed at the intervening wall.

"What—who's there?"

"Nothing to worry about, Mister Breem. Just rest and when you feel better we'll get you some breakfast."

Martin nodded slowly, then hiccoughed and lay down on his side to face the intervening wall, hugging his bruised arms to his chest.

"I tried," he said, just as Fisher and Rose were about to leave. He did not move as he spoke. "I tried to see the doctor for help, but I couldn't find him. He wasn't there."

"I'm sure you just missed him," Rose said.

"No, he wasn't *there*. There was no office. It was like he'd never *been* there. It was empty. Why wasn't he there?"

"I just spoke with Doctor Wy this evening," Fisher offered. "He's *definitely* still there. You must have gotten off on the wrong floor. Now, go to sleep, please."

They waited, but Martin Breem said nothing more.

Once outside the room Fisher could hear the telephone ringing, and its soft trill immediately put his teeth on edge. He winced and waited for Rose to answer it. She did so with a put-upon sigh, then after a lazy moment listening pushed a button and handed the receiver to Fisher. "It's Wy. He's checking in. Again."

"Hello, Doctor Wy."

"Who's in the lab tonight?"

Fisher hesitated. "Pardon?" How could he already know about Breem?

"Which patient is there tonight?"

"Oh, um...It's Sanderson." He looked at Rose but her expression was inscrutable.

"Good, good. I have Sanderson on a new permutation of the drug. I'm hopeful he sleeps through the night on this one."

"He may, but he looks awful. Tonight his skin—"

"A side-effect, nothing more. Once it's working I'll worry about fine-tuning it. How long has he been asleep?"

"About two hours."

"And how are his readings?"

Fisher tabbed through the consoled software until he found the sensor readings.

"A little more erratic than usual but still within the normal range. He's in REM right now."

"Good. Watch him closely and report anything new to me at once. I have strong hopes this configuration will be the key."

Fisher hung up the telephone. Rose shook her head; he already knew what she was thinking.

The bulk of the nights in the lab were spent monitoring the polysomnograph, which recorded not only the subjects' heart rate but brain activity as well. The results were recorded in a series of jagged lines across the bottom of the console display, and Fisher was able to mark off any anomalies that he noticed. Despite the signs Doctor Wy warned him about he had never seen anything out of the ordinary, and as a result spent much of his time catching up on his reports and charting previous nights' sessions. He had to match the audio and video footage with the graphs and mark where any changes in one were reflected in the other. It was simply a matter of adding flags to the graph each time something occurred, and then noting an explanation in the supplied field. The work was tedious but quiet, and as he did it Rose often spent her time cleaning the remaining two rooms and preparing them for their next occupant. She was hampered by Breem's presence though in Room Three, and her nervous pacing put Fisher on edge.

"I'm going to have to wash that bedding again. It probably stinks now."

"I'm sure it will be okay," Fisher said. "It's only for tonight. The room would have been empty anyway."

"It *does* seem a waste of space to be testing them all one at a time. I can't believe Wy doesn't think we can't handle even two at once."

"It's not that we can't handle them," he said. "It's that Doctor Wy doesn't want them in contact with each other. He says it will taint the experiment. I don't think he wants them discussing their symptoms."

"Do you think that's it, though? That that's the reason?"

"What other reason could there be?"

She shrugged her shoulders.

They both turned at the sound of something falling outside the control room, but as Fisher recoiled Rose stood and walked out to see what had happened. There was a shadow briefly across the doorway but no doubt it was Rose's own. Nonetheless it took Fisher's heart a few moments to stop racing. As it did so Rose returned to the control room.

"Well I can't see anything out there. Maybe those guys across the street dropped something outside?"

"Possibly," Fisher said.

There was a pause.

"Hm. That's weird," Rose said. "The camera in Room One isn't working."

Fisher walked over to the console and tried to call the room's details up but when he hit the command to display the video feed the picture was black. Fisher checked the connections; the feed was good—the camera was sending information properly but the computer wasn't receiving it.

"Try switching to the other rooms," Rose said.

Fisher tabbed through Room Two's and Three's feeds and saw the ghostly image of a made bed and then of one unmade and slept in. Back to Room One, there was nothing.

"That *is* strange," Fisher said, leaning closer. "If the cameras weren't working, we'd get an error. That fact alone—"

Rose's finger pointing to the screen interrupted him.

"Did you see that?"

"What?"

"*That*! Look!"

Fisher did look, and at first didn't see anything in the black display. Then, glimpses of something indistinct appeared faintly in the darkness.

Fisher scratched his head. He'd never seen a camera fail that way before. Then, the darkness parted further and Fisher saw a strange shadow in the room. It stood still, hovering over Sanderson. Something about its shape niggled at the back of Fisher's mind, something that coiled the anxiety in the small of his back, and when it sprung he had to cycle through the video feeds once more to confirm his fears. The bed in Room Three was unmade, but there was no one occupying it.

"Breem is in with Sanderson," he said.

Rose ran to the door while Fisher tried to study the readings. The screen of the polysomnograph was flickering wildly, drawing thin blue and red lines across the entire width of the display as rows of white corrupting code scrolled upwards. "I don't understand," was all Fisher could think to say, his brain tripping over the incomprehensible events.

"Fish! Come here!"

Fisher went to the door and saw Rose standing by Room One, looking through its tiny window.

"Rose, what's happening in there?"

She struggled for words. "It's—I can't—"

Fisher raced over and lightly pushed her aside to look through the window, but he too struggled to comprehend what he saw. Thick black smoke covered the ceiling, spewing from the unconscious Sanderson's gaping mouth. It billowed out in waves and continuously rose to join the cloud amassed above that was slowly circling the room. There was a faint humming noise but Fisher couldn't be sure he wasn't imagining it. Beneath the darkness stood the muttering Breem, oblivious to the blackness creeping downward.

"We need to get him out of there," Fisher said, desperately trying to make sense of what he was seeing. "Doctor Wy never wanted them so close to each other."

"Why not? What's happening?"

"I don't know. We need to get him out of there now and worry about the rest later." Fisher put his hand on the doorknob and then recoiled. It was vibrating. Rose cupped her hands and looked through the window in the door.

"Hurry, I think he's having a seizure!" she said, and opened the door.

There was a drone as though insects were swarming. The sound pierced Fisher's head, the sensation like knives cutting through his skull. Rose ran into the room toward Breem, who had fallen to his knees and was rocking, releasing choked moans. Fisher covered his ears and called Rose back but she didn't seem to hear him. Above them the dark cloud swirled faster, swelling and contracting as though it were breathing. From that darkness split two protrusions like thick fingers; they slowly stretched toward the floor behind Rose while she held Breem's shaking body. As she turned to Fisher, screaming something he couldn't hear, the darkness behind her began to solidify and take shape. Fisher yelled and frantically pointed to where the two figures were forming but she didn't understand. The shapes were barely four feet tall, thin and childlike, and as they reached their arms toward her the cloud descended further, the storm brewing. Breem's lips moved as though he were silently incanting, each word causing further tumult above. Fisher screamed "Get out

of there!" as loud as he could, louder than he thought was possible—so loud his panic flared white-hot. But it came too late.
Rose looked behind her, and everything slowed down in Fisher's
mind. The two figures reached her and when they lay their dark
hands upon her there was a bright flash like lightning sparking and it blinded Fisher for an instant, leaving an after-image
burned on his retina like a photograph. He saw laughing children, but the laughter was without warmth, and as he blinked
the image away he saw those two dark shapes fall apart, disintegrating in thousands of tiny shadows like flying insects. She was
gone in an instant, and he saw remnants of what she had been as
they bobbed along the surface of the dark swirling clouds above.
Then they sank out of sight forever.

Fisher shook as he closed the door. He could still see through
the window though, see the cloud churning as its turbulence
settled. Sanderson had ceased moving as the endless spewing of
darkness filled the room. In the shrinking space near the floor,
Breem continued his inaudible speech, bent as though in prayer.

Fisher paced, his hands over his ears to block the noise but
it didn't stop his heart from racing furiously, the pounding filling his head. He didn't know what to do or understand what he
had witnessed; Rose had disappeared so quickly, so impossibly,
that it left him numb. The droning noise worsened the sensation,
creeping through the bones in his hands to fill his head with
rough cotton. Everything was dull and out of sync, as though he
had fallen asleep and in his dreams was no longer part of what
he surveyed. Fisher saw Breem through the door's tiny window,
saw his face turning a deep crimson. The muscles in the man's
throat stood out as though he were commanding the darkness
above to stop. Fisher almost believed it was working. The spin
of the dark cloud orbiting the room slowed as the effort exerted
by Breem increased. His entire face shook, beads of sweat running down his cheeks. Breem poured every breath out to stop
the thing, and as his kneeling body began to waver the tumul-
tuous rolling of the cloud began to ebb. Soon it came to a full
stop, settling upon the ceiling like a calm pond, and then Breem
collapsed onto Sanderson's bed in a heap. Fisher took hold of the
door handle to retrieve Breem and Sanderson's lifeless bodies.
If he could get them to safety...but before Fisher could open the
door streams of dark shapes swarmed from the cloud above and
with them came a sickening noise that filled Fisher with terror.
Everything the darkness touched was consumed in a flurry of
bright flickering sparks. The electronics in the room were the

first to go, devoured in seconds, then the stands and wires. Fisher removed his hands from his ears to bang on the door, but the sound paralysed him with instant dread. There was nothing he could do but watch as the finger-like projections of darkness descended on the unconscious body of Breem. There was a bright flash and he was gone. Left behind was an image burned into Fisher's retina of Breem being joyfully beaten by a crowd of leering strangers.

Fisher's head throbbed. He didn't know what to do. He couldn't take his eyes from the thundercloud in the window, terror weighing his limbs down. There was a ringing in his head he feared might be his brain about to burst until he recognized the sound. He managed to turn away from the small window and quickly made his way back to the control room. The telephone there continued to ring, as though waiting patiently for his return. He shook as he picked up the receiver and held it to his ear. He did not speak. He did nothing but listen and stare at the door to Room One and at the small dark portal in its frame.

"Fisher? Are you there? This is Doctor Wy."

Fisher's eyes began to water.

"There's been—We had—"

"What's happened, Fisher? Is there something wrong? You were supposed to call me."

"There wasn't time. It's Rose and—and Sanderson. He's—and Breem, he—"

"*Breem* was there?" Doctor Wy's voice shook as he spoke. "Did he come into contact with Sanderson? I told you to not let anyone in." Fisher couldn't say anything. All he could hear was the sound of a windstorm, and that terrible droning that could no longer be blocked. "Fisher, you must listen to me now. The experiment is a failure. I should have known better; some things cannot be controlled. It's my mistake and I have to clean it up. Stay there; don't do anything. I'm going to make a call and send someone right over."

"But," Fisher was dizzy from confusion; "I don't understand. What's happening?"

"There's a darkness, Fisher, that is slipping into the world through the dreams of the weak. A force of corruption, of entropy, that is taking this world apart to feed itself. I thought —naively it seems—that there might be some way to control it, to slow it, perhaps even reverse it. But I see that was a mistake. I thought I could plan for everything, but one cannot plan to thwart entropy. By its very nature it's unpredictable. I only hope

I can stop this in time. Whatever you do, stay there until some-one arrives. I—I'm sorry about this, Fisher."

But Fisher could not hear those words. They were over-whelmed by the sound of droning. He dropped the receiver to the floor and tried to rub the pain from his temples. "It's okay," he chanted. "It's going to be okay. Doctor Wy is sending someone." On the desk were his headphones and he put them on, desperate for anything that would block the noise from getting inside his head. He turned the volume of the white noise machine up as far as it would go but it was no use. It did nothing to mask that hor-rible droning. Fisher threw the headphones to the floor, nearly weeping, and watched them break into plastic pieces, scattering them. Unwillingly his eyes moved to the polysomnograph which was still drawing Room One's feed across the console screen. The peaks fluctuated so wildly it was a solid wall of color, yet how was it possible when Sanderson had ceased to be anything but some sort of gateway?

Amid the noise around Fisher was something sharp and sudden, yet he could not place it, not until it repeated. He stepped from the control room to the sound of an echoing creak and saw the door to Room One had bowed out, its window a spider web of cracks, barely containing what lay behind it. Dark flying things swarmed, splinters popped off the frame and landed a few feet way. Where was the help Doctor Wy promised him, Fisher wondered? He had to escape the lab before what was amassing inside Room One broke free.

Fisher ran to the front door and tried the handle but it would not budge. He fumbled the key from his pocket, almost drop-ping it in his heightened state of anxiety, yet when he tried it he found it would not fit the lock. He scrambled back to the control room, throwing everything aside until he found Rose's keys on her desk. He ran back but it made no difference; the door would not open, no matter how hard he shook it. Desperate, he tried the front windows but found they too were locked. Outside them, on the other side of the fogged and dirty glass, a pair of figures moved slowly back and forth. He banged on the windows to get their attention.

"Help me!" Fisher screamed. "You've got to get me out!"

If something was said in response, he couldn't hear it. There was only the sound of glass and wood continuing to break behind him, and then the horrible droning became something far worse, something like the screeching of machinery. He was afraid to turn and instead banged his numbed fists harder against the window, but the figures did not pause. Fisher pressed his face against the glass and saw two pale thuggish faces scowling at him through the haze as they had so many months previous, though they had traded their suits for coveralls. They were adding small shadows to the growing pile in front of the window, like bricks to a wall.

Fisher screamed, afraid to turn and face what was coming for him. It sounded of storms and mistakes and regret. Yet in the window he could see a reflection, a reflection of the swarm that advanced upon him. Fisher could not speak. The noises the cloud made—the sight of those insect-like things swarming as one—were nothing compared to what he saw within the darkness that enveloped him. There was a series of flashes like sparks in a roaring surf. They lit his face as he stared into the dark swirling void and saw something else moving towards him. There was a sound, like hoof-beats, pounding in his ears, and then there was nothing. No noise of any kind. Just an image waiting to develop.

LAST WALTZ

Jason S. Ridler

"You dead yet?" said a Slavic crow on a low hanging branch, chewing on a cigarette butt.

"Been working on that one a while," Fritz said, laying corpse-still on a concrete bench, shattered bottles blossomed into broken petals around him, guitar in its case at his feet like an epitaph unsung.

"Seems like you need some help."

"Maybe so, maybe so."

The crow fluttered. "I could stitch you out some, tear off a few slices. Gotta make me a nest to catch me some honey. I'm good. I'm a doctor."

Fritz snorted. "Even dirty Dr. Crow gets more action than me. Heh."

"Might take a load off you, too, slim. Seems like bunch of things weighing you down like a tractor."

The guitar case glared at him, cracked and torn. "I don't know. What are you without dreams?"

The crow inched closer, wings out for balance. "But what are you with dead ones still rotting inside you? Dead dreams are poison. Let me bleed the wound. What else you planning on today? A sold out show at the Gardens? Busking for dollars? Waiting for the runaway muse?"

Fritz snickered. "Have at me."

Dr. Crow dove his beak into Fritz's head quick, sharp and deadly. Heavy wings flapped until he reached the treetop, and in his mouth was a whisky bottle. He dropped it, letting more shard flowers blossom. "I can't build a nest with devil piss! What the hell were your dreams made off?"

Fritz burped red froth. "Monsters made of whisky and rye, devil kisses and sex with angels. All shimmer, no core and such and such." He exhaled smoke. "You take the drowning man out of the sea, he's just another sailor. The spotlight was addicted to his disgrace. So when you can't hack through another pack, drink through another day, when the tremors are all you got left ...well, try and steal some more, Dr. Crow, but I doubt there's anything left." He coughed yellow-red foam.

Dr. Crow sneered. "So. You think there's no music unless you're drowning?"

Fritz's chin jabbed his chest, as if the strings above his skull were snapped.

"Idiot." Dr. Crow dived and then tore out the Texas mickeys, tall-boy six packs, and wine boxes until a sour mash river ran out of Fritz's mouth and rushed into the soil, turning the green to brown.

Dr. Crow pecked the latches to the guitar case, then returned to his perch. "Go on," he said. "I've drained the worst. Now give me something worth stealing."

Fritz was bone pale. He coughed red wetness into his fist, words dribbling out in whispers. "It would be a lie."

"Then lie," said Dr. Crow. "Or I'll peck that guitar to kindling."

Fritz's body shivered, hands all nerves and trembles.

"That's it."

The dull-sheen Telecaster should have been a feather but weighed a ton. Fritz draped it across his knees and they cracked, heavier than God's balls.

"Now what?"

Dr. Crow cawed. "Make a chord. Then another. Then another. Build me a fucking nest, you self-defeating jackass."

Skeletal fingers formed an E minor, while Fritz cleared his throat of froth. "But you spilled it all."

"No. Give me your last drop."

"It will stink like a dead man's asshole."

"But it'll be true."

Fritz gulped brine and blood, heart mere leaves rustling in the wind, as his jagged fingers strummed and the words fought through the paste gluing his teeth shut in the cold air.

"Empty bottle of broken down dreams and everything ain't resplendent. No poet of the underground, no underdog hero winning the final round, a wasted neverwas husk of ancient dust. And a crow demands his nest."

Pain snickered through his brain as Dr. Crow darted into his head, then back up to the tree with strong loops of rope from a hole in his skull. He weaved a nest of brain that pulled Fritz into the air. "Go out fighting, my friend," said Dr. Crow, and Fritz strummed above the ground, the sound of that guitar bringing lady crows from sunnier skies to sink into the brooding nest above. All the while, Fritz's legs waltzed with the wind above the shattered glass garden, a blue smile stitched on his now silent face.

SYMPATHY FOR THE DEVIL

Nancy Kilpatrick

They treated him like a monster. Everybody did. And he didn't deserve that. He didn't do anything. Nothing at all. He wasn't responsible, it was the others. He was the victim here. A *real* victim. All this nasty business because of that stupid woman...It was so wrong.

The nurse arrived and went about the work of nursing, sans comfort. This one was young and fairly pretty, with brown hair and eyes, though a little plump for his tastes, but she did the things the other nurses had been doing over the last week since he's regained consciousness into this living hell. She took his temperature, blood pressure, heart rate, all that from the automatic readings so that she didn't need to have any physical or verbal contact with him. Yeah, he was a pariah.

"I'd like my pillow fluffed," he said, not because he needed it fluffed—that wouldn't matter. He just wanted to see how she would react.

Her head jerked up as if she hadn't heard a sound in ages. Without even a glance in his direction, she moved to the side of the bed, pulled the pillow out from behind his head, made a great show of pounding it into a new shape, then, carefully, pushed him forward with latex-gloved fingertips on his shoulder as if touching him might infect her in some way. He couldn't even feel it through the fabric of the hospital gown, but that, too, didn't matter. In fact, it was a plus.

Once the pillow was in what she deemed to be the right position, she moved his shoulder back. Without a word, she hurried from the room as if he might have the audacity to ask for something else and she had to get out of earshot fast.

"Bitch!" he muttered to her back. "Every last one of you!"

Now that he was back from the dead, so to speak, he was bored. Seriously bored. It was just a question of when they'd let him out of here. He could use a drink. And a cigarette. Neither one was possible in this place. The only thing that cut the boredom was the pain. He didn't think he'd ever been in such physical pain, not even as a kid when his asshole stepfather beat the crap out of him for killing the neighbor's cat. That was nothing compared to this.

At least he had a morphine drip and he could self-regulate. With both arms and legs in casts, he had to gum the clear plastic tube hanging beside his head. He did that now, only to find that nothing came through the tube. He glanced up; the morphine release syringe hanging on a tripod next to the bed was empty and the stupid nurse hadn't changed it. But she wouldn't, would she? None of them would. They were punishing him. They were like sheep, sentimental slobs, soap opera addicts so pathetic they'd hang on every word of a sobbing woman. But he was the victim here. The *real* victim. Look at his body, broken, bandaged from head to toe! And now, craning his neck had caused pain to slice through his shoulder and back as if a hot rod had been plunged into his muscles. Yeah, and look how they treated him.

"Hey," he yelled. "Hey! Somebody get in here and turn on the damned TV, will ya?" But nobody came, of course. Why should they? They blamed him for the accident. Well, damn them to hell, it wasn't his fault!

When he woke up, the TV was on. His eyes focused on the small screen. A soap. Right. It would be. The bed next to his was empty, had been, as if they didn't want anybody too near him. Fine with him. They could all go to hell.

"Mr. Hammersmith."

His head jerked around. "Who the hell are you?"

The old woman smiled one of those beatific smiles that only the old and nearly toothless can manage. "I'm Mrs. Shade."

"Shade? Like window shade? Or are you shady?"

She laughed, one of those sweet-old-lady laughs that most people seem to love. Harmless old lady. Annoying old lady.

"What are you doing here?" he demanded.

"Oh, I'm just a volunteer, Mr. Hammersmith. I visit people in hospitals and other institutions, those who have no one else visiting them. People alone often feel a bit hopeless. I just want to help."

"Yeah, well, I don't need or want your help, but you could change the channel." He nodded towards the TV where some woman was crying and a man was holding her. Yeah, right. Real life. Bullshit!

As Mrs. Shade switched channels, stopping at a game show, she said, "Mr. Hammersmith, I have the feeling that you're lonely."

"So much for your feelings, lady. Not lonely. Not at all."

That damned smile again. "Well, I came by when I discovered you'd not had any visitors or even next of kin who might phone or visit. Everyone should have someone who cares what happens to them."

"Ha! Like you care. You're just an old bat with nothing to do before you die." He could have laughed but he wasn't in the mood. "Look, lady—"

"Mrs. Shade."

"I'm just recovering from a bad accident and want some peace and quiet so if you don't mind—"

"Oh, I wouldn't deprive you of that. Certainly not. I'm sure you're in a great deal of pain and—"

At her words, a fierce and fiery snake shot through his spine. His mouth opened involuntarily and a cry slipped out. He rode the pain for the long moments it slithered through his spinal cord, desperately biting on the clear tube for morphine that was not there. "Damn those bitches!" he yelled when he could articulate it. "Fill the goddam morphine!"

"Here," Mrs. Shade said, "let me help you. I'll get the nurse."

She trundled out of the room at a snail's pace, which he saw through his fog of agony, returning with the young nurse. While he writhed internally, they chatted as if he wasn't even there, and certainly not in extreme and relentless pain.

"And I worked as a nurse before I retired, but that was a dozen years ago. My, this apparatus is much more complicated than in my day. Do you have children, Laura?"

The nurse named Laura smiled and said, "Yes, a toddler. He's twenty months and getting to be a handful."

"Oh, that's the age! I remember my daughter at two..."

And on and on they nattered while the nurse took her damned time changing the morphine syringe in the machine. Finally she was done and the two douche-bags walked out the door together. But what did he care. He gummed the tube and saw a couple of drops flow down into the needle stuck into the vein just above the cast covering his left arm. The drug kicked in at last and he exhaled wearily.

The old woman poked her head back in the door and said, "Is there anything else you need before I go?" That stupid smile again. "I'd be happy to bring you books and magazines."

He didn't even bother answering her, just closed his eyes and bit down on the tube again.

"You'll have to appear in court," the lawyer was saying, staring only at the papers and not at his client.

"Why? I didn't do anything. It wasn't my fault."

The lawyer, whose name he thought was Lawson or Lawrence or something like that had been appointed by the court to represent him. Not that an innocent man needed representation but, as they say, the man who represents himself has a fool for a client, and he was no fool.

The lawyer paused for a moment, barely glanced at him, then said, "Be that as it may, the law is the law, and you'll need to appear in court for sentencing. Your history of impaired driving won't help but I expect your injuries could work in your favour when I ask for a continuance. If that's denied, perhaps the judge will take your estimated recovery time of a year into account when sentencing."

"Right!" He snorted. Damned lawyers and judges. What did they know about pain? It was all so wrong.

"As I've told you, the law stipulates two to five years for involuntary manslaughter but the judge has discretion to reduce that, depending on circumstances. If we're lucky, you might serve six months, or no time at all in jail, especially if you can show remorse."

"Why should I be remorseful? I didn't do anything wrong."

The lawyer looked at him blankly, licked his lips, and then went back to his papers.

"Alright, Mr. Hammersmith, let me go over with you again how—"

"We've already been over everything. Twice. That's enough. Get out!"

The lawyer had a look on his face that said he wasn't used to being talked to this way. He sighed, gathered the papers atop his briefcase and slid them inside, clicked off his expensive-looking pen, then stood. "We'll continue another time, when you're feeling up to it." He made his way out of the room as one of the orderlies came in with a food tray.

"Supper time," the cheerful young punk said. Arms full of tattoos, skin studded with metal, hair in one of those mini-Mohawks, the color bile green.

"Jesus! How come they let people like you work here?"

The punky kid's smile turned to a scowl. "Maybe because I'm caring and sympathetic, even to sociopaths?"

"Go to hell!"

"If I do, Mr. Hammersmith, I'm sure I'll meet you there. You probably run the place."

At that, another pain shot through his spine. But, dammit, he wouldn't show this kid he was suffering.

The punky orderly placed the tray on the table and moved the table so it stretched across the bed, then uncovered today's lousy meal. He glanced at Hammersmith. "Too bad you're in pain. But, at least you're alive."

The pain left him speechless so that he couldn't respond.

"I'll be back in a few minutes to feed you," the orderly said, turned and walked out.

Once the pain subsided, he caught his breath. The nauseating smell of mushy, micro waved food filled his nostrils and cut off any sense of hunger. Just as well. By the time the punk orderly returned to feed him, the food would be cold, just like it was every meal, every day. They were all blaming him.

This was so wrong.

"Mr. Hammersmith. May I call you Evan?"

"Who in hell are you?"

"I'm Reverend Francis, of St. Margaret's, the church down the street. Mrs. Shade mentioned you and I just stopped by to see if you needed anything."

Great. Now they were hell-bent on saving his soul. Like he had one. "I don't need anything, Reverend. Wasted your time coming here."

The minister smiled and took a seat. "It's never a waste of time to minister to one of God's children."

"I'm not a child and I don't believe in God. Or the devil, unless that's me, which everybody seems to think I am. What I do believe is that earth is a hellhole."

The minister smiled patiently. "Well, whether or not we believe in God, he believes in us."

"I don't think your God believes in me, unless he's a sadist. I'm the victim and I'm being treated like a criminal."

Reverend Francis had clearly heard statements like this before. "God forgives all, even if the people around you don't, or can't."

"What's to forgive? I was in an accident. My body is broken. Maybe your God can forgive everybody who's blaming me for something I didn't do, but I can't."

The minister paused. "You were driving that night."

"Yeah, of course I was. And?"

He paused. "I believe you'd been drinking."

"I'd had a glass of wine. Is that a sin? I guess it is in your books."

"You're alcohol level was far over the limit."

"What is this, the Inquisition? I had a bit to drink, like people do. What's the harm?"

"The harm is that a woman was seriously injured, with brain damage, and her child—"

"Look, that stupid woman crossed against the light. That's not my fault."

"Mr. Hammersmith, under God's law, when one takes responsibility for his actions—"

Pain zapped through his arms and legs, starting at the base of his spine and shooting out as if he'd been electrocuted. He barely had time to yell, "Get out. Now! Get the hell out of here!"

He was only vaguely aware of the minister leaving. Pain racked him, zigzagging, alternating sharp then dull, the signals hopping along his nerves to the endings then back again until he could hardly breathe.

It seemed to go on for minutes but he knew it could only be seconds. The pain had been growing worse each day since he'd regained consciousness. All the broken bones from when he flew through the windshield and into the air then slammed against the tree. Everything broken. He'd lost consciousness quickly and that saved him from knowing about it then, but now... Now that he was 'recovering', the pain just kept intensifying and all the morphine in the world wasn't enough.

He chewed on the drug drip anyway, trying to get enough into his system to allow him to lose consciousness, even though the tube wouldn't give more than his daily dose, which he'd reached. His throbbing head fell back against the pillow. Everybody was wrong. *He* was the victim, not the stupid woman who walked in front of his car. Not her stupid kid, and at least the kid died fast and didn't suffer, not like he was suffering.

If that religious guy was right and there was a God, he saw no sign of him. And besides, if there was a God, any God, then people should know that and stop blaming him for something that wasn't his fault anyway. It was *her* fault, not his. What a sick world.

"I've brought you a few magazines, Mr. Hammersmith." It was that old lady again, hobbling into the room, placing the magazines on the bed beside him.

"Yeah, well, you may have noticed I can't really hold a magazine to read it, can I?"

She looked a little befuddled, as only old people can. "Oh. Well, maybe I can read to you."

He sighed heavily. "Look, lady—"

"Mrs. Shade."

"Right. Look, thanks for the magazines but no thanks. Just go. Don't come back."

Instead of leaving, Mrs. Shade took a seat by the bed. She reached out a hand and touched his torso, about heart level, where his rib bones were broken. Through the sheet and the hospital gown he felt heat flowing into him.

"What in hell are you doing?"

"Just making contact, Mr. Hammersmith. Heart contact. I wanted to feel your heart beating."

"Take your hand off me, lady, or I'll call for the nurse."

She smiled that sickly-sweet smile again and said, "Oh, Mr. Hammersmith, I'm not sure she would come, are you? I really do understand that they've been treating you like a monster. But then, they blame you for the accident."

She removed her hand and suddenly a ferocious pain stabbed him in the chest. The fierceness of such a knife-edged attack left him breathless, unable to speak, to scream, to do anything but lie as if comatose while the nerves in his chest exploded. Maybe he was having a heart attack!

Sweat broke out from every pore and his muscles trembled. He was going to die. This time, the pain would kill him, he just knew it. Well, damn it, bring it on! He didn't mind dying. He minded physical pain.

Through the ceaseless agony, he heard the old woman say, as if reading his mind, "No, Mr. Hammersmith, you won't die. Not yet. You're still relatively young, with much life left in you. This too will pass."

He'd gotten through enough of the physical torment that he could snarl at her, "Pass? You think this will pass? It's not passing, it's getting worse."

"Things get worse before they get better."

"Take your fucking platitudes and get out!" he gasped, his vision still blurred, but the pain seemed to be easing a little. He caught a few deeper breaths and the trembling subsided. As his vision cleared, his body shivered from cold; his hospital gown was soaked.

"Let me help you, Mr. Hammersmith. That's what I'm here for."

"I-don't-need-help," he growled between teeth still clenched against the attack.

"Don't you? It seems to me that you do. I know Reverend Francis was here yesterday. And I know you sent him away too. But really, this isn't getting better, its worse, isn't it? And most of your pain is because you don't accept your part in what happened."

How dare she? The old bat was hitting him when he was down. That's the only reason he could think of that he was even listening to all this BS.

"You know, lady, it's a good thing I'm trapped in this hospital bed. If I wasn't, I'd have kicked you out on your ass by now!"

"Mr. Hammersmith. Everyone is guilty of something. It's just a question of fessing up. It's that simple. Admit your part in things and life becomes easier. For you, for those around you. It's a simple exchange, really. You give something, you get something."

He wanted to yell at her, no, *scream* at her. He longed to be able to leap up out of this bed and throttle the old bag!

"Really, Mr. Hammersmith. I don't think you have anything to lose by admitting that you drove drunk, that it wasn't your first accident while drunk, and that you are directly responsible for killing a child and severely and permanently injuring her mother. You have a lifetime of cruel, callous and unconscious acts, monstrous acts that have resulted in pain and suffering for others. It's a fact, all of it. Admitting it can only easy your pain. Give yourself a break, Mr. Hammersmith. Do that, and others will give *you* a break."

He longed to be free of these casts so he could throw her out the window! But suddenly the bad sensations returned, without warning, turning his body electric again with high-voltage sparks of blinding, searing pain. He could barely stay conscious. His body shuddered, close to convulsing, staggering through immobility, unable to stand the onslaught.

"Admit your responsibility, Mr. Hammersmith, and the universe will open new doors. One thing in exchange for another. That's a rule of life; the old goes out, the new comes in, and change occurs. You'll be a different person, I guarantee it."

It was as if one of those doors opened inside him, one clear and pain free. He saw a door in his mind, one with a transparent window that beckoned: 'Enter here'. Something was on the other side of that door, something better than this and he thought: *What the hell, what the hell, what the hell...! I've got nothing to lose. Anything's worth a try. At the very least, if I tell her what she wants to hear, she'll go away.*

"Okay, okay, I did it! Alright? Did you get what you want?"

"Did what?"

"I was drunk. I had drinks."

"And?"

"And what?"

"The woman."

"Okay, I didn't see her. Or the kid. Maybe I saw the kid, I don't know. Okay? Is that it? Is that what everybody wants to hear? Satisfied?"

"I think the universe is satisfied, Mr. Hammersmith."

He gummed the morphine tube and found it empty again. "Shit!" he yelled.

Mrs. Shade looked at the self-regulator, then stood. "I think the tube might just be twisted. I'll fix it for you."

While she worked on the machine, she said, "You know, admitting guilt is really only the first step."

He bit the tube. Nothing. Then, finally, a couple of drops.

"There is still the question of reparations."

Before he could respond, in a split second, as if a magnet had sucked the iron from his body, the pain disappeared. He blinked in disbelief. "What the...?" His body hadn't felt this light, this pain free...ever! He began a laugh that plunged to his gut and soon turned uncontrollable. "I don't believe it. It's gone. The pain is gone!"

He turned to the old woman. "It's gone," he said again, feeling his face stretch into a smile of astonishment. "You were right. All I had to do was take responsibility for what I did and now I'm free."

She reached over and patted his chest with that warm-, like-fire hand. "I'm happy the physical pain has dimmed, Mr. Hammersmith. I think things have resolved the way they should and you're now where you deserve to be. Admitting guilt. Free of physical pain. Now there's only restitution."

He laughed, almost crying in relief. For the first time since he'd regained consciousness, his body felt alive, real, pain free. He just might recover after all.

Mrs. Shade hobbled to the door and he called out after her, "Hey, lady, good tip."

With one backward glance, she grinned. "My pleasure. And I'm so pleased to have met you, Evan Hammersmith. Oh, and by the way, have you guessed my name?"

He felt confused. "Guessed your name? I don't get it. Your name is Shade, right? Mrs. Shade?"

"In one sense it is, Mr. Hammersmith? My daughter is Gheena Lewis, nee Shade, and Suzy Lewis was my granddaughter."

His breath caught. The woman and kid he'd hit.

He thought for a moment, quickly rearranging the letters of her name in his mind but he didn't get far with that before he noticed her grin looked oddly toothy. He realized that what he was seeing didn't really resemble teeth. These were sharp and pointed, a mouthful of daggers. Not just that, but her face was morphing before his eyes. The sweet-old-lady look altered as if the lines imbedded in her skin ran together, drawing a roadmap of deeper lines gouged in flesh that took on the quality of parched, abandoned earth. The whites of her eyes disappeared completely until the entire eye was red with a black glow behind. The dry, crinkly skin of her arms, her hands, her legs, all of it distorted until she became something *other*. Gruesome, grotesque. Terrifying!

His throat constricted and his skin turned clammy. His heart fluttered madly in fear. He registered surprise: fear, an emotion. One he did not remember ever feeling. Like lava racing down a mountainside, a range of scalding emotions washed over him in fiery waves, as intense as the physical pain that had vanished. Guilt, grief, remorse, horror, self-loathing... Responsibility. A lifetime of responsibility for a lifetime of irresponsible actions, for all the pain and sadness he had caused others and the negativity he had spewed into the world.

"What's happening to me?" he cried.

And in an instant, as the demon before him laughed and glanced at the morphine drip, he knew. She had changed the syringe.

"What did you drug me with? What?"

"You wouldn't know the chemical name, but it's a drug used for torture. Oh, and the effects? They seem to be permanent. Fitting, don't you agree?"

Whatever invaded his bloodstream forced back the physical pain and filled him with emotional pain of equal weight. Killing emotions that sliced him to ribbons and left his mind reeling. Emotions he did not know he was capable of; he had no knowledge of how to cope.

"It's that deal-with-the-devil thing, Evan Hammersmith. And the devil got her due!"

The demon laughed, the sound grating, rubbing his anorexic soul raw.

The thing that retreated, eyes gleaming like the fires of hell, whispered in a voice that caused shivers up his spine and sent his mind reeling in terror, "Welcome to *my* Hades, Evan Hammersmith. Prepare yourself for a long and well-deserved stay!"

Evan sensed his reason slipping down a bottomless well. Finally, he saw clearly why everyone else despised him because now he hated himself. Self-loathing left him hopeless. Despicable, inhuman, unlovable, he longed for release from this unbearable dark weight of who he was. If he could move, he would jump out the window to his death, but he could not move, and would not be able to for a long, long time. Time. It stretched before him: hours, days, weeks, months, years of scalding emotions, agony, and no relief in sight.

He screamed for help, but no one came. There would be no sympathy for this particular devil.

THE NEEDLE'S EYE

Suzanne Church

Lise held the needle up to the light. A single drop of vaccine nestled between the twin points, glistening amber. She hesitated, hating the cure for the slow ravages of Retiniapox. But she'd seen the horrible devastation the scourge could bring. Entire villages wiped out. Bodies doused with bleach and left to petrify in the sun, as no one would risk the dangers of burial or cremation.

Her patient, a young girl, wailed on the cot, held down by her mother. The cot's canvas, once green and now a drab shade of grey dotted with splotches of blood and fluids, groaned under the pressure of two bodies pressing down. The stench of it wafted up, adding to the reek of sweat and fear that permeated the medical station.

The girl's mother wore a bandage over her left eye from her own inoculation. Red and yellow blotches stained the white gauze; the eye would never function again, but her chances of contracting the virus had dropped by sixty-eight percent. Lise had vaccinated the mother only moments before, yet it felt like hours. *So many eyes ruined.* When she'd signed up for overseas medicine, she had prepared herself for the horrors of makeshift facilities and understaffed clinics, but nothing could have prepared her for Retiniapox. Back in university, medicine had called to her, with its noble pursuits and its promise to help, to cure. Now she felt like a crusader, storming through a new dark age with a bifurcated needle instead of a sword.

"Où est ton Papa?" Lise asked about the father's whereabouts in the hopes of distracting the girl while the Alcaine numbed her eye.

The mother shook her head.

I shouldn't have asked. They come from the northeast, where the last outbreaks were reported. Choosing silence over further reassurances, Lise began the scratching. Two strokes left and right, pressing the serum with both points just below the surface of the cornea. The girl squirmed and shrieked, more from fear than pain. She shouldn't be able to feel the needle. Two strokes up and down and the amber liquid disappeared into the layers of her eye. Lise pressed gauze over a closed lid and taped the dressing down.

Next.

A young man, about the same age as Lise's beloved Rideau, lay down on the cot. She tied his arms in the restraints, sanitized her needle, and gathered another drop of serum.

Sweat poured down Rideau's back. The Hazmat suit made the dry heat unbearable. He leaned over his next patient simultaneously cursing and thanking the layers of PVC separating him from the virus.

The woman's body wept from countless pustules, most concentrated on her face, neck, and chest. Her eyes had liquefied the previous day; always the first casualty. A biological weapon of war, the virus had been designed to blind its victims, rendering an opposing army helpless. Nature, in its random cruelty, had mutated the pathogen to a deadly cousin of Smallpox since its introduction in the battle of Baqa el Gharbiyya.

The woman moaned, unable to scream, throat clogged with erupting sores.

"Bientôt," he said. *Soon, it'll end.* One in a thousand would survive the illness. About three in ten would succumb despite vaccination, a high price to pay after trading sight in one eye for hope.

He readied a dose of morphine to add to her IV. A seizure gripped the patient in the next cot. Arms and legs flailed, knocking Rideau off balance. He fell onto the woman. His arm brushed across her neck and chest, ripping open a swath of pox. In his haste to push himself back up, he twisted the morphine syringe in his hand.

Pop. Rideau started, stunned, terrified, at the unmistakable sound of a suit breach.

He hurried for the rinsing station, searching for the suit's weakness. The needle had poked through a smear of pus. Contamination. *No, I must think positive.* Other doctors had endured a suit breach without a hint of infection. Some more than once.

He showered the suit with bleach until the buzzer sounded. Next he stripped, set the bleach to half-dose, and cleansed himself. Caustic welts erupted on his skin and he dared not open his eyes, though they stung mercilessly. At the buzzer, he lunged blindly for the eye wash and rinsed the bleach from his face.

In two hours he would learn the true effectiveness of his inoculation; whether the trade of sight in one eye for his safety had been fair. He headed for the quarantine tent and scribbled a note on the chalkboard outside, "Rideau, needle through suit, Wednesday, 1027 hours."

Inside, he clung to thoughts of Lise, fleeing this room of despair for better times.

He remembered the previous Saturday, bringing the thought to the front of his mind, reliving its exquisite beauty.

He rested on their cot, watching her run a sponge along her arm. She turned to face him and said, "Like what you see?"

He smiled. "Always."

The air in their tent hung dry and cloying, like laundry at the bottom of a hamper. His skin was slick with sweat. He sat up and the sheet fell from his chest, pooling around his waist. Part of him wanted to grab her in his arms, make love to her again, but watching her bathe electrified him; his muscles twitched with desire and bliss.

The lights dimmed then returned to their yellow murk. "The generator needs filling," *she said.*

"I'll get to it. Are you finished with the water?"

"Not quite."

"Hurry and come back to bed."

She lifted another sponge full of water along her thigh and the excess dripped slowly back into the basin she had placed below. "I think we've wasted enough time today."

"Wasted?" He crossed his arms against his chest. "Is that what you think of our time together?"

She glanced out the mesh window. "The queues have started already."

He clicked his tongue against his teeth. "I shouldn't have to take a number to be with my own wife."

She shook her head. "Pardon. I've so much on my mind."

He tugged at the sheet, wrapped it around his waist and approached her naked body. As she dabbed the sponge along her neck, he followed her movement, kissing her hand and then her neck.

"Rideau...."

He turned her around to face him.

She trembled in his arms. "What is it?" he said.

"I'm late."

He traced the line from her chin to the base of her neck. "The clinic can wait."

"No. I'm pregnant."

He dropped the sheet and pressed his hands against her belly. "Vraiment?"

She nodded.

He pulled her close. Her trembling intensified and he pressed her chest against his, feeling her heart beating in synch with his own.

"The clinic's no place for a baby," *she said.*

"Kiss me." *He found her tongue with his, absorbing her passion like cracked earth soaked by rain.*

When their rhythms eased and her breath slowed, he said, "We'll put in requests for transfer. They'll grant yours on medical grounds and I'll meet you in Montréal as soon as I'm able."

"I won't leave without you," *she said.* "We're in this together."

He kissed the back of her neck. "We should dress."

"Rideau!" Lise peered through the quarantine tent's plastic window. "What happened?"

"A needle through the suit."

She pushed at the tent flap, and poked her head inside.

"Stay out!" he snapped.

"I won't come any—"

"Close the flap, Lise. I couldn't live, knowing I contaminated you."

She backed outside, glanced at the chalkboard, and then her watch. "We'll know in another twenty minutes."

"Twenty-three."

"I'll wait."

"No," he said. "Get back to the clinic. The time will move quickly if you're busy."

She touched the tent fabric with her right hand, willing it to turn into his skin so that she might comfort him. With her left, she pressed at her belly, at the tiny person growing there. *Not now. I need him more than ever. Please, God, protect him.*

"Go on, Lise."

"Je t'adour," she said.

"Moi, aussi," he responded.

Biting back her grief, she hurried to her work.

For the longest thirty minutes of her life, she vaccinated patient after patient. Every other woman was with child. Her mother had once said to Lise, "When you're pregnant, it seems that everyone around you is, too. That's the way of the world; people making babies, loving along the way in their own manner. Enjoy every minute of this special time. I never felt as much a woman as when I carried you inside me."

A pregnant woman with near-black skin lay on the cot. With her arms at her sides, she waited for Lise to tie her down. Her eyes full of fear, she closed the left one, indicating that was the eye she wanted vaccinated. As Lise moved closer, the vaccine held between the needle's twin points, the woman's belly shuddered. The unmistakable shape of a foot protruded against the skin. Lise laughed, nearly choking on the sound of it. A smile passed briefly along the patient's face and then terror filled it once more.

With careful and deliberate strokes, Lise scratched the vaccine into the soon-to-be mother's eye.

Glancing at her watch, she returned with a kit and a Hazmat suit to the quarantine tent. She stripped to her underwear and tugged at the thick plastic, yanking it over her sweating body. Sebastian had offered to examine Rideau. Though tempted to dodge the duty, she stuck by her resolve to do it herself.

With her suit sealed, she lifted the tent flap and entered the dark space. She touched Rideau's cheek with her gloved hand and stared at the red blotches blossoming in the white of his good eye. Soon it would weep the toxins building in his body.

She choked back a sob.

"I know," he said.

"I brought vaccine. If I scratch your good eye it will reduce the severity of the symptoms."

"I'll spend the rest of my life blind and scarred by the pox. How could you love such a man?"

Tears erupted, a river of sadness. In the suit, she couldn't wipe at them. "I would love you blind and deaf with no legs. I will keep on loving you. Don't make me raise this baby alone."

He was silent for a long time. Lise listened to her breath in the suit, the loud echo of life, reminding her that she was healthy. For now.

While she waited, his empty, vaccinated eye stared out, still clear and unmarred by red blotches. She wanted to kiss it, to press her lips against him and show him that life was worth living. *"S'il te plaît."*

"Don't beg, Lise. I can't bear it. You're right. I want to be a father."

He sat up awkwardly, and kissed the plastic of her face plate. "Do it."

She kissed him back and then gently pressed him down onto the cot. Two restraints hung from her belt. She pulled the first one free, her hands shaking beneath the thick layers of plastic.

"Tie them tightly," he said. "I don't want to accidentally infect you."

She strapped him down, doubling over the fabric then clipping the clasps together. Welts criss-crossed his body—burns from the bleach wash. She ran a gloved hand along his skin, hating the way it stuck to his body, agonizing over the barrier between them.

"Don't hesitate. You've done this hundreds of times. I'm only one more patient." With that, he stared at the ceiling, his eye full of resolve and bravery.

Holding her breath for a long time, she let it out and dropped Alcaine into his right eye. While she waited for it to numb, she slowly and carefully opened the vial of serum and dipped in the bifurcated needle. Her skin stuck to the inside of the suit. The smell of her breath, overpowering in the small space, reminded her of the coffee she'd shared with Rideau only hours before. The memory lifted the dam on another flood of tears.

"I'll never forget your beautiful smile." His voice cracked, as though he hadn't spoken in a lifetime. *"Je t'adour."*

Her vision, distorted by her anguish, turned his face into a streaky blur. She tried to find him through the waterfall, blinking frantically. With time, his blue eye came back into focus and she leaned in close with the needle.

Her every instinct told her to pull away, flee from this madness. Finding her inner resolve, thinking of the needs of their unborn child, she focused all of her energy into steadying her wavering hand. She whispered, "Forgive me."

Rideau picked at the wax in his ears. The long hours, by jeep, then train, then plane, had exhausted him and clogged his remaining senses. He'd never realized how loud transportation could be. Now he stood in the customs line, the last hurdle between him and his family, and listened to the conversations all around. A couple discussed in whispers how much to claim on the duty form. A child complained about the cold. How many of them stared at him, saying nothing? Victims of the pox were rare in Canada, and survivors rarer still. How many times had he brushed his fingers along his pocked cheeks and wondered how hideous he had become?

On that fateful day, after she'd vaccinated his good eye, they'd agreed that, for the safety of their child, she should return to Montréal as soon as possible. So when his fever had broken, they had said their good-byes. In her absence, he had truly understood the meaning of despair.

The long months in the hospital had passed with sickening slowness. His illness had relapsed four times before he was finally well enough to leave the biohazard tent. Weak from so much time on his back, he was forced to take even more time to build up his strength for the journey home.

A lifetime had passed, Théophile's lifetime.

When his turn came, his aide led him ahead to the customs officer. Documents were produced and with a loud stamp, he was sent towards his future.

The aide asked, "Is someone meeting you?"

"My wife. Lise."

"Wonderful."

"And our new son, Théophile."

"Will this be the first time you've seen him?" The woman's voice faltered. So many idioms were based on sight.

"Yes," he answered, before she apologized for the comment.

Their shoes clicked on the hard floor, echoing along the narrow corridor. Then the whoosh of automatic doors and the noise of a crowd. All around him, cries of "Pleased to meet you," and, "Welcome home," erupted from a sea of unseen faces.

And then the touch of fingers he remembered and the whisper of her breath against his neck.

"I've never been so happy to see you, my love," she said. "Would you like to hold your son?"

She handed him the baby. Rideau steadied himself for the boy's cry, at the sight of this horribly disfigured stranger. But the boy cooed instead.

"He's been wondering when his father would come home to spoil him."

"I brought presents," he said as he felt the soft nose and chubby cheeks. "For both of you."

She squeezed his hand, then nudged him to take her arm.

"What does he look like?" he asked.

"Healthy and handsome," she said. "Just like his father."

LOOKER

David Nickle

I met her on the beach.

It was one of Len's parties—one of the last he threw, before he had to stop. You were there too. But we didn't speak. I remember watching you talking with Jonathan on the deck, an absurdly large tumbler for such a small splash of Merlot wedged at your elbow as you nodded, eyes fixed on his so as not to meet mine. If you noticed me, I hope you also noticed I didn't linger.

Instead, I took my own wine glass, filled it up properly, climbed down that treacherous wooden staircase, and kicked off my shoes. It was early enough that the sand was still warm from the sun—late enough that the sun was just dabs of pink on the dark ocean and I could tell myself I had the beach to myself.

She was, I'm sure, telling herself the same thing. She had brought a pipe and a lighter with her in her jeans, and was perched on a picnic table, surreptitiously puffing away. The pipe disappeared as I neared her. It came back soon enough, when she saw my wineglass, maybe recognized me from the party.

I didn't recognize her. She was a small woman, but wide across the shoulders and the tiniest bit chubby. Hair was dark, pulled back into a ponytail. Pretty, but not pretty enough; she would fade at a party like Len's.

"Yeah, I agree," she said to me and I paused on my slow gambol to the surf.

"It's too bright," she said, and as I took a long pull from my wine, watching her curiously, she added, "look at him."

"Look at me," I said, and she laughed.

"You on the phone?" I asked, and she dropped her head in extravagant *mea culpa*.

"No," she said. "Just..."

"Don't fret. What's the point of insanity if you can't enjoy a little conversation?"

Oh, I am smooth. She laughed again, and motioned me over, and waved the pipe and asked if I'd like to share.

Sure I said, and she scooted aside to make room on the table. Her name was Lucy. Lucille, actually, was how she introduced herself but she said Lucy was fine. I introduced myself. "Tom's a nice name," she said.

The night grew. Lungs filled with smoke and mouths with wine; questions asked, questions answered. *How do you know Len? What do you do? What brings you to the beach when so much is going on inside?* It went both ways.

Lucy knew Len scarcely at all. They'd met through a friend who worked at Len's firm. Through the usual convolutions of dinners and pubs and excursions, she'd insinuated herself onto the cc list of the *ur*-mail by which Len advertised his parties. She worked cash at a bookstore chain in town and didn't really have a lot of ambition past that right now. Which tended to make her feel seriously out of her weight class at Len's parties or so she said; the beach, therefore, was an attractive option.

She finished my wine for me, and we walked. I'd been on my way to the water's edge and Lucy thought that was a fine idea. The sun was all gone by now and stars were peeking out. One of the things I liked about Len's place—it was just far enough away from town you could make out stars at night. Not like the deep woods, or the mountains. But constellations weren't just theoretical there.

"Hey Tom," she said as the surf touched our toes, "want to go for a swim? I know we don't have suits, but..."

Why not? As you might remember, I've a weakness for the midnight dunk. We both did, as I recall.

I stepped back a few yards to where the sand was dry, set down my glass and stripped off my shirt, my trousers. Lucy unbuttoned her blouse, the top button of her jeans. I cast off my briefs. "Well?" I said, standing *in flagrante delicto* in front of her.

"Get in," she said, "I'll be right behind you."

It didn't occur to me that this might be a trick until I was well out at sea. Wouldn't it be the simplest thing, I thought, as I dove under a breaking wave, to wait until I was out far enough, gather my trousers, find the wallet and the mobile phone, toss the clothes into the surf and run to a waiting car? I'm developing my suspicious mind, really, my dearest—but it still has a time delay on it, even after everything...

I came up, broke my stroke, and turned to look back at the beach.

She waved at me. I was pleased—and relieved—to see that she was naked too. My valuables were safe as they could be. And Lucy had quite a nice figure, as it turned out: fine full breasts— wide, muscular hips—a small bulge at the tummy, true...but taken with the whole, far from offensive.

I waved back, took a deep breath and dove again, this time deep enough to touch bottom. My fingers brushed sea-rounded rock and stirred up sand, and I turned and kicked and broke out to the moonless night, and only then it occurred to me—how clearly I'd seen her on the beach, two dozen yards off, maybe further.

There lay the problem. There wasn't enough light. I shouldn't have seen anything.

I treaded water, thinking back at how I'd seen her...glistening, flickering, with tiny points of red, of green...winking in and out... like stars themselves? Spread across not sky, but flesh?

I began to wonder: Had I seen her at all?

There was no sign of her now. The beach was a line of black, crowned with the lights from Len's place, and above that...the stars.

How much had I smoked? I wondered. What had I smoked, for that matter? I hadn't had a lot of wine—I'd quaffed a glass at Len's before venturing outside, and I'd shared the second glass with Lucy. Not even two glasses...

But it *was* Len's wine.

I'd made up my mind to start back in when she emerged from the waves—literally in front of my face.

"You look lost," Lucy said, and splashed me, and dove again. Two feet came up, and scissored, and vanished. Some part of her brushed against my hip.

I took it as my cue and ducked.

The ocean was nearly a perfect black. I dove and turned and dove again, reaching wide in my strokes, fingers spreading in a curious, and yes, hungry grasp. I turned, and came near enough the surface that I felt my foot break it, splashing down again, and spun—

—and I saw her.

Or better, I saw the constellation of Lucy—a dusting of brilliant red points of light, defining her thighs—and then turning, and more along her midriff; a burst of blue stipple, shaping her breasts, the backs of her arms. I kicked toward her as she turned in the water, my own arms held straight ahead, to lay hold of that fine, if I may say, celestial body.

But she anticipated me, and kicked deeper, and I'd reached my lungs' limits so I broke surface, gasping at the night air. She was beside me an instant later, spitting and laughing. No funny lights this time; just Lucy, soaking wet and treading water beside me.

"We don't have towels," she said. "I just thought of that. We're going to freeze."

"We won't freeze," I said.

"It's colder than you think."

"Oh, I know it's cold. We just won't freeze."

She splashed me and laughed again and wondered what I meant by that, but we both knew what I meant by that, and after we'd not-quite tired ourselves out in the surf, we made back for the shore.

I wonder how things went for you, right then? I know that you always fancied Jonathan; I know what happened later. I hope you don't think I'm being bitter or ironic when I say I hope you had a good time with him. If he misbehaved — well, I trust you did too.

Shall I tell you how *we* misbehaved?

Well—

In some ways, it was as you might expect; nothing you haven't seen, nothing you haven't felt, my dear.

In others...

Through the whole of it, Lucy muttered.

"He is," she would say as I pressed against her breasts and nibbled on her earlobe; and "Quiet!" as I ran my tongue along the rim of her aureole... "I said no," as I thrust into her, and I paused, and then she continued: "Why are you stopping, Tommy?"

This went on through the whole of it. As I buried my face between her legs, and she commented, "Isn't he, though?", I thought again of Lucy on the shore, under the water. "Too bright," she moaned, and I remembered my visions of the sky, on her skin.

And as I thought of these things, my hands went exploring: along her thighs, across her breasts—along her belly...

She gasped and giggled as I ran my thumb across her navel...
and she said, "Tommy?" as my forefinger touched her navel
again...and "What are you doing?" as the palm of my hand,
making its way along the ridge of her hip-bone...found her navel
once more.

I lifted my head and moved my hand slowly aside. For an
instant, there was a flash of dim red light—reflecting off my
palm like a candle-flame. But only an instant. I moved my
hand aside and ran the edge of my thumb over the flesh there.
It was smooth. "Tom?" she said sharply, and started on about
unfinished business. "Shh," I said, and lowered my face—to the
ridge of her hip-bone, or rather the smooth flesh inward of it.
And slowly, paying minute attention, I licked her salted skin.

I would not have found it with my crude, calloused fingertips; my tongue was better attuned to the task. I came upon it
first as a small bump in the smooth flesh: like a pimple, a cyst.
As I circled it, I sensed movement, as though a hard thing were
rolling inside. Running across the tiny peak of it, I sensed a line
—like a slit in the flesh, pushed tightly closed. Encouraged, I surrounded it with my lips and began to suck, as I kept probing it
with my tongue. "I'm sorry," she said, and then , "Oh!" as my
tongue pushed through. It touched a cool, wet thing—rolling on
my tongue like an unripened berry.

And then...I was airborne...it was though I were flying up, and
falling deep. And I landed hard on my side and it all resolved,
the world once more. Icy water lapped against me. And Lucy
was swearing at me.

I looked at her, unbelieving. She looked back.

She, and a multitude.

For now I could see that what I'd first thought were star-
points, were nothing of the sort. Her flesh was pocked with eyes.
They were small, and reflective, like a cat's.

Nocturnal eyes.

In her shoulders—the swell of her breasts—along the line of
her throat...They blinked—some individually, some in pairs, and
on her belly, six points of cobalt blue, formed into a nearly perfect
hexagon. Tiny slits of pupils widened to take in the sight of me.
The whole of her flesh seemed to writhe with their squinting.

It didn't seem to cause her discomfort. Far from it; Lucy's own
eyes—the ones in her head—narrowed to slits, and her mouth
perked in a little smile. "He is that," she said, "yes, you're right."
And it struck me then: those strange things she was saying
weren't intended for me or anyone else.

She was talking to the eyes.

"He can't have known," she continued, her hand creeping down to her groin, "and if he did, well now he knows better."

I drew my legs to my chest and my own hands moved instinctively to my privates, as the implications of all these eyes, of her words, came together.

These weren't her eyes; they were from another creature, or many creatures. And they were all looking upon me: naked, sea-shrivelled, crouching in the dirt.

Turning away from her, I got to my feet, ran up the beach and gathered my shirt and trousers, and clutching them to my chest, fairly bolted for the stairs. I pulled on my shirt and trousers, hunted around for my shoes, and made my way up the stairs. At the top, I looked back for the glow of Lucy. But the beach was dark.

The eyes were shut.

You and Jonathan were gone by the time I came back to the house.

I wasn't surprised; Len had switched to his Sarah Vaughan / Etta James play-list, and I remember how fond you are of those two. And it was late. The party had waxed and waned during my excursion with Lucy on the beach and those who remained were the die-hards: Ben and Dru, sprawled on the sectional, finishing off a bottle of shiraz; Dennis, holding court in the kitchen with Emile and Prabh and the dates they'd not thought to introduce —at least not to me; maybe a half-dozen others that neither of us wouldn't recognize if we met them on the street. Len's party had proceeded without me.

I wasn't surprised, and I wasn't unhappy about it. Skinny dipping on the ocean and fucking on the beach are two activities that hardly leave one presentable to polite company. Best then to wait until the polite company had moved along, leaving only the depraved ones.

I made for the bathroom—the second floor bath, which yes, I know, was a *faux-pas* at Len's parties, particularly late into the evening. But there was a small crowd around the two-piece off the kitchen, and I needed to tidy up sooner. so I slipped upstairs and made for the master bath. Which, happily, was vacant. The lights flickered on as I stepped inside and I slid the pocket door shut, and confronted myself in the long mirror opposite the showers.

I didn't think I took that long; just splashed water in my face, ran a wet comb through my hair, shook the sand out of my shirt and tucked it in properly before giving myself another inspection. By my own reckoning, it couldn't have been more than five minutes. But the hammering on the door said otherwise.

It was Kimi, Len's Kimi.

In a week, she'd be on a plane back to New York, done with all of us, gone from Len's circle for good. That party, she was on the verge of it. I slid open the door and apologized. "You shouldn't be up here," she said, "not this time of night," and I agreed.

"Ask forgiveness not permission? That it, Tommy?" she said and brushed past me. She had been spending time in Len's rooms, and it had gone about as badly as it did toward the end. You could tell. Do you remember that time Len had us all on that boat he'd hired for the summer? And she came hammering on our cabin door—with that fish-hook stuck in just below the collar-bone? And when you opened it, she was so quiet, asking if you knew where they kept the first-aid kit on the boat because "Len isn't sure." You knew something awful had happened, I knew something awful had happened. We talked about it after we got the hook out and the wound cleaned and bandaged and Kimi, smiling brightly, had excused herself and skipped back to the cabin she and Len were sharing. What did you say? "One day, that armour of hers is going to crack. When it does, she'll either leave or she'll die."

It was a good line; I laughed as hard as you did.

Well there in the upstairs bath, the armour was cracking. And Kimi wasn't dead. But she wasn't leaving either. She leaned against the vanity, arms crossed over her chest. She was wearing a short black skirt. Her shoulders, arms, and legs were bare. There were no visible bruises. No fish-hooks either. She studied me, maybe looking for the same things.

"You go for a swim?" she said finally. "You look like you went for a swim in the ocean."

"Guilty."

Her eyes flickered away a moment as she waved a hand. "Nobody's guilty of taking a fucking swim. And it's a good look for you." Then she looked again, reassessing. "But you didn't just go for a swim."

"You were right. I took a fucking swim," I said, and started to laugh, and she got it and laughed too.

"How's your night going?" I asked. She made a little sneer with her lips—as if she was trying to fish a piece of food out of her teeth. Put her bare feet together on the slate tile floor, made a show of inspecting the nails.

"Len's very tired," she said.

I raised my eyebrows. "Oh dear. That doesn't sound good."

"It's not as bad as that."

"If you say so."

She looked at me. "Are you hitting on me, Tommy?"

I said I wasn't.

"Then why the fuck are you still here?"

There was an answer to that question, but not one I could really articulate—not the way she was looking at me then. I wanted to talk to her about Lucy, about the eyes...I thought—hoped—that she would be able to help me parse the experience somehow. Or failing that, help me put it away, someplace quiet.

But her armour was cracked. She had nothing to offer me. And although I wouldn't know for sure until a week later—she wasn't leaving that night, she stayed the whole time—she was almost certainly planning her escape.

So I left her to it. "I'm very tired too," I said, and stepped into the hall.

That one didn't get a laugh. The bathroom door slid shut behind me, hitting the door-jamb hard enough to quiver in its track.

"You're still thinking about *her*," said Kimi through the wood. "Well give it up, Tommy. It's obvious to everybody. She's done with you."

Oh, don't worry. I know you're done with me. I'm done with you too.

I joined the conversation in the kitchen, or rather hovered at its edge. Dennis had stepped away, and now Emile was talking about Dubai, which was hardly a new topic for him. But the girls he and Prabh had brought were new. They hung on every word. I leaned against the stove, poured myself the dregs of a Chardonnay into a little plastic cup and swallowed the whole thing. Prabh found me a Malbec from Portugal and poured a refill.

"Yeah, you look like shit," he said. "Bad night?"

"Not exactly bad," I said. "Strange. Not exactly bad."

Prabh nodded and turned back to his girl. She was very pretty, I had to hand it to him: tall, with streaked blond hair and a dancer's body. Twenty-seven years old, no older. I'd turn back to her too.

So I kept drinking, and Prabh kept filling my cup, and after awhile, I'd moved from the periphery of the conversation to the juicy middle. And there, I asked as innocently as I could manage: "Any of you know Lucy?"

Shrugs all around. I showed a level hand to indicate her height. Another to show how long her hair was. "We don't know her, Tom," said Emile, and Prabh poured me another glass. "Maybe you want to sit down?" asked one of the girls.

It was an excellent suggestion. I made my way to the sectional in the living room with only a little help here and there, as necessary.

Really, I don't think I made *that* much of a spectacle of myself. But I had had too much to drink and I'd had it all too quickly. I was speaking extemporaneously you might say. So I concluded it be best not to speak at all.

I fitted myself into the corner of the sectional. Dru and Ben a few feet to my left, made a point of staying engrossed in one another—and as soon as it was polite to do so, got up and found spots at the dining room table. And I was left to myself.

By this time it was well past midnight. You know how that is. It's a time when you start asking questions about things that in the light of day you wouldn't consider twice. It's a time...well, we both know how it goes, in the dark hour.

I was left to myself.

I began to feel badly about leaving Lucy on the beach. I wondered if I might have handled things differently. I worried that I might have impregnated her, or caught a venereal disease. Briefly, I worried that some of those eyes might have migrated from her skin to mine—if I'd caught a case of leaping, burrowing and uniquely ocular crabs. If I closed my own eyes, would I see a thousand dim refractions of the room from the point of view of my belly?

The notion made me laugh—a little too loudly, I think. Dennis, reeking of weed and vodka cooler, just about turned on his heel at the sight of me and fled back to the deck. But it got me back wondering at the nature of Lucy's peculiar disease, if that's what it was. If not she, then who was looking out through those eyes? And so, in circles, went my thoughts.

The front door opened and closed once, twice, five times. Water ran in the kitchen sink. Lights dimmed in rooms not far from this one.

"Hey Tom. How you keeping?"

I looked up and blinked.

"Hey Len," I said. "Haven't seen you all night."

He nodded. "I've been a rotten host."

Len was wearing his kimono, that red one with the lotus-design. He'd lost a lot of weight—you couldn't mistake it, the kimono hung so loose on him. His hair was coming back in, but it was still thin, downy. He sat down beside me.

"You met Lucille," he said.

"How did you know?" I asked, but I didn't need to; as I spoke, I saw Kimi over the breakfast bar in the kitchen, putting glasses into the dishwasher. She'd told him about our conversation in the washroom. He'd put it together.

"Yeah," said Len, "you were on the beach. Two of you. Had yourself a time, didn't you Tom?"

"We had ourselves a time."

Len put a bony hand on my thigh, gave it a squeeze of surprising strength, and nodded.

"Now you're drunk in my living room, when everybody else has had sense to get out. Too drunk to drive yourself, am I right?"

That was true.

"And you don't have cab fare, do you?"

I didn't have cab fare.

"You're a fucking leech, Tom. You *smell* like a fucking leech."

"It's the ocean," I said.

Kimi turned her back to us, lowered her head and raised her shoulder blades, like wings, as she ran water in the kitchen sink.

"Yeah, we know that's not so," said Len. "You smell of Lucy." He licked his lips, and not looking up, Kimi called out, "that's not nice, Len," and Len chuckled and jacked a thumb in her direction and shrugged.

"Did she leave?" I asked. "Lucy I mean."

"Miss her too now?" Did I miss her like *you*, he meant, obviously.

"I just didn't see her leave."

"What'd I just say? *Everybody else* had the sense to get out."

A plate clattered loudly in the sink. Len shouted at Kimi to *be fuckin' careful with that*. Then he coughed and turned an eye to me. His expression changed.

"You saw," he said quietly. "Didn't you?"

"I saw."

He looked like he wanted to say more. But he stopped himself, the way he does: tucking his chin down, pursing his lips...

like he's doing some math, which is maybe close to the mark of what he is doing until he finally speaks.

"Did she tell you how we met?"

"Friend of a friend," I said, then remembered: "Not just a friend; one of your partners. And then you just kept inviting her out."

"Always that simple, isn't it?"

"It's never that simple," I said, "you're going to tell me."

"It is that simple," he said. "Lucille Carroll is a high school friend of Linda James. Linda isn't a partner now and I won't likely live to see the day that she is. But she did work for me. With me. And she used to come out sometimes. And she brought Lucille one day. And not long after, Linda stopped coming around. Lucille still shows up." He sighed. "Simple."

Kimi flipped a switch under the counter and the dishwasher hummed to life. "I'm turning in," she announced, and when Len didn't say anything, she climbed the stairs.

"It's not that simple," I said when Kimi was gone. Now, I thought, was the time when Len would spell it out for me: tell me what had happened, really.

"And she doesn't like to talk about it," was what he said instead. "It's private, Tom."

What came next? Well, I might have handled it better. But you know how I hate it when my friends hide things from me. We both remember the weekend at the lake, with your sister and her boys. Did I ever properly apologize for that? It's difficult to, when all I've spoken is God's truth.

But I could have handled it better.

"It's not private," I said, "it's the opposite. She's the least private person I've met. The eyes..."

"Her skin condition you mean."

"You do know about them." I may have jabbed him in the chest. That may have been unwise. "Maybe you like them? Watching everything you do? Maybe they flatter your vanity..."

Len shook his head. He stopped me.

"You know what, Tom? I'm sick of you. I've been sick of you for a long time. But I'm also sick, and I'll tell you—that clarifies things for a man. So here's what I see:

"You come here to my house—you moon around like some fucking puppy dog—you drink my wine...the friends of mine you don't fuck, you bother with your repetitive, self-involved shit. Jesus, Tom. You're a leech."

"I'm sorry," I said, because really—what else do you say to something like that? To someone like Len, for Christ's sake?

"Yeah," he said. "Heard that one before. Lucy's a special girl, Tom. She's helping me in ways you couldn't imagine. And it has nothing to do with my fucking vanity. Not a fucking thing. Lucy's my...assurance. And she's always welcome here."

"I'm sorry."

"I got that. Now are you okay to drive yet, Tom?"

I wasn't. But I said sure.

"Then you get out of my house. Get back to your place. Stay there. I don't think you should come back here again."

Yes. That's why you hadn't seen me at Len's after that. He cast me out—into the wilderness—left me to my own devices.

I wasn't avoiding you.

Far from it.

Lucy wasn't that hard to find.

She had a Facebook page, and I had enough information to narrow her down from the list of those other Lucy Carrolls who said they were from here. So I sent her a note apologizing for being such an asshole, and she sent me a friend request and I agreed—and she asked me to pick a place, and that's where we met. It's the Tokyo Grill in the Pier District. I don't think we ever went there, you and I. But at 12:15 on a Tuesday in June, it's very bright.

Lucy wore a rose print dress, not quite as pale as her skin. She had freckles and her hair was more reddish than brunette. Perhaps it was the effect of wearing a dress and not a pair of jeans, but she seemed more svelte on the patio than she did that night on the beach. *Her* eyes were hazel.

Do you remember how I courted you? Did you ever doubt that I was anything but spontaneous? That when I laughed so hard at that joke of yours, it was because I thought it was the funniest thing I'd ever heard?

You didn't? You should have. I'm not good at everything in life, oh that I'll admit. But I am good at this part. I am smooth.

And that's how I was at the Tokyo Grill that Tuesday.

Lucy wasn't sure about me and she made that explicit pretty early. I'd seemed nice at first, but running off like that...well, it had been hurtful. It made her feel as though there was something wrong with her, and as she made explicit somewhat later on, there wasn't anything wrong with her.

"It's not you—it's the rest of the world," I said, and when she took offense, I explained I wasn't making fun.

"The world's an evil place. Lots wrong with it. Look at...think about Len, as an example."

"What do you mean?"

"Well. How he treats people. How he uses them. Like Kimi."

"He's an important man," she said quickly. "I imagine it takes a toll. All those clients he's got to look after." She sighed. "Clients can be very demanding."

"Clients." I made a little smile. "That's a good word. Len has clients like other people have friends."

Yes, I suppose I was being dramatic. But Lucy didn't think so; she laughed, very hard, and agreed.

"So what about you?" she asked. "Are you client or friend?"

"Something else."

I explained how Lucy wasn't the only one I'd offended with my bad behaviour that night—and again, I layered contrition on top of itself, and doing so took another step to winning her over.

Working through it, I could almost forget that Lucy was a woman containing a multitude—that as she sat here opposite me in the Pier District, the lids up and down her body squinted shut like tiny incision scars against the bright daylight.

Like clients.

I had to forget. Because I couldn't mention them; Len was right—she didn't want to talk about it. She may not have even been capable.

And keeping silent on the subject, and knowing of that alien scrutiny, resting behind translucent lids...

I couldn't have done what I had to do.

Lucy's next shift at the bookstore was Wednesday afternoon, so she had the rest of the day to herself, and as we finished our sashimi, she made a point of saying the afternoon shift meant she could stay out as late as she liked.

So we took a walk. We found my car. We drove back to my apartment. And behind drawn blinds, we stripped off our clothes and lay down together on fresh white sheets.

Oh dear. I can tell you're upset—not by anything I've done, but what you think I'm about to do: relay some detailed account of how it was for Lucy and I, rutting on the very same sheets where you and I lolled, those long Sunday mornings, when... well, before you came to your senses is how you might put it...

I'll try and be circumspect.

Lucy talked through it all, same as she had on the beach: those half-formed statements: "He's the same," and "The third floor," and "I do not agree." Of course, she was talking to them —fielding questions: *Is he the handsome fellow from the beach? On what floor is this fellow's apartment? Don't you think he's a bit much —being too...*

too...

To which she answered: *I do not agree.*

I'd drawn the curtains in my rooms, to make it dim enough for the curious eyes to open without being blinded—and sure enough, this is what they did. As I ran my tongue along her shoulder-blade, I found myself looking into a tiny blue orb, no bigger than a rat's. It blinked curiously at me as I moved past, to the nape of her neck, and there, in the wispy curls at the base of her skull, I uncovered two yellow eyes, set close together, in the forest of her hair. Were they disapproving? I imagine they must have been, affixed on Lucy's skull, less than an inch from her brain. I winked and moved on.

"Tell them," I whispered into her ear, looking into a squinting, infinitely old eye fixed in her temple, "that I understand."

"He understands," she murmured.

"Tell them I'm not afraid."

"He's not afraid."

"Tell them," I said, before I moved from her ear to her mouth, and rolled her onto her back, and slid atop her, "that I'm ready."

And the rest of it?

Well, I did tell you I'd be circumspect. Suffice it to say...just as poor old Len would, not long after...

I *entered* her.

You looked good at my funeral. You and Jonathan both. The dress you wore—was it new? Did you buy it especially for the occasion? It would be nice to think that you had.

In any event, I must say that Jonathan was very supportive of you. He held your hand so very tightly through the eulogies. Had you needed it, I'm sure he would have provided a handkerchief; if it had rained at the graveside, he'd have held the umbrella. He seems that sort of upright fellow. A real keeper.

You look great now, too. You have a lovely smile, you always have, and the shorter haircut—it suits you. It really frames your face. I can't hear what you're saying, here in Emile's house in

town, over the dregs of what I recall as being an acceptable cab-
franc from Chile.

Still, you're laughing, and that's good. You've left Kimi and
poor dying Len behind. You're cementing new friendships...
with Prabh and Emile and, perhaps, Lucy?

Perhaps.

It's impossible to say of course—I haven't been at this long
enough to learn how to read lips, particularly with that damned
brooch in the way. I never could guess your mind on this sort of
thing. But you seem...open to it, to this new friend who works the
cash in your favourite bookstore. You are. Aren't you?

Ah well. I must learn patience here in my new place. After all,
Lucy will tell me everything—in due time, in a quiet moment,
when the lights are low:

*She says she misses you. She says she can't believe she let you go.
Now that you're gone.*

She says that she and I will be great friends.

And then, if all goes well...if you and Lucy really do hit it off...

I can't promise, other than to say I'll do my best. I'll try not to
let my gaze linger.

COWBOY'S ROW

Christopher K. Miller

Rex Wheeler loved Hell-driving, didn't mind going all the way to Cayuga to catch a show. He knew about reverse spins, hi-skis and precision drifts. He knew about skids, drifts, jumps and tight formation manoeuvres. Of course he only knew *about* all these. He couldn't actually *do* any of them. Really, he couldn't even parallel park.

Rex was a smart driver who knew that Hell-driving ain't real driving, the object of which is to arrive at one's destination in a consistently safe and timely manner, and in which real success is based not on sharp tactics, but on good strategy, and that the most important strategy (beyond not driving shit-faced drunk, dog tired or hopping mad) is to try to stay as far away as possible from all the other bad drivers on the road. Assume that everyone around you is disabled, distracted, delusional or suicidal, and you will not be far wrong.

He had many ways of maximizing his road space, of avoiding man's primordial tendency to travel with the herd. But his favorite method was to choose unpopular routes. And that is why, instead of being squeezed along on highway 7, trying to pass seniors tooling along at thirty under the limit with their left turn signals flashing and flashing, and playing road roulette with oncoming traffic eager to pass dawdlers of their own, Rex was sailing along alone in the dark on county road 13, listening to his favorite country rock station.

Rex lived in Maryhill and worked evenings in Guelph as an animal husbandry technician for United Breeders. The job could be tough, especially in the fall when the bull's libidos began to wane. Rex used the drive home to relax and unwind.

On AM radio, Toby Keith sang his first big hit. On the horizon, a harvest moon like the ghost of a pumpkin rose behind dark clouds.

Rex turned on his high beams, cutting a bright swath through surrounding bush, and illuminating blacktop split by a single solid yellow line. He liked how County Road 13 seemed to wind through the country with no clear purpose. At night, with its rounded surface, blind curves and narrow gravel shoulders, it was like riding on the back of a snake.

"I should've been a cowboy," sang Rex. He needed this drive. His father had always taught him to stand up for himself, to treat others with respect, and to know when to do which. The lessons hadn't always been easy either, and neither was living them. It had been a bad shift, a *real* bad shift. There had been an *incident*. Now, soothed by the song, the wind, and the road unfurling, he went over it in his mind.

Rambo hadn't gone for the AV (Artificial Vagina) even with a new trained steer to coax him. And prepping him for digital manipulation had just pissed him off more. He'd recommended giving the big Holstein the day off. But there were back orders on his semen and at two-hundred-and-seventy dollars a half-gram straw, management hadn't wanted to see any slacking. Rambo could fill a *lot* of straws.

The seminal vessels of a bull are situated on either side of the pelvic urethra. Through the walls of the large intestine they feel like symmetric bags of grapes. Rambo had snorted when he'd begun to gently palpate the gland on the right. The gland on the left had been swollen and warm, and Rambo had bellowed falsetto and bucked against the bars of the tight stall when he'd applied a small amount of pressure to it. "Seminal vesiculitis," he'd said withdrawing his arm, beginning to peel off the glove. "You've been pushing him too hard. Don't matter how hot his wrigglers are now. My boy here needs a break."

Rambo had grumbled as if to concur.

His boss, Mr. Hornsby, from the safety of the raised cement walkway dividing the rows of dirt-floor stalls, had carefully folded a silk hankie that he'd been cleaning his glasses with and returned it to his breast pocket. Then he'd said, "Use the electro-ejaculator."

His mother's lifelong belief in and example of treating all God's creatures with kindness had afforded a gentle but enduring lesson. Just thinking about this device, even now, made his knees weak and his prostate ache. The thing resembled a giant copper-tipped 30-30 round. But attached black electrical cables made it look like some high-tech implement of torture—which wasn't far wrong. Vocalization is an indicator of pain in bulls, and the bulls tended to get pretty vocal when the ejaculator was applied.

The lights of an oncoming vehicle stabbed up over the crest of a hill. Rex turned off his high beams before returning to the day's events.

He'd pulled the long latex glove on up to his armpit. "I've been in and around bulls for thirty years," he'd said, "And I'm telling you, you pump current through those glands now, you're gonna rupture something." Then he'd slapped Rambo high on the rump. "And your million dollar man here is hamburger."

Rambo had lowed, raising and dipping his head between vertical crossbar restraints as though nodding.

"Why don't you pull one on," he'd said to Hornsby, tossing the spent glove into a waste receptacle. "See for yourself what I'm talking about."

Rambo had responded to the suggestion by raising his tail and dropping a nine inch pie.

"That won't be necessary," Hornsby had replied, blanching. "I've made my decision."

It'd satisfied him to see Hornsby's pinched expression, to see him shrug his hands up almost into the sleeves of his virgin wool suit jacket. He knew the man had never had an arm in a bull in his life, had no business supervising the harvests. Who wears Brooks Brothers to the pens anyway? The man was a bean counter.

His reverie was broken by fast approaching headlights in his rear view. Rex flipped it up to reduce night glare and eased to the right. A pickup truck shot by on his left and then cut in front of him. As he pulled away, the driver slid open the back window and pushed something out. Rex flicked on his high beams to see that it was only the driver's arm. The guy was giving him the finger.

Asshole. A flash of hot irritation caused him to step on the gas, then to open his own window and return the gesture. The world is so full of assholes. The thought took him back.

"Now see here Mr. Wheeler," Hornsby had said, "It's not your call to make." Hornsby had sucked in a breath as if to inflate his confidence before continuing. "You know the drill. Sanitize the ejaculator. Check the battery." Hornsby had blown air into his cheeks while staring down at Rambo's steaming shit. "Clean the animal's rectum. Stick it in and make it happen. I'll expect at least 150 ml."

He'd fantasized grabbing his boss by the scruff of the neck and shoving his *head* in Rambo's rectum. This had helped keep him from saying or doing something he'd regret. This had enabled him to walk away.

"You know you aren't the only one with skinny arms and soft hands," Hornsby had shouted after him. "You know you can be replaced."

He'd stopped and turned, pleased to see his boss take a step backwards. "Go ahead," he'd said. "Find someone else to do it then. Ask your secretary for all I care. But you injure this animal, and I hope you remember what I told you. Because I sure will."

Rounding the next bend, Rex saw that the truck that had cut him off had pulled off to the side. Because the shoulder was only a few feet wide, half of it still stuck out on the road. He sped up to veer around it, cutting it close. Engine trouble, he hoped.

But it was not engine trouble. In his passenger side mirror he saw it pull back out onto the highway as soon as he'd passed. Rex slowed and then held his speed steady. He didn't want to give the appearance of running. So it didn't take long for the other driver to catch him. Headlights lit the interior of his car and danced in his side mirrors. He lowered his rear view. In it the Dodge grill emblem loomed. The way its ram's horns curled out in a V reminded him of fallopian tubes in diagrams of the female reproductive system.

As it crept closer, vibrations from the big V8 hemi began to rattle his spine. Battered by the tailgating truck's engine noise and its driver's sporadic blasts on the horn, the song on the radio became irritating, just confusing background noise. Rex turned it off.

The urge to injure the other driver began to gnaw at his guts. He thought about pulling over and just going to town on the guy, beating the living crap out of him, or even getting the crap beat out of himself as long as he could land a few. Even getting in just one good nose shot on the immature asshole behind him, taunting him and playing games with his life, would make any reciprocal pain a pleasure to endure. And the longer the guy rode his bumper, the more he yearned to punish him, the more he longed to make him hurt.

The way he had longed to make Hornsby hurt when Rambo screamed. Probably Bill Slater, the only other qualified man on duty, had also refused. Because the guy Hornsby had gotten to do his dirty work wasn't even certified, just a glorified stable boy who didn't have a clue about the electro-ejaculator. Or maybe that'd been Hornsby's plan, his way of getting back at him for refusing. Rex squeezed the wheel to keep his hands from shaking.

The driver of the truck dropped back, but then accelerated forward as though to ram him, honking his horn before stepping on the brake. He did it again, and then again. Each iteration seemed to raise his temperature a little, the way a jack raises a car. His hands were now slippery on the wheel. It took a moment for him to realize that the pitched swearing ringing in his ears was his own.

When the driver of the truck switched on his high beams, the world dissolved in feverish red; the red that goads bulls and makes them charge; the red that had tinged the vial of warm semen that Hornsby had called him into his office in order to wave in his face while Rambo keened down in the pens.

"220 ml," Hornsby had bragged. "When was the last time you collected two-twenty? Guess I'll stop sending a boy to do a man's job."

He'd replied through teeth clenched so tight his ears ached. "There's blood in your collection. I'm calling in the vet."

Hornsby had frowned and then held the sealed vial up to his fluorescent ceiling fixture. "You're fulla' shit, Wheeler. You're just jealous."

He hadn't meant to yank on the jack cord so hard. Hornsby's phone had dinged and rattled and hopped across his desk, knocking over a mug of cold coffee and ploughing pens, paperwork and a framed picture of his wife over the edge and down onto the floor.

Hornsby had leapt to his feet, dug his fists into his hips, and then cocked his head to make a show of listening to Rambo's far off bullish crying. "Thing sounds healthy enough to me," he'd said.

Rex had spoken slowly, meticulously, as though stalking down each word. "You better pray that they can salvage those glands Hornsby—that they don't have to put my boy down."

He'd just begun to punch in the vet's number when Hornsby darted around the desk and unplugged the phone. "Now see here Wheeler. We don't have the budget to call in a veterinarian every time you get a whim. This time you have gone too far. You have crossed the line. You're not calling anybody! I plan to report your insubordination—and your threats. You are suspended until further notice."

The driver of the truck began to flash his high beams: on-off-on-off-on-off. Over and over: too bright to see, then too dark to see—an assaulting rhythm that wouldn't let his eyes adjust, and that triggered in him a blinding apoplectic seizure.

The sole of his steel-enforced Kodiak work boot thumped down onto the brake, much the way its toe had earlier flown up into Hornsby's groin: without direction, as of its own accord, the way a motor-reflex jerks your hand away from a stove before you even realize it's hot. It had landed with a solid squish, almost a splat, tearing a trouser inseam and lifting the natty accountant up onto his toes. There comes a time when a body's need to hurt another trumps all consequences.

In the shrieking of tires, Rex could feel the stutter of his ABS seeking traction, his chest pressing and his hips lifting against the straps of his torsion-locked seatbelt as his body strained for the dash.

Behind him, headlights dipped, veered left and then right, and then disappeared. He stepped off the brake.

Hornsby had gone down hard too, curled up like a sow bug right between his oak desk and his calf's leather couch. He'd plugged the phone back in and spoken to the vet while Hornsby and Rambo made similar background noises. After he'd hung up, Hornsby started to puke. So he'd fetched him his trash can. Then he'd gone down to the pens and stroked Rambo's neck and forehead until the vet arrived.

Except for the chirping of crickets and the distant barking of a dog, the world rested. With the truck gone, the road behind looked so empty that Rex began to wonder if he hadn't imagined the whole thing. Of course he knew what had happened. The driver had jammed on his brakes, realized he wouldn't be able to stop in time and tried to swing around. But cranking his wheels left while into a skid had caused him to ski right, right off into the ditch.

Rex turned his radio back on. On it, a stupid couple urged potential blood donors to register on-line. Clouds parted for the moon, letting it paint surrounding fields in starlight golds and shadows. Rex slowed, then stopped, and then performed a perfect three point turn.

If not for the smoke, he might have passed right by. The truck appeared to have tipped onto its side after leaving the road, and then slid into a short wire fence demarcating a field of clover before rolling onto its roof.

Rex pulled over and punched 911 on his cell. His hands were shaking. His whole body began to tremble as though he were freezing. "Been a real bad accident on County Road 13 just outta Guelph around fire route fourteen-ninety," he said through clenched teeth. "Gonna need fire and ambulance I guess."

A woman had answered. She sounded bored, or maybe stressed. She seemed to be questioning and instructing him all at the same time.

"I gotta run," he said, and lumbered down onto the field.

It was an old truck he now saw, rusting out on the bottom. Upside down it looked smaller than it had in his rear view. Oily, grey smoke billowed from beneath the hood, picked up by a westerly breeze.

Inside the truck's cabin the driver was pressed up against his side window, making it hard to see much else, to see how bad he was. Rex could hear his high-pitched wailing.

Something stung his hand when he touched the door handle. At first he thought it was heat from the engine fire that had conducted into the truck's body. But the pain was intermittent, arriving in buzzing once-a-second jolts, like clockwork. Then he saw. The wire fence the truck had pushed, snagged and pinned was electrified, probably low impedance to cut through all the high surrounding vegetation. Pretty good kick to it too, probably for horses. "Sure wish I'd thought to bring my gloves," he said to the night.

The weight of the truck had warped the struts and the top of the driver's door was buried in the field. Pulsating current burned his hands and filled his boots and legs with sand as he tugged. But no way could he open it. He stumbled around to the passenger side. There, the wailing grew louder. He now saw that it was not coming from the driver. It was coming from a car seat. A tiny upside-down face, its mouth locked in the rictus of a howl, stared out at him through wide, yet incongruously thoughtful, eyes. The face of a little girl.

He grabbed the door handle and yanked. Again the fence tortured him. Again the door would not open.

Far off, a siren sang, and then faded.

He tried to yell. "Close your eyes honey!" But his voice was still hoarse from his earlier rage. "Close your eyes." But the eyes stayed open. Smoke began to leak into the cabin. The little girl coughed, and then continued wailing.

He kicked the window with the same toe he'd planted in Hornsby's crotch. The window cracked. He kicked it again, and again, harder. When his toe punched through he dropped to his knees and tore at it with his hands. Shards and slivers of glass glued to safety laminate splintered and cut into his fingers and palms.

He had to snake in and twist to sit in the window of the overturned truck. Fumes and smoke stung his eyes. Wicked metronomic jolts spanked him through aluminum window trim. Hands burnt and bleeding, he fumbled between the seats for the belt release.

Once freed, the inverted car seat and its tiny passenger dropped into his lap with unfortunate precision and unexpected force, causing him to gasp and fold, to gag and cough, causing him to suspect that he would soon barf the way Hornsby had.

"Save Melinda. Save Melinda," said the driver as though he'd been saying it forever. "Save Melinda. Save Melinda." He had a Newfoundland accent. It sounded like he was saying, "Save me Linda."

It was hard to crawl all the way into the truck with the car seat and child on him, harder still because the child, now grounded by him, shared in the punishment of the fence, but that instead of pushing away, she screamed and pulled at his hair and beard and gouged at his neck and face like one drowning. In such cramped acrid quarters it was hard to separate the freaking child from her car seat and then from his face, and then to shove her out to safety.

"Save Melinda. Save Melinda." The driver from the Rock continued his lilting plea, even after the girl was out. "Save Melinda. Save Melinda." It had become his mantra.

Rex now saw that the driver was just a kid, but a big kid, a *real* big kid—too big for the side window. He figured kicking out the windshield would be easier than reaching across the big strangely sprawled kid to try to press the door open with his legs, and that, even if he could kick open a door, this might weaken structural support and cause the cabin to be crushed. Sitting awkwardly on the interior roof light with his back against the sliding rear window through which he'd earlier been given the finger, he stomped outward with both his heels.

With the windshield booted out, heat and black smoke from the fire under the hood rushed in as though having planned the attack.

Holding his breath, Rex squirmed out. Then, blind, on his stomach in steaming clover, broken glass, and finally his own vomit, he turned and groped through electrified moulding... until he found a leather belt.

"Save Melinda. Save Melinda," said the kid, making no effort to save himself.

The hood of the truck was like a grill. But there was no other way then but for him to dig his knees into the ground and wedge his back up against it in order to gain enough purchase to pull the kid's slack weight through the jagged hole in the windshield. Heat fused cotton to skin as electricity snapped through his buttocks, thighs and knees on its persistent ground-ward course. Smoke saturated his lungs.

And he was being whipped by his father in their woodshed. But instead of the belt, his father was using a bullwhip, a bullwhip with long black electrical cords like those on the ejaculator attached to it. He wondered what he'd done to deserve this and if it was because his father was senile and staying in a home that he was using a bullwhip instead of the belt—or if maybe it was because he himself had the belt. He could feel it cutting into his hands as he tried to pull it away.

And his mother was ironing his clothes. He could smell the hot fabric, and bacon grease. It made him dizzy to think about why she'd iron his clothes in the woodshed with bacon grease so long after her death from breast cancer.

So he dragged the belt away from the woodshed, away from his aging father's whipping and his dead mother's cooking, out onto a moonlit field. And when a waif of a girl crying "daddy daddy-daddy-daddy" flew over to grab hold of it and cling to it and he could find neither the breath nor the words to tell her that everything was okay now because no one was hurting anyone, he dragged her too.

"Save Melinda," said the belt. "Daddy, daddy!" said the girl.

He dragged them both. Across clover and burdock and milkweed he dragged them, dragged them until the field opened up and he fell and sat gazing into a crackling campfire with his arm around his summer love roasting hotdogs and marshmallows and laughing and singing to a wailing sad guitar while up on the river colored lights from many boats bobbed and spun and swept smooth black water that flowed aimlessly nowhere.

SAFE

Brett Alexander Savory

When the sun started melting, no one seemed particularly bothered. No one except Clark.

"Todd, check it out," Clark says, points at the sky.

"What?" Todd says, and looks up. The two are on the sidewalk of a busy street. Cars and bees buzz by. Summertime.

"The sun," Clark says. "The sun. Look at it."

Todd glares. "What about it? It's the sun. Big whoop." He bites into the street meat he'd bought from one of the vendors downtown.

Clark stops walking. Todd keeps going. A few steps later, Todd realizes Clark isn't beside him. Wiping at his mouth with a ketchup-stained napkin, he turns around, says, "Come on, man, we'll be late. Get your skinny ass in gear. Quit staring at the sun. You'll burn your retinas out."

Todd turns, keeps walking and chewing.

Later, they're on the outdoor patio of a café, sitting with the girl both Clark and Todd want. Neither of them know of the other's desire.

Todd says, "So Jane, Clark tried to burn his eyes out of his stupid head by staring at the sun on the way here."

Clark says nothing, glances up into the sky. Then, after a moment's reflection: "I'm actually pretty concerned about the fact that when I look up into the sky, it looks as though the sun is melting—like yellow-orange paint that's been heated and is dripping down a light blue canvas."

Jane laughs. Clark does not. Jane stops laughing. Unlike Clark and Todd, she is fully aware that they both want her. "You're serious, aren't you?"

Clark lifts his head again skyward. Jane follows his gaze, shielding her eyes from the full force of the sun's brilliance. A man riding by on his bike lifts his head. Sees nothing. Carries on.

"I don't see anything weird about the sun, Clark," Jane says. "Honest, I don't."

Clark nods his head slightly, blinks rapidly, taps his fingers on the wooden table.

Beers arrive. Todd drains his in four gulps. Clark's sits untouched. Jane sips.

A breeze stirs, sending a lavender scent across the table from Jane to Clark. Clark inhales it, smiles. Wonders how the underside of her forearm would feel cupped in his hand.

When Clark gets home that night, he posts on his blog: "The sun is melting. Has no one else noticed this?" Only one person responds, a friend of his from high school with whom he has recently lost touch. A girl named Bernice. Bernice writes: "Clark, the sun is not melting. You probably have a brain disease and are dying. Maybe it's cancer. A horrible way to go. When you're dead, can I have your cat?"

The next day, Clark is supposed to meet with Jane and Todd for dinner. Instead, he calls them and lies, says he's caught some kind of bug. Needs to stay home and rest up.

After making his calls, he draws back the curtains in the living room of his one-bedroom apartment. The feeble light from the melting sun drizzles in, settles across the hardwood floors grudgingly.

It's easier to look at the sun today; it's become hazier, its edges more indistinct.

Clark thinks about what it means, what he can do about it. Wonders why newspapers, TV, and the Internet aren't buzzing with headlines about The End of the World.

Clark closes the curtains, makes coffee, bacon, and eggs. Dips toast into the runny centres. Waits for nightfall.

Last night, he didn't look up at the stars. He was afraid of what he might see. Tonight, he braces himself, walks over to the living room window when he sees the dark red and purple light bleed away to black beneath the curtains. Glances at his watch: 8:49 p.m.

Heart fluttering madly, stomach in knots, he reaches out to yank the curtains aside, but stays his hand. Lets it drop to his side.

He walks to the cordless phone, picks it up from its cradle, dials. His cat brushes up against his legs, meows for food. It's two hours past its feeding time. When Jane picks up, Clark is scooping food into the cat's bowl.

"What's up?" Jane says. "Thought you were sick."

"I am. Listen, can you come over? Just don't bring Todd, alright?"

"What's that noise?" Jane asks.

"I'm feeding the cat."

"You mean the cat you're going to leave to Bernice when you die of brain cancer?"

"You saw that?" Clarks says. "What kind of thing is that to say to someone?"

Clark closes the lid on the plastic food container, walks back into the living room, stands in front of the curtains. Afraid of them. Wanting to be as far away from them as possible.

"So did you hear me? Don't bring Todd," Clark says.

Jane replies, "Sure, no problem. Should I bring something? I'm not sure what you want me to do over there."

Clark hears something in her voice. "No, it's okay. Just bring yourself. I want to show you something. Actually, I want to show *myself* something, but with you here in the...um, in the room, I guess."

He feels a certain distance grow between them just then. "Todd can be a bit of a douche sometimes and I think it'd be cool if we spent a bit of time together without him, you know?"

"Oh, yeah, well...okay, sure. Sounds good." Clark hears her voice warm again. "I can be there for 11:30. Good with you?"

Clark says, "Good with me, yeah. Thanks, Jane. See you soon."

Once he's hung up, Clark goes to his computer, pulls up his blog, types: "Bernice: The sun *is* melting. I do not have brain cancer. I am not dying. You cannot have my cat. I never really thought of you as a friend."

At 11:37, Clark's phone rings.

"Hi, Jane," Clark says.

"I'm right around the corner, fella. Get ready to buzz me in."

Clark says, "Roger, that."

"Oh, and I know you said not to bother with anything, but I brought wine. You know, in case you want to get me drunk and take advantage." Jane laughs. Clark does not.

"I'm ready to buzz you in. Todd's not with you, is he?"

Jane's tone changes. She sounds embarrassed, a little hurt. "I was kidding about the take-advantage-of-me thing, you know."

"Yeah, I know. Sorry, I'm a little tense is all. Wine will be great. Red?"

"Yeah. Red."

Clark's apartment buzzer rings. He presses a button beside the door.

The curtains push on Clark's back like a firm, cold hand. He cannot turn around to look at them. He walks over to the door, stands there with his hand on the knob, waiting, fiddling with his watch.

Enough time passes that Clark thinks Jane has changed her mind, turned around, gone home. Left him in this cramped apartment, the weight of the curtains pressing on him, crushing the wind out of his lungs.

What could possibly be taking so long? Christ. It's just a few flights of stairs. And if she took the elevator, which she probably did, then she'd be—

Three soft raps on the door.

Clark turns the knob quickly and yanks the door open hard, startling Jane.

"Sorry, sorry," Clark says, reaches out for the wine, plucks it from her hand. "Come on in, don't worry about your shoes, lemme take your coat." He disappears into the kitchen, leaves the wine on the counter, comes back down the hall, opens a closet, puts her coat on a hanger with shaky hands.

"Clark, calm down. What's going on? What's—"

"The, um...the sky. Remember the thing about the sun yesterday? When I said it was—"

"Yeah, melting. That was pretty weird, Clark, I have to admit."

"Look," Clark says, walks over to the couch—the farthest piece of furniture from the curtains and the window—and plunks himself down. "I know it sounds ridiculous, but...it happened again today. The sun looked even hazier, more indistinct. Like someone is smearing it across the sky."

Jane says nothing, just stands by the doorway. She looks over her shoulder at the door, and Clark thinks, *We're really not very close at all, are we? She doesn't trust me. Not one bit.*

She takes two tentative steps into the living room, then a few more, and finally sits down on the arm of the tattered couch. She puts the palms of her hands together, pushes them down between her thighs at the knees. Takes a deep breath. But she doesn't say the kind of thing Clark thinks she's going to say. She says, "What do you want me to do, Clark?"

"What?" Clark says. "What do you mean? I don't understand."

"How can I help you?" Jane asks. "What do you want me to do?"

Clark hears sympathy in her voice, a genuine need to help, but he also hears condescension, as though she's speaking to a six-year-old who doesn't want to sleep with the light off.

"I dunno," Clark says, after thinking about it for a moment. "I just wanted you to...well, it sounds crazy, I know, but I wanted you to be here when I looked out the window tonight. At the sky. At the stars."

"In case of what, Clark? In case the stars are melting, too?"

Silence. Clark casts his eyes down, fiddles some more with his watch. The room is suddenly too hot. The curtains loom over him, leering.

Clark looks up. "I guess I shouldn't have asked you to come."

"Probably not," Jane says. "But I'm here now. If you want me to stay, I will." She glances at the kitchen, cracks a little grin that lifts one side of her mouth. "Wine or no wine at the Restaurant at the End of the Universe?"

Despite the dread gnawing at his insides, Clark returns the grin, says, "Wine."

Jane disappears into the kitchen. Clark hears her rooting around in drawers, looking for the corkscrew. *I like that she doesn't ask me where it is*, he thinks, unsure why this appeals to him.

Jane returns with two full wine glasses, hands one over to Clark—who promptly drops it on the floor. Glass shatters, wine splashes their feet and pant legs.

"Fucking shit," Clark says, sighs, moves toward the kitchen to get paper towels. He returns, leans down and, with shaking hands, mops up the mess while Jane carefully picks up the bigger chunks of glass, brings them to the kitchen garbage. She returns to the living room. Clark brings the soggy paper towels to the garbage, washes his hands, heads back into the living room—

—and the curtains have been pulled completely aside, exposing the sky.

Clark tries to avert his eyes; he wasn't ready for this yet. *Christ, at least let me get a glass of wine or two down my fucking gullet before springing it on me,* he thinks. But it's too late; even though he only catches a glimpse, his mind picks up all the information needed. *The stars are melting, too. Blurring. Smeared across the night like wet white paint on a black wall.*

"Close it, Jane," Clark says, his voice low, head turned to one side.

"Oh, come on, Clark, just look, would you? There's nothing wrong with the sky. The stars are fine." She turns from where she's pulling the last section of curtains open, walks toward Clark. She reaches out a hand, puts it gently on his arm, moves her other hand to his cheek, cups it, turns his face toward the window. He shuts his eyes tight, refuses to open them.

After a few moments of her palm on his cheek, warm, her breathing near his ear, steady, he opens his eyes, but does not look out the window; he looks directly at her. "Where's your wine?"

"I left it in the kitchen. I'll get you a new glass in a minute, okay?"

Clark nods, swallows hard. In his peripheral vision, he sees the alien sky. Senses it pushing into his skull, trying to pull his eyes toward it.

"I don't..." Clark says. "I don't want to look, Jane. Okay? I don't want to see it. I know you don't see what I see. But I can't *not* see it, alright? And it scares the almighty fuck out of me."

"Okay, Clark. It's fine. Just relax. Relax." She strokes his forehead, moves her hand up and down his arm, soothing.

A long time seems to pass, then; Jane soothing his nerves, his breathing coming under control, his hands shaking less and less until they're almost steady again.

"Clark?"

Clark concentrates on breathing, eyes still closed.

"I know you like me, Clark."

Clark makes no effort to deny it. "I've liked you for a very long time, Jane."

"I know. I like you, too. Very much."

Jane leans forward, kisses Clark gently on the lips. He returns the kiss, moves his hand to cup the underside of her forearm, squeezes the flesh there.

When he finally opens his eyes, Jane's face is a wet streak across his vision—eyes too big and stretched down her face; lips sagging, dribbling down her chin, her neck; nose a bulbous pool of flesh; forehead running down to cover it all like egg yolk.

Clark pulls away fast, knocks over a stereo speaker behind him. Jane stumbles back, too, surprised at Clark's reaction. "Clark, what's...what's the matter? I thought—"

The phone rings. Clark cannot convince his legs to take him over to it. He stands, frozen. Rooted to the spot. In his peripheral, the sky continues to melt, more white than black now, but fast becoming grey, the two mixing together. The city lights below snuffing out, the high-rises becoming drenched and sodden with the fallout.

The answering machine clicks on. Clark's greeting plays, then Todd's voice erupts from the tiny speaker: "Yeah. Clark. You fuck. I know she's there. She told me where she was going. Told me you didn't want me over there. Fucking dick. Traitor. Some friend. Some fucking friend."

Clark's head spins. He teeters, falls against the nearest wall. Jane moves closer to him, hands out. Not much left of her face, most of it dribbled onto her blouse now. No skull beneath the flesh. At least no recognizable human skull. It fazes in and out of familiarity, never settling on any one form.

"I know we never talked about it, Clark," Todd continues, his voice less manic, more controlled than before. "But you knew, man. You had to have known how I felt."

I don't know what you are, Clark thinks, staring at what used to be Jane, his mind grasping for any kind of decision, anything that smacks of control. *I don't know what you are. I don't know what you want and I cannot help you. Whatever you need, whatever it is, it's not up to me. I do not recognize you.*

"Pick the phone up, pig. Pick it up, you dick."

Jane moves closer, bends down, hands reaching out, that alien skull hovering like a splintered moon, trying to cohere into something worse than it already is.

Jane's hands close on Clark's shoulders; he lashes out with a fist at her skull. Something like blood runs from the middle of her face. A hand comes up to stem the flow. She mutters something, but Clark cannot understand her words anymore. They sound like mush to his ears.

I don't understand you. I don't understand you. I do not recognize your face. You're not Jane. You're not Jane.

Clark gains his feet, continues punching the skull, advancing on it, heedless of the rest of the body, focusing entirely on the white shock of bone sprouting from the shoulders. Jane trips over the coffee table backward, falls to the floor. Clark hears a thick crunching sound.

"Consider us finished, man," Todd says, voice more resigned than angry now. "Consider our fucking joke of a friendship terminated, okay? Don't call. Don't email. Don't even think about me anymore, alright?" A brief pause. "Because I sure as shit won't be thinking about you."

There is a soft click. The answering machine beeps once. Red light blinking in the dark. More dark than Clark has ever experienced in his life.

He turns and very deliberately looks out the window. The sky is completely black. Not a speck of light left. Absolute pitch.

Void, Clark thinks. Shudders. *Empty.*

He looks back down at whatever is cracked and bleeding on his floor. Skull shattered. A pool of liquid spreading out slowly behind it, creeping toward the couch leg.

Clark feels a calmness come over him, then. His heart settles, limbs no longer vibrating with adrenaline. Breathing under control. *I'm going to be alright. Whatever happens. I'll be fine. Whatever is happening to me, it will pass.*

Clark walks slowly to the window, opens the sliding glass door that leads onto his balcony. A gentle breeze dries his sweat, pushes hair off his cheeks. He closes his eyes, breathes in deeply. Opens them, head lifted skyward.

Nothing. As though stars never existed. *Alone*, he thinks. *Alone. Hidden.*

A memory comes to him, then. Of hiding as a child. In a fort built of furniture. Lights out, only a flashlight gripped in his tiny hand, leading the way through the maze of overturned couches, chairs, end tables.

One word in his mind: *Safe.*

After what feels like several hours, Clark turns around, steps inside his living room, shuts the sliding door behind him.

He walks to where Todd's body lies crumpled, one leg up on the coffee table, the rest of him splayed out on the floor. Unnatural.

Bleeding face. Back of his head caved in.

When Clark cries for him, tears come out, but the grief does not.

THE CARPET MAKER

Brent Hayward

The man from personnel held open his office door and indicated, curtly, with his free hand, that Patrick should enter; as Patrick did so, the man said, in low and threatening tones, "Mr. Troy, you understand we are not running a whorehouse?"

Chagrined, Patrick took a seat. The chair was creaky and uncomfortable and very small. He faced a huge wooden desk. Air in this dank basement office smelled sour and stuffy and he shifted in the chair. Black mould grew on the cement walls, by the baseboards. Over the big desk, a single bare bulb cast huge shadows.

He looked down at the carpeted floor as the door squealed shut behind him.

Walking softly, the man from personnel returned to his place. His own chair—deep green, leather, high-backed—glistened in the light as if it were a living thing. The man put his hands on the desktop, locked his long fingers together, and waited.

Patrick cleared his throat. "Well," he said, "I can understand why you said that. But let me explain." Leaning forward, elbows on knees, he took a deep breath, focussed again on a spot between his sneakers. He could distinguish a muted pattern of red, gold and black. Fleurs-de-lis swam in the depths of the worn pile.

"Mr. Troy?"

"Yes..." He could even *smell* the carpet now, the ages it had laid here, the vanished lives come and gone, passing through this room. "You see, it's just that my wife and I—"

"Look how you've dressed your daughter."

Following the direction of the pointing finger, Patrick was startled to see that the wall to his right had become a window, of sorts—had it always been? Was this a one-way mirror? Had a curtain been lifted?

"How—?"

Words failed. He was looking at the waiting room, where he had left Samantha, moments before.

But that room was on another floor, on another side of the building altogether.

Samantha sat between two tired-looking teenagers, a boy and a girl, her thin legs stretched out, one ankle crossed over the other. At least she had taken off the stilettos. On the way uptown, the shoes had been hurting her feet, she'd said. With her head tilted back, so that her neck was taut, smooth—her throat curved and muscled—Samantha's hair hung down, out of sight. Patrick couldn't see the make-up—the foundation and blush, the blue eye shadow and lipstick—that Kendra had applied to Samantha's face before he brought her here, but that sequined dress, clinging tightly to her thin, boyish body, changing tone from deep red to small lakes of cerise as she breathed, made him wince.

"My wife is..." Now he met the gaze of the man from personnel and the disapproval he saw there caused anger to bloom in him, and it felt like a release. "Look," he said, "my wife is not a happy woman. We know this isn't a whorehouse. You should be careful what you say to me."

His outburst was ignored. "Where is your wife now?"

"Kendra is, uh, she's busy. She couldn't make it."

The man from personnel continued to stare for a long time. Shadows moved, like bruises, over his face. Finally, though, his expression seemed to soften. He brushed at his black moustache with one curled knuckle. "We have to be careful here, Mr. Troy. I thought we had agreed to the utmost discretion. I thought you understood our position."

"I thought so too. I'm sorry about the dress."

"Mr. Troy, we are trying to operate a business. That's all. This is a cutthroat world. We want to provide quality carpets at affordable prices." He smiled a thin smile.

"Carpets," Patrick echoed, nodding. "I understand."

"And, Mr. Troy, though I honestly can't fathom why you dressed your daughter like that"—the man's eyes glittered— "she is by all means hired."

Patrick did not know what to say. He did not even know what to feel, whether relief or remorse. "Thank you," he mumbled.

"Now let's fill out the forms, shall we, and forget about this unfortunate incident?" The man from personnel bent to open a drawer, and Patrick heard the sound of wood moving on dry wood, and then the rattling of documents that he would shortly sign to complete the sale.

Samantha's clothes—her ridiculous shoes, her gaudy and sequined dress—were quickly stuffed into a paper bag by a woman in a dull twill suit. Like the man from personnel, this woman did nothing but scowl at Patrick. Her skin was stretched so tight over her cheekbones that tiny blue veins showed, patterns of cracks in fine china. She handed Patrick the bag and nodded as he took it, am almost imperceptible movement, then took him firmly by the arm with a surprisingly strong grip, guiding him towards what was—he realized with some additional shock—the rear exit of the building.

"Do not worry about Samantha, Mr. Troy," said the woman as they made their way through a large kitchen: ceramic-tiled floor, sinks along one wall and, between them, truncated pipes of gas mains that protruded from the sea-green walls like accusing fingers. "The food here is wonderful and the rooms are always comfortable. I assure you that Samantha will make new friends. At lunchtime, all of our young workers sit together in the sunlight, eyes closed, faces turned toward the sky, as if they have founds peace. This is a sight we have come to love."

He stopped, turned towards the woman, confused. "Sunlight? But where, where do they sit? Where could they go?"

The door was opened, unanswered questions sucked out into the night. Rain diffused the city lights. Car tires hissed on nearby wet roads. Blowing in, the rain was cold and reflected neon on the wet tiles at their feet.

"Tell her to write." Patrick clutched the bag to his chest like a life preserver. He could smell the perfume; Kendra had splashed Samantha liberally with some cheap brand this morning, after the fight.

With little choice, Patrick stepped outside. The metal door clicked shut.

Standing atop a landing, in an alley, stunned for a moment by memories, Patrick was soon soaked. A car horn blared, waking him, as if from a dream, and he blinked, letting the rain patter his face. He took a deep breath. The segment of street that he could see at the far end of the alley was busy with people hustling to get somewhere dry, hustling with trucks and cars and buses that appeared and disappeared abruptly.

A set of cement stairs, strewn with garbage, led down from where he stood.

A black metal dumpster, looming.

Before Patrick made it to the street, the paper bag had darkened, shifted, and fallen apart in his hands. The shoes spilled away from him, splashing into a silvered puddle where they lay sideways in the rainwater like tiny, capsized boats. Struggling to keep hold of the reeking dress, Patrick stepped into the water and bent, one hand outstretched.

He did not pick up the stilettos.

Instead, he kicked out, spraying water up his own leg, nearly falling as one shoe clattered along the sidewalk and was immediately picked up by a passing man in a long dark coat who did not so much as look into the alley where Patrick stood, feet apart, breathing hard, fists at his sides.

He went back to the dumpster to toss in the dress. When he saw the ink stain on his hands, like blood, he realized that he could not remember having signed any documents. He tried not to dwell on this, but he was frightened as he walked the length of the alley to the street. No, he could not remember signing any documents, nor could he remember any features of the woman who had shown him the door. He could no longer even remember details of the altercation with Sam, when he and Kendra had told her, just today, what they had decided.

As Patrick turned onto the busy sidewalk, his vision kaleidoscoped through drops of water, but he knew this effect was not from the rain.

He did not have enough change for the bus, which he thought was rather ironic, since he'd just sold his daughter, so he walked home, a twenty minute trip, and decided this was for the best, for by the time he got back to the apartment the knot that had been tightening in his chest had loosened.

He went slowly up the stairs, as if there were a force repelling him, and passed two derelicts, asleep on two different landings. One of them had pissed himself. The urine was as dark as stewed tea and smelled like ammonia.

The door to his apartment stood ajar. Dark inside, but Kendra often kept their place dark, either watching TV or sleeping on the couch. Suddenly he felt drunk; his head buzzed, reeled. He pushed the door open with one foot and let it hit the inside wall. He staggered in.

From the gloom of the bedroom, dressed in a torn and yellowed nightgown, Kendra appeared, knuckling her eyes. "Make a little more noise, why don't you?" Her voice was hoarse. The apartment smelled of cigarettes and stale food and traces of the lingering perfume. Dishes filled the sink. The coffee table was strewn with ashes and papers, and a good deal of the floor was covered. Neither he nor Kendra had ever been good at cleaning; Samantha had done most of the work.

"Well, that's it," he said. "They were absolute freaks. Thanks for your support." Then, louder than he had meant to: "For god sake Ken, why did you dress her like that? They gave me a hard time."

Kendra scratched at her hip. "You're getting the floor wet."

He flicked on the light. His hands shook. When he looked back, Kendra had vanished. He went to the bedroom doorway and, with one hand either side of the jamb, tried to breathe regularly.

She lay on her back on the bed, arms above her head, legs open. He could see the dark patch of her pubic hair. He and Kendra had not made love—had not held each other or kissed—in over a year.

"I asked you," Patrick said, his voice tremulous, "why you dressed her like that."

Kendra stared up at the ceiling. "Did they give you any money?"

He licked his lips. "No."

"Don't try to make me feel any worse than I do. We both agreed to this. Samantha *wanted* to get out of here."

There had been times in the past when their daughter had screamed at them both, *I hate you, I hate you*, and she had run away twice, coming home once by herself, another time with two police officers who had found her at an arcade. Recalling his daughter's vehemence, and his own anger at the policemen's questions, Patrick stepped closer to the bed and reached out. "Ken?"

"Don't fucking touch me," his wife replied.

Patrick went to the post office daily to see if any cheques had come in and to see if Samantha had written, but nothing came: no cheques, no letters. After a week or so, he returned to the building where he had brought Samantha, feeling nauseous and edgy. It was still raining.

He waited for over an hour in the lobby. Behind the taciturn male receptionist were two disintegrating wall hangings. Patrick was finally met by the stern-faced woman who had given him Sam's shoes, and he recalled the strange absence he had felt after the previous encounter with her. He scowled. "Where is she? And where is our money?"

"Mr. Troy, your daughter is fine. We can't force her to write if she does not wish to. This is a transitional period for her. Please be patient. As for the cheques, if you'll read the contract, you'll see that we keep two weeks in hand. Next week your money will start to come in."

"Can I talk to her? Can I see her?"

"Mr. Troy, I really suggest that you go home and read over the contract. I will relay your regards to Samantha. Now, we are very busy here. Many parents participate in our program. If there's anything else we can do for you, be sure to make an appointment."

The cluttered apartment seemed to be filling with litter. Every surface of the room was covered by paper plates and cups and plastic vials, cardboard and magazines, the detritus of their lives. He wondered how he and Kendra could generate so much refuse, especially since Kendra, who had always, relied on Valium, had begun to take more and more of the pills and was sleeping through the long and silent days. As for himself, between running to the post office, where he would invariably find the box empty, and trying to fill bogus prescriptions in drugstores all across town, on foot, the days also passed and he spent little time at home. Yet garbage continued to accumulate.

Whenever he did return, exhausted, numb, Kendra would be in bed or on the couch, her eyes staring at nothing, and when she spoke, her voice was slurred, slow:

"We wore uniforms to school," she told him.

He stood with a vial of Ambien in his hands.

"Tunics were a dark blue. I was always called into Mr. Hornstein's office. I must have been ten years old."

"Jesus Christ," Patrick said. His breath came in short gasps. He felt like he was on the verge of an anxiety attack. His insides boiled then went preternaturally calm, as if he were suddenly rendered hollow. A buzzing, in his ears. "What are you talking about, Ken? Why are you telling me this?"

"And Mr. Hornstein used to cane me. Across my knuckles, with a wooden ruler. Twice he bent me over his knee and lifted my skirt."

Before he knew what he was doing, Patrick had stepped over to where his wife sat and, awkwardly, hit her across the face. His open hand knocked her hair forward and she fell silent.

Amid a rush of cascading images, Patrick remembered his wife's face when they had first met. He remembered her smile, her laugh...

Slowly, without another word, Kendra stood and went into the bedroom.

Patrick watched her go. He sat heavily on the couch where she had been. His hands operated remotely; he had no control of them. He watched them as they lay in his lap.

He might have slept then. When he did manage to open his eyes—perhaps at the creaking of floorboards, or the rustle of papers—he saw Kendra's brass hairbrush coming down swiftly toward his head.

This time he stood in the reception area for over two hours before anyone came to see him. Under the cap, his head throbbed. Seven stitches had closed the gash and the doctors had shaved a good deal of his scalp.

Again, the receptionist was no help. And, again, it was the stern-faced woman who eventually came out to talk to him.

"Where's our money?" he said, but he didn't sound as tough as he wanted. "You have our daughter and we haven't got any cheques from you at all."

The woman frowned. "May I have your name, sir?"

"Don't give me that shit." Ice had formed in his blood. "My name is Patrick Troy. My daughter's name is Samantha."

"Wait here a minute, I'll speak to the manager."

The woman turned and left.

At a loss, Patrick waited.

A short time later, the receptionist's telephone rang. When Patrick looked over, the receptionist gestured towards the receiver. Frowning, Patrick walked over to the desk and answered the call.

"Hello?"

The receptionist watched him.

"Mr. Troy?"

The voice was that of the man from personnel. Patrick said, "What the hell is going on here?"

"My wife tells me you seem angry."

"Your wife? Yes, I'm fucking angry."

"She says you want your money. Well, Mr. Troy, I have your daughter's file here with me. Samantha Troy. Twelve years old. Extensive bruising down her left thigh and on her left biceps. Swollen tissue around her right eye."

"What are you talking about?"

"Your daughter, Mr. Troy."

"What the hell have you done to her?"

"Us? We merely try to help. You know that she was admitted in this condition."

"I will go to the fucking police," he hissed.

"You won't, Mr. Troy. We both know that. Now listen, according to our records, Samantha's contract expired over two months ago. She was sent home."

The walls receded and the floor dropped out from underneath Patrick's feet. He clenched the receiver. "Two months ago? Are you insane? We just signed her up!"

"Don't raise your voice to me. I have dealt with many fathers like you before, many parents. Some of them sent their children into mines, others forced them into bordellos, or onto the streets. Not to mention a litany of more horrific and unmentionable fates."

"We did the best we could. But I don't need to justify myself to you. Tell me where my daughter is."

"I told you. She's gone home. I ask you to do the same. Goodbye, Mr. Troy."

"Wait—"

The line went dead as the receptionist's hand fell onto Patrick's shoulder, firm, squeezing. Patrick's knees buckled, all strength gone. He hung up, and was escorted outside.

Patrick got drunk that night. He drank a twenty-six ounce bottle of vodka, sitting, ruminating in the dark while Kendra slept on the couch. When he finished the bottle, he stood and woke Kendra by kicking at the couch pillows.

"God damn you," he shouted, swaying over her. "This is all your fault! Where is that fucking contract?"

"My fault?" Kendra had not bathed in weeks. Her hair was stringy and greasy, her eyes sunken. She was falling apart. "I never saw any contract so leave me alone, you bastard. Let me sleep."

Knee deep in garbage, struggling to stay on his feet, Patrick felt both fists clench. He lunged forward, and the world went black.

FOXFORD

Sandra Kasturi

Furred shapes move in the darkness near the platform, wait-ing for the last train. Fog muffles their sharp barks.

Eleanor made it onto the last Express heading back to Oxford from London just in time, despite Frankie and Bill's nonsense at the Fox's Head pub—leaving her with the bill and then scurry-ing off in a fit of laughter as if they were teenagers. Eleanor had been working on her thesis in England for a year now, and she would have thought her half-sister might have grown up a little since she'd been away, but Frankie was still her usual childish self. And now she was dragging Bill along with her, their new relationship excluding everyone but themselves. Their visit was almost over, but Eleanor had already had enough.

She fumed silently as she thought about the scene all over again. She'd only had a vodka and orange at the pub, for good-ness sake, but somehow Frankie and Bill had managed to down several pints and squeeze in a bottle of champagne as well. Then Eleanor had gone to the loo, only to find them vanished on her return, and there was the barmaid presenting her with the bill. She could hear their giggles outside, fading as they ran off. A hundred and twenty pounds! That must be...what? Nearly two hundred dollars?

Surely not that much, she thought.

Her whole life with Frankie was filled with similar scenarios. The past year in Oxford had been glorious with its silences and lack of drama.

The train swayed and Eleanor dozed, grinding her teeth like she hadn't done since she was living at home.

She really should have known better. The whole day had started unpleasantly, and even though she was used to it by now, she was still surprised at how miserable she was in the presence of her half-sister. In Oxford, she'd finally felt like she belonged somewhere, and here was Frankie ruining it, like she ruined everything. And Bill was worse.

Frankie and Bill were both terrible guests, Eleanor's small flat rendered even smaller by their tiresome boisterousness and complaints about water pressure, English food and the fact that hair dryers and shavers didn't fit into the outlets.

"I told you it was a different voltage system," said Eleanor with a sigh, but Frankie had gone back into the bedroom to sulk. Eleanor lay back down on the narrow sofa and wondered again what had possessed her to agree to this two-week visit. But she knew—it was their mother, still recovering from Frankie's father's death, who desperately needed some peace and quiet, even for a short while.

I need to get them out of the flat, thought Eleanor. *Or I'll kill them both. London. I'll take them to London.*

"I'd love to go to London," said Frankie on hearing the proposal. "But don't you have more research to do?" She stood in front of the window, brushing her silvery blonde hair.

"Well, yes," said Eleanor, "but I can do that tomorrow. Or the next day."

"I didn't think Nervous Nelly wanted to brave London again after the Heathrow craziness." Bill grinned maliciously at Eleanor.

Eleanor looked at Frankie. Eleanor had e-mailed her and their mother to let them know she'd arrived safely in England, but she'd only mentioned her hatred of Heathrow and London's crowds when she and her mother were e-mailing privately later. Would her mother have told Frankie? Or had Frankie read her mother's e-mail? It wouldn't surprise her. And Frankie, of course, would have told Bill.

When did he get so nasty, she thought. *Was it always like this, or is it just this trip? Maybe it's Frankie. The two of them together.* She looked away, tried to ignore him.

"Come on, Bill. You know Eleanor doesn't like crowds. Or new places." Frankie smirked at her.

"Oxford is hardly new to me anymore," said Eleanor. "And neither is London. It would be silly for you to come all this way and not see London properly," said Eleanor, still not looking at them.

"Very silly," said Frankie.

"Very silly, very silly, very silly!" shouted Bill. He grabbed Frankie by the hands and twirled her around in the cramped room until they nearly fell on top of Eleanor on the sofa, laughing. Bill pulled Frankie to him and started kissing her on her thin mouth.

Eleanor stood up quickly and said, "I'm going to run a few errands. I'll meet you at the train station at 11:00 if you want to go. If you're not there, I'll go to the Bodleian and do some work. You two can do whatever you like."

"Ooooh, we can do whatever we like," said Bill, looking down at Frankie. "Did you hear that?"

Frankie pulled his head down to hers again.

Eleanor dressed in the bathroom, grabbed her purse and slipped out the door. They were unbearable. She and Frankie had never been close. Eleanor had been ten years old when her mother remarried, and Frankie had been born a year later. She'd felt completely disconnected from the pink, squalling creature, and retreated further into the books she loved. And Bill...Bill had been so nice in Toronto during grad school; she had even thought at one point he would be something more than a friend. She'd had no idea that he and Frankie had even met, much less become involved. When Bill said he'd dropped out of the graduate program and wanted to visit, she'd felt her heart lurch. That was before she'd known Frankie was coming too.

Bill had turned into a real Biter. That's what her mother had called men like him, her Welsh accent still strong.

"Nell, lovey, watch out for those men, they're real Biters." Eleanor wasn't quite sure what she'd meant, but had avoided entanglements on principle. Until Bill...and even then it had just been a friendship. He probably hadn't even realized that she'd once had other ideas. Now, in England, she was glad it hadn't come to anything. Biting Bill.

And Frankie...Frankie had been a Biter from birth.

The train picks up speed and dives into thickening fog that is rolling in from the north, turning the falling darkness a silvery grey, through which strange shapes move, keeping pace.

To Eleanor's surprise, Frankie and Bill did meet her at the station, and the hour-long ride up to London was uneventful. She didn't sleep like she usually did in trains, only managing a kind of fitful doze, the clacking of the wheels echoing like the snap of teeth as she drifted in and out of peculiar dreams. The other two had chosen a seat ahead of her, and Eleanor heard their whispering every time she lurched into wakefulness.

Paddington Station was a crowded nightmare, but Eleanor plastered a falsely serene smile on her face and walked ahead of the other two. They skittered forward to catch up, and she could have sworn she saw a look of disappointment on Frankie's face. Perhaps they had been looking forward to abandoning her in the crowd and then teasing her mercilessly about it later?

I've been living in Oxford for a year, Eleanor thought. *Do they really think I can't even manage some minor travel on my own? Idiots.* She smiled. A genuine one, this time. She caught Frankie looking at her again, a puzzled frown on her face.

"Let's go on the London Eye," said Frankie.

"Oh, our Nelly-Nell doesn't like heights, does she?" said Bill.

Eleanor, who usually didn't, perversely said, "I think I can manage."

Bill, clearly smelling blood, grinned and said, "Oh, yes, *let's.*"

Eleanor beamed throughout the entire whirling ride on the London Eye, pointing out landmarks, much to the others' obvious annoyance. Frankie looked like she had bitten into a wasp.

"Tell you what," said Eleanor back on the ground, "I want to have a look at some historical buildings and do a lot of boring stuff. Why don't you two go shopping and we can meet up later? Maybe at a pub?"

Frankie looked like she was about to protest, but Bill interjected: "Sure. I know just the place. It's called the Fox's Head. Victoria Road, near Queen's Park station. I read about it on the internet. Think you can find it?"

Eleanor was more than tired of both of them. It was only another three days and they'd be gone. She could manage. She looked at Bill. "I live in England, Bill. It's no problem. I'll meet you at the Fox's Head at six o'clock"

"Sure," said Frankie.

"Whatever," said Bill.

"Bye, then," said Eleanor, and walked off. Only another three days.

The fog has completely blanketed everything for miles, but Eleanor is oblivious to it. She sleeps even more deeply, the sound of the train's wheels turning into sharp barks in her dreams, the train furring over into a river of steel grey foxes speeding north-ward, carrying her with them on their backs, like a queen being brought to her rightful throne.

Eleanor loved her solitary hours in London. She decided to become the complete tourist and wandered the streets looking into shop windows and even ventured into Harrod's where she allowed the perfume girl to spray her with an exotic musky scent. She took a ride on a double-decker and bought a map and a paper at a news agent's, finally settling down to a proper cream tea in a forgotten little café and enjoying herself hugely, despite not having seen any of the important things—the Tower Bridge, Big Ben, the Beefeaters. Well, she was here for another year at least. There'd be plenty of time for that.

"Will there be anything else, dear?" asked the elderly café lady.

"No thank you," said Eleanor. As she looked up, she saw something in the corner of the shop—something furry that darted quickly out of sight. "Er, I'm so sorry, but you don't have mice, do you? I thought I saw..."

"Well, dear, sometimes you can't avoid 'em in big cities, you know. But mostly the foxes do take care of 'em," said the old lady.

"Foxes?"

"Yes, dear. London has red foxes everywhere."

The train slows, and Eleanor wakes with a start at the change in its rhythm. The lights in her carriage have dimmed, and several flicker. Outside is nothing but darkness and fog.

She looks at her watch. It is very late.

"That can't be right," she says. The trip back to Oxford should only have taken an hour.

The train slows further. A tree branch brushes against her window, and Eleanor jumps. Why would anyone plant trees so close to the track?

The train comes to a halt. Eleanor can almost distinguish the platform outside, and a sign that says "—xford," and then some-thing else underneath it.

Oxford, she thinks. She picks up her purse and moves toward the door. The rest of the train carriage is empty. Frankie and Bill are nowhere in sight.

Having asked at the Tube station and consulted her map, Eleanor found Queen's Park on the Underground without difficulty. Victoria Road, lined with knobbly, still-bare plane trees, was only another block away and the Fox's Head was right on the corner.

The pub's weathered sign swayed as the wind sprang up. It was a bit odd—Eleanor had expected one of the famous red foxes of London—but the sign had the painted head of a big grey fox, teeth showing, red tongue hanging out lasciviously. Its eyes were bright and full of mischief.

Frankie and Bill were already at a table, barely visible in the dim interior, two pints in front of them.

"Eleanor," called Frankie, and waved her over. "Did you have a nice day?" she asked as Eleanor sat down.

"Lovely. Have you been waiting long?"

"Not long," said Bill, casting a sly glance at Frankie. "See anything good?"

"Not much. The usual tourist stuff. Maybe a fox. Just walked around a bit," said Eleanor. "I'll have a vodka and orange," she said to the barmaid.

"*What* did you say? A *fox*?"

"Yes, London has foxes everywhere, didn't you know? Hence the pub, I guess. But they're red foxes, not grey ones," said Eleanor.

"Oh, yes, *hence*," said Frankie.

The barmaid returned with the vodka and orange.

"Excuse me, but could you tell me why you have a grey fox on the sign? I thought it was only red foxes in London," said Eleanor.

"Well, it is, usually," said the barmaid. "The landlord got the sign from up in Wales. Says it's one of the *milgwn*."

"Mil-what?" said Frankie.

"*Milgwn*. It's a Welsh word. Means these enormous grey foxes up in Wales that have magical powers or some shite." Another punter caught her eye and the barmaid moved off.

"Aren't you Welsh?" asked Bill.

"Our mother is," said Eleanor.

Frankie chimed in, "My father isn't. But Eleanor's father might be. She doesn't know, of course, since she doesn't know who her father is, poor lamb."

Eleanor looked at Frankie calmly and said, "No, I don't." Frankie actually looked faintly ashamed and studied her pint carefully, a red flush moving up to her ears. "I have to go to the loo," said Eleanor. She got up and went to find the toilets.

When she got back, they were gone. She paid the bill, champagne included, which they must have had while waiting for her. She could hear their laughter outside—actually, just Bill's laughter—but decided to ignore it. She'd go back to Paddington Station and then Oxford on her own. She'd had enough of their selfishness and bad manners. If they got stuck in London on their own for the night, so be it.

"Nasty little Biters," she muttered, doing a passable imitation of her mother's Welsh accent.

Outside, it wasn't quite full dark. Eleanor kept thinking she saw movement out of the corner of her eye, but when she looked there was nothing. There seemed to be more shadows in the alleys and along the sides of buildings than there should have been, all of which were blurred along the edges, as if they had fur.

From Queen's Park to Paddington, Eleanor didn't see Frankie or Bill anywhere, but what did it matter? They could go their own way. She'd be rid of them soon, and they'd be going back to Canada. Maybe she wouldn't move back home after her second year at Oxford. Maybe she'd just stay permanently. She smiled at the thought.

Paddington Station wasn't crowded. She fed her return ticket through the machine, and the turnstile opened. The lights flickered and the very air grew dimmer.

A man in a conductor's uniform shouted, "Last train to Foxford, departing now from platform seven!"

Eleanor ran up to him. "What did you say? Oxford?"

"This is the train you want, ma'am," said the conductor, and handed her into the carriage. His accent was thick and barely intelligible.

Eleanor sat down in the last seat. Up ahead she spotted a silvery blonde head and a dark one, close together, whispering. Frankie and Bill had made the train after all.

"All aboard to Foxford," said the conductor, but Eleanor was already nodding off.

Eleanor steps onto the platform. It is very cold and she can't see much in the fog. Frankie and Bill must have gone ahead. The platform doesn't look anything like the one they'd left from that morning. She walks up to the sign. Part of it is obscured, but she can still make out that it says "Foxford," not "Oxford." She inhales sharply. She has taken the wrong train and now she is lost in the dark. She squints at the sign again. Eleanor can't read the smaller writing underneath, but she does recognize it. It's Welsh.

Her watch isn't wrong—she's been on the train for hours. She's in Wales. Eleanor shivers. As she stands there wondering what to do, the train starts up and speeds off into the darkness without her.

From somewhere in the fog comes a series of sharp barks.

The fog swirls and pulses. Eleanor clutches her purse, and stands very still. The barks come again, closer.

The fog in front of her parts, and standing there is one of the most enormous foxes she has ever seen. It is almost the size of a small pony. It gives that high, barking yip and looks right at her. More foxes emerge from the fog, though none are quite as large as the first.

The great king fox barks again, and the other foxes surge toward her, a relentless grey tide. Eleanor shuts her eyes. She feels them against her legs, fur hot and coarse. They mill around her, noses touching her knees. She waits to be torn and eaten, but there is only quiet.

She looks down. She is stranded in a sea of furred creatures, all of them eerily silent, looking at her expectantly. She lowers one hand to them. The king fox steps forward and licks her. His tongue is rough and warm. The other foxes shrug closer. They lick at her legs and feet. Wherever their tongues touch, she *changes*. Her shoes disappear, her skirt vanishes, her skin turns dark, furring grey.

Eleanor drops her purse and falls to all fours. The foxes lick her clothing away, until she is new-minted, a clean animal, grey coat gleaming as the fog lifts and the moon comes out.

She sniffs the air. She can smell two-leggers close by. A male and a female. Some part of her wants to remember something, but she pushes it aside. She lets out a bark and surges to the head of the pack, next to the king fox. He barks at her in return, and all the *milgwn* brethren flow forward, together in joyous pursuit, teeth white, red mouths open and ready.

My Body

Ian Rogers

I had seen enough darkness in Sycamore to last me a life-time. Once I got home I planned on turning on every light in my apartment and sitting in the middle of the living room floor, as far away from the shadows as I could get.

It was Sunday night and I was driving toward the bright lights of the city. I had the gas pedal pressed to the floor and the radio cranked to an oldies station out of Barrie. I also had the dome light on. It made driving a little difficult, and I got a few disapproving honks from the one or two other drivers on the road, but I needed it.

The Platters came on singing that heavenly shades of night were falling, and I switched off the radio. I turned off the dome light, too, and that's when I saw her.

She was standing at the side of the road. I thought she was a deer at first, the way the headlights reflected off her eyes. Then I saw her dress. I expected her to dart out in front of me, but she just stood there. A little girl about seven or eight years old.

My foot lifted instinctively off the gas pedal, and the car decelerated. As I cruised by, I looked out the passenger window. The girl turned her head at the same time and our eyes locked. We looked at each other for only a moment, but I clearly saw the blank expression on her face flicker to one of intense gratitude. It was like a spotlight snapping on. I put on my blinker and pulled over.

The girl came running up as I stepped out of the car.

"Please," she said. "No one would stop."

The girl brushed at her cheeks with the back of her hand, and I could see she had been crying. She was wearing a coat with a fur-lined collar over her dress. The dress had some sort of print pattern on it, but I couldn't make it out in the dark. She didn't seem to like my staring, and pulled her coat tight against her body. A red leaf was stuck in her wavy brown hair. She brushed at it absently, but it stayed put.

"What are you doing out here?" I asked. "You lost?"

I looked up and down the highway. There were no other cars on the road, or parked on the side of it, and I felt a brief sensation of unreality standing there with a little girl who should have been at home in bed. It was a school night.

"I don't know where I am," she said dismally.

"Are you cold?" I took a step toward her, and she took a step back. "I'm not going to hurt you, kid. I stopped so I could help you. Where are your parents?"

"I don't know." She looked around like her mother and father might come wandering out of the woods at any moment.

"What's your name?"

She hesitated a moment, then said: "Millie."

"Millie?"

"It's short for Millicent."

"Hi Millie. My name is Felix. Felix Renn." I held out my hand and Millie looked at it distrustfully. "It's okay, I'm not going to hurt you." She still wouldn't take my hand, not that I blamed her. "Do you live around here?"

"No," she said. "I live in Toronto. In Rosedale."

I nodded. My office was in the next neighborhood over, in Yorkville. "Did you drive up here with your family? You and your parents? Maybe your brother and sister?"

"I don't have a sister," Millie said.

"Do you have a brother?"

She nodded. "Mom drove Pete to hockey. It was her turn. Dad took me to the mall for dinner. He went to the food court to buy us french fries. He said Mom would kill us if she knew, but I said I wouldn't tell."

"Where's your father now?"

Millie shook her head slowly. "He told me to come with him, but I didn't want to. I wanted to stay and watch the kittens."

"The kittens?"

"In the window," Millie said. "At the pet store. I always visit the kittens when we go to the mall. They remember me," she added defiantly, as if I might not believe her.

I nodded. "I'm sure they do. Which mall did you go to?"

Millie shrugged. "The mall. The same one we always go to."

"Do you know where you are right now?"

Millie shook her head. Her lower lip trembled and her eyes blurred with tears.

She was scared, and I didn't want to scare her more by telling her she was, at present, about eighty kilometers away from home.

I went over to the edge of the shoulder. The land sloped down to a drainage ditch that ran between the road and the woods. There were no streetlights on this stretch of the highway, and the spaces between the trees were very dark. I took a step down the slope, mostly to see if I could do it without flinching. This new aversion to the dark was looking dangerously like it could turn into a full-blown phobia, and quite frankly I was too old for a nightlight in my bedroom. I took another step.

"Don't," Millie blurted. She came toward me, then remembered that she was afraid of me, and moved back. "The man who looks like Daddy is out there."

I thought I had misheard her. "Your daddy is out there?"

"He's not my daddy," Millie snapped at me. "He *looks* like Daddy. That's why I went with him. He said he knew where Daddy was."

"What did this guy look like?"

"Like my daddy," she said. "I told you."

I bit my lip. "Was he short or tall? Did he have long hair or short—or was he bald?"

"He's almost bald, like my daddy, but he has some hair. It was brushed across the bald part."

"Do you remember what was he wearing?"

"A grey coat. It was long, and it had a belt."

"Like a trench coat?"

Millie shrugged. "He had a bag, too. A big one. Like the kind Pete uses to carry his hockey stuff."

I nodded.

"He said he knew where Daddy was. So I went with him. He said Daddy was looking for me, and he was getting angry because he couldn't find me. But I didn't go anywhere. I was still watching the kittens."

"Where did the man take you, Millie?"

"Outside, to the parking lot. I got scared. I started to cry. The man told me to stop, but I couldn't. He started shaking me. Then he hit me with something. He hit me right on the head. It hurt so much." She brushed at the leaf in her hair again, but still couldn't dislodge it.

"What happened after that?" I asked.

"I don't know. It was dark and hot. I tried to move, but it was too tight."

"Too tight?"

Millie nodded. "I couldn't move my arms or legs. I heard a loud buzzing sound and then I saw the man looking down at me. I was in the bag. He put me in the hockey bag. I kicked and kicked, but he wouldn't let me out. He kept pushing me down. Then I managed to get out. I didn't know where to go. I wasn't in the parking lot anymore. All I could see was trees. I ran and ran until I came here. I waited for someone to stop but no one did. Until you came."

I nodded, taking this all in. Millie was lucky. I didn't want to tell her how lucky. She was unlucky too, in that she had an idiot for a father, one who thought it was perfectly fine to leave a young girl alone in a mall while he went off to buy french fries. But that wasn't Millie's fault. At that moment, I wasn't sure who I wanted to get my hands on more, Millie's dad or the pervert who had abducted her.

Her abductor was closer, at least for the moment. He wouldn't stick around for long if he had any kind of survival instinct. Millie had gotten away from him, and he must have known she would eventually find an adult who in turn would contact the police.

I looked off toward the woods again. It was a clear night and the stars were out. A quarter moon brooded over them like a fretful mother. I could see about five feet into the trees, but no more. I didn't want to go in there. There could be anything in those woods. I hated myself a bit for thinking that. There was cautious and there was cowardly, and I was starting to get the two confused. If I couldn't sort them out soon I'd have to hang up my spurs and quit the private eye racket, maybe open a beauty salon.

"All right, kid," I said, turning back to Millie. "Let's get in the car. I'll drive you to the nearest police station, and then we'll figure out how to get a hold of your parents."

"No." Millie shook her head firmly. "I'm not supposed to take rides with strangers."

I almost said, You don't seem to have a problem wandering off in the mall with them. Instead I said, "I told you who I am, Millie. I'm Felix, remember?"

"You're still a stranger," Millie said. As if to emphasize this, she took another step backward. I was a real smooth talker with the ladies. At any age.

I put my hands on my hips and looked up at the quarter moon. The dome light of the night sky. I didn't have a lot of options here. Stuck between a car and a dark place. Millie wouldn't let me drive her to the police, and I couldn't leave her at the side of the road while I went to get them myself. I took out my cell phone and wasn't surprised to see there was no signal out here in the willywags.

I went over and opened the trunk of the car. I dug around in my luggage until I found my gun in its clamshell holster. Millie watched raptly as I clipped it onto my belt at the small of my back and covered it with my jacket.

"Are you a policeman?" she asked.

I should have lied and said yes. Maybe it would have gotten her into the car. Curse my honest soul.

"No," I said. "I'm a private investigator."

"What's that?"

"Someone who investigates things privately."

Millie made a face.

"I do some of the things a policeman does, but I don't work for the police."

She pondered this for a moment. "Like Batman?" she asked.

"Sort of. Except I don't wear a cape and utility belt."

"And your car's not as nice as the Batmobile."

"Thanks, kid."

"Pete likes Batman. He has all the movies on DVD. I like Spider-Man better, because sometimes he makes jokes."

"Yeah, Batman is more the serious type," I agreed.

"Do you have a badge?"

"No, but I have a license."

She looked disappointed. I didn't blame her.

"Are you going to arrest the man who took me?"

I wasn't sure what I was going to do. I was in a strange and difficult situation, and that was really saying something for me. The cases I worked on, I usually tried to avoid police involvement. Now I was in a position where I would have danced naked in the middle of the highway to get their attention. Irony, thy name is Felix.

"I'm going to take a look," I said noncommittally. "And you're going to stay here."

"Can't I come with you?" Millie said, and huddled deeper into her coat. "It's scary out here."

"Better to be scared than in danger." I didn't know if I believed that myself. Not when I looked toward those woods. "I think you've had enough of both for one night, huh?"

Millie lowered her eyes and didn't say anything. I went around the other side of the car and opened the front passenger door. "I know you don't want to get in the car, but I'll leave it open just in case you change your mind, or if you get cold. Okay?"

Millie nodded mutely without raising her eyes.

"I'll be back as soon as I can."

I went down the slope, jumped over the drainage ditch, and started toward the woods. Right before I stepped into the trees I got an idea and called back to Millie. "If you need me, honk the car horn, okay?" She nodded and I turned back and stepped into the inevitable darkness.

There was a harsh wind blowing through the woods that hadn't been there, or that I hadn't noticed, out on the highway. It made it seem like the trees were moving around me on all sides, keeping pace with me, running ahead of me, running behind me. It was like nature's equivalent of a funhouse hall of mirrors. I felt frightened and disoriented. I made myself keep walking because I knew if I stopped, I wouldn't be able to start again. Someone would find me the following morning curled in a ball on the ground, rocking slowly from side to side. If they found me at all.

Millie was waiting back at the car for me. I wanted to go to her, but I couldn't do that. I didn't have any kids of my own, and I didn't plan on having any in the foreseeable future, but a sense of responsibility had descended upon me just the same. It happened the moment I pulled off the road. Millie wasn't my child, but she was someone's child. Her problems were my problems. Her fears were my fears.

I lengthened my stride and quickened my pace, and when the wind blew the trees again, I forced myself to turn and look at them straight on, pinning them, and my fear, in place. The branches swayed mockingly; leaves blew around in heavy gusts. The trees were not moving. All was right with the world. Except for the little girl alone on the highway and the man who abducted her somewhere in these woods. I kept moving.

I held my hands out in front of me so I wouldn't run into anything. I could barely see them. It was like they weren't even connected to me, like they weren't even my hands. I began to breathe faster, and it had nothing to do with the pace I was keeping. I was starting to feel disconnected from my body. I told myself it was my body. Mine. I lived in it. I hadn't left it. It was still mine. I was here. In these dark woods. In my body.

Dry leaves crackled under my shoes like brittle laughter. The wind hooted and whispered.

I tried to focus on another sound, one that I was just now becoming aware of, an almost musical babbling. A river. Distant, but not too far away. I attuned my ears to it like a radio dial fixing on a frequency, and followed it. I didn't know if the river was where I wanted to go, but the sound of it grew louder as I got closer, and pushed out the sound of the wind and the leaves.

I came out of the trees and into a clearing. No river, but there was a tumbledown cabin with dark windows and a slate chimney. A pickup truck was parked under a carport that looked ready to collapse with the next deep breath. Stacked on the other side of the cabin was a towering pile of firewood.

I walked across a field of tall grass, looking for the road that the pickup would've taken to get to this place, but I couldn't find it. No surprise there. I couldn't see much of anything.

I stood on the cabin's front stoop and debated knocking. I decided I wasn't ready to alert my presence to anyone yet, and went over to the carport.

I put my hand on the pickup's hood. It was warm. I continued around to the back of the cabin. The river sound was louder back here, the cheerful babble of water rushing over rocks. There was another sound mixed in with it. A splashing sound that wasn't as regular as that of the river. It came intermittently. Splash. Splash, splash. Nothing for a few beats. Then splash, splash, splash.

I went down a grassy slope to a screen of trees and peered through them. I could see the river. And a man crouched on the bank with his back to me. He was scooping handfuls of water and splashing them on his face and chest. He was wearing a long coat. It might have been grey, it was too dark to tell, but I could see a belt hanging loosely around his middle.

I took a step forward, started to say "Excuse me," but my foot got caught on something buried in the leaves, and the words stuck in my throat. I tried to pull my foot back, but whatever I had snagged it on wasn't letting go. I brought my other foot forward and it got caught up in, too. I started to fall forward. I got a hand out in front of me and landed on the ground propped on one side like a man doing a crooked push-up. I twisted around and saw something glinting at me in the moonlight. A coil of metal was wrapped around my left foot. Barbed wire from an old fence. I pulled my foot toward me and the barbed wire came with it, along with a couple pieces of rotten wood posting. I was lucky the wire had only snagged my pant leg rather than my skin. I was able to get it unhooked without cutting myself. No tetanus shots for me. Now if I could only find a diet that worked.

By the time I finally regained my feet, the man at the river bank had stood up and was now facing me. He didn't say anything. I didn't blame him. It was not my best entrance. I was just glad there were no women around.

"Hi there," I said, brushing myself off. "Good evening."

"Good evening," the man said, in almost the exact same register as my own voice. I couldn't tell if he was mimicking me or mocking me. I got the impression it was both. The man was tall, about six two, and he may have been bald, but I couldn't tell for certain. He was rail-thin and it made him look taller. The trench coat he was wearing made him look even taller still. Add it all together and he looked about seven feet tall.

"Good evening," the man said again, and started toward me. "Good evening. Good evening."

Something was wrong with him, I thought, and not just because he was washing his hands in a river in the middle of the night. I could see stains on his jacket and on the clothes he wore underneath. I couldn't tell exactly what it was, but I had a hunch it wasn't Smuckers raspberry jam.

"Good evening," he said again.

I went for my gun, but it was too late. I had let Mr. Good Evening get too close. He sprang at me. I sidestepped him and dashed into the trees, drawing my gun from its holster. At the same time I felt a tug on my foot. An annoyingly familiar tug. I had enough time to think, *The goddamn fence*, and then I was falling down again. I put my hand out as I had done before, except I was holding a gun this time and it went flying into the brush. It made a rustling sound as it landed, then it was gone. I could search for three hours in this dark and not find it. I didn't have three hours.

Mr. Good Evening was on me then, his knee driving into my back. One of my arms was wedged beneath me, the other flailed uselessly to the side. He pressed down on my spine and gripped my head in both of his hands. He had huge hands and my head was like a walnut between them. His fingers probed my face like a bowler looking for the fingerholes in his ball.

I sunfished up and down, but couldn't get him off me. I snapped one of my legs back like a mule, but hit only air. I tried the other and struck something. Mr. Good Evening let out a loud grunt and got off my back. He stumbled away and I went with him. The leg I had kicked him with was the one wrapped in the coil of barbed wire. The barbed wire that was now embedded in the fork of his crotch.

He took another step back, and I was dragged along with him. Those barbs were really sunk in deep. I sat up, planted my hands on the ground, and jerked my foot back. The barbs tore loose and Mr. Good Evening let out a high-pitched scream that wavered in the night air. It went on and on.

The scream dissolved into a bubbly growl and Mr. Good Evening came at me again, flexing his hands. As he leaned over me I came around with a right cross that connected solidly with his temple. Mr. Good Evening exited stage left.

I went back to the barbed wire still wrapped around my foot. It was connected to pieces of the rotten posting, and I tried to use them to uncoil the wire without cutting my hands or my foot. By the time I managed to free myself, Mr. Good Evening had recovered his *joie de vivre*. He shambled toward me, listing a bit from the shot I had given him. That buoyed me up a bit. I might be afraid of the dark, but I could still clock a child abductor with the best of them. Mom would be proud.

He crouched over me and reached for my throat. I let him.

My hands were tucked in at my middle. I was still holding the two pieces of posting with the length of barbed wire strung between them. The moment he started to squeeze, I pistoned my arms forward and wrapped the barbed wire around his throat. He took one of his hands off me and tried to pull the wire away. Big mistake.

I couldn't see the blood at first, but I felt it. Hot wet droplets landed on my face, first in a slow patter, then a drizzle. Mr. Good Evening took his other hand off my throat and rose up slightly from his crouch. Not much, but enough for me to get a foot between us. I planted it firmly in his stomach and kicked out. He landed on his back and lay there, clutching at his throat with both hands and making a choking, gobbling sound. He pulled himself into a sitting position, and in the light of the quarter moon I saw it.

I had gotten his jugular. Blood was spilling out between his fingers in an alarming stream. I thought of the small boy with his finger in the dyke. There hadn't been much hope for him either.

Mr. Good Evening tried to stand, went down on one knee, tried again, and went down on both knees. He slumped further and further forward until he had to take one hand off his throat to prop himself up. It looked like an invisible weight was pressing down on his back, driving him down until he lay flat and unmoving on the ground.

I went over to the river bank and crouched next to the duffel bag. The zipper was pulled down. I reached in and spread it open. There wasn't enough moonlight to show me everything, but I could see enough.

The white dress stained with maroon blotches that I had thought were some sort of print pattern. The thin holes in the material where the knife had gone in. For a moment I thought there was a small animal in there with her, but it was only the fur-lined collar of her jacket. Her head was nestled against it. There was a red leaf in her hair.

I turned to my right and Millie was standing there.

"So this is your body," I said to her.

"Yes," she said. "That's my body."

I reached down and plucked the leaf out of the dead girl's hair. I looked over at Millie, but she was gone. I held the leaf on the palm of my hand. A gust of wind picked it up and dropped it in the river. I watched the current take it away, then I stood up and went to look for my gun.

THE SHRINES

Gemma Files

Photo: A rubble sculpture on the Leslie Street Spit. Five layers, the bottom two made from three-hole cinder blocks, then a two-hole block (jaggedly broken) and two partial blocks of one hole each, plus one more three-hole block. On top is a lump of concrete with rusty wires jutting from it; the wires have been "shaped" to suggest hair flowing in the wind, while the lump itself has a grey suggestion of features, open-mouthed, in profile.

Dear Darrow: Yesterday I went out to the Spit and saw the Shrine you'd made, that awful thing. All those honest gifts defiled, just to cobble together a poisoned offering for some nameless god to choke on. All those other Shrines broken up for parts, heaped like garbage—a middle finger made from other people's dreams, doubled, quadrupled, up-thrust towards silent heaven.

No secret at all about how I knew to go there; I found the article about the place when your landlord let me in, pinned to your bedroom wall.

New Gods of Leslie St.
On the Spit, Some Torontonians are Building
a Religion Even They Can Believe In
By Gregg Polley, Bite Daily

The first, built from broken bricks and cinder block, stands less than a metre tall, sides and roof forming a stage for a jumble of obscurely significant items: A ceramic Easter egg, a box of baby teeth. *A votive card to St. Martha, guardian against distractions. In front, a ceramic cast of the soles of someone's feet around which have been sprinkled brightly colored marbles seems to indicate where prospective pilgrims should stand, if they want to view this odd little diorama for maximum impact. There's even a "spire" made from half an orange traffic cone, like a Church of Oz raised by Munchkins.*

But this isn't Macchu Picchu, or Angkor Wat. This "sacred" structure, like the fifty surrounding it, sits square on the shores of Lake Ontario—a little-trod part of the Leslie Street Spit.

"A lot of people don't even realize the Shrines are here, because they're in this kind of nook, hidden from the road," notes Jensen Cort, crew leader with the Toronto and Region Conservation Authority, which manages the park.

The collection of towers looks like a primitive city fallen into disrepair, its miniature buildings fashioned out of construction debris fetched from the shoreline, where crashing waves have weathered bricks and cast iron into found art. The grass around it is revealingly trampled, indicating a steady stream of visitors. A few feet away, a garter snake slithers through another of the follies.

"We're standing on tons of rock with just a little soil on top," Cort says, unsurprised. "This place is like one big hibernaculum."

According to him, the entire spit was created over many decades by clean fill and construction waste being dumped to form a promontory, with adjacent lagoons and ponds. Now the place teems with wildlife: Foxes, raccoons, hawks and the many rodents they prey on, plus the nearby water-bird colonies Cort's team looks after.

Dear Darrow: Three weeks since we'd last spoken. I can still play the conversation back in my head, almost word for word—

"Mom," you said, "you're a smart woman. That's why it kills me you're letting this crap pull you down to...their level. All these other idiots."

"Like what, like Dad? *That* kind of idiot?" I gave an angry sigh. "He would've said he died in a state of Grace—that means something. The way Gran and Granddad's kindness means something to *me*, whether it comes with the Church attached or not. You don't spit on somebody for offering you sympathy."

"*You* don't. Besides—didn't do him much good, all that happy Christ-crap, did it? In the end."

"You don't know that."

You turned away. Threw back: "Yeah, well...neither of us does, actually. That's kind of the point."

What's "funniest" about all this, in retrospect, is that when Frank and I first married, I was definitely the Godless one in our relationship: Raised with no religion at all, taught only that Christianity was one more mythic system, one more set of stories people tell themselves at bed-time to distract themselves from an impending, inevitable headlong plunge into darkness. We used to joke about it, uneasily, whenever we ran across nursery rhymes like this:

Goosey goosey gander, whither shall I wander?
Upstairs, downstairs, and in my lady's chamber.
There I met an old man who would not say his prayers;
I took him by the left leg and threw him down the stairs!

"Thus perish all apostates!" I'd say, and you'd giggle. Too young to know what I was talking about.

That last fight ended when I told you that you were free to believe any damn thing you wanted, or not. But what I resented was being browbeaten for choosing not to tell people who believed something I didn't that they were idiots to their face—certainly not Frank's parents, whose grief over his death (Jesus talk set entirely aside) was just as sharp and valid as my own, or yours.

Dear Darrow: Most aneurysms have no cure, or reason. Your father died because people die; that's just what happens. There's no right or wrong to it. No good or bad, except as it applies to you.

I didn't tell you that then, because I knew you wouldn't believe me. But you would have grown out of it in time, this impossible hunger for accountability. I believe that devoutly, or try to. No one can stay that sad, that angry, forever.

No one human.

The towers stand above a shoreline littered with great slabs of broken sidewalk and tangles of re-bar, as though announcing the Shrines' presence to those approaching by water. Closer to the road, a meandering, human-scale walkway has been laid down with discarded bricks. At one end, the entrance closest to the road is framed by tree branches festooned with bits of cloth and paper on which questions, statements—invocations?—have been scribbled, like improvised prayer flags.

A subsidiary wall of sculptures lines both sides of the walkway, all of them decorated with bits of broken ceramics, doll parts, toys, metal hardware, feathers, pine cones, ornamental grass.

No one seems to know precisely when the charmingly rustic village of Shrines first took shape, or who started it. But the more compelling question might be, why?

Obviously, this is a place of meaning, somehow sacred to those who've lovingly gathered up Toronto's detritus, fashioning it into votive folk art.

Wanting to meet a few of them, we settle in to wait.

Dear Darrow: Shall I tell you a secret? It was always the *despair* at the root of all your anger which really got to me. That black bile. The way, after Frank's death, you tore through life as though wedged alone inside your own coffin, the four roughly hewn wooden walls of your own death's inevitability. And what you really wanted was for everyone else to willingly crawl into that box, right along with you. But some people do insist on hoping.

I certainly know how annoying *that* can be.

So don't think I can't understand how much that article must have upset you. So infuriating, those happy little idiots with their DIY deities. Setting up their stupid hopes like idols, watering the seeds of dream with prayers—and you wanted to show them, what? That it's all a lie, softly told? That everything lets you down?

Did you really think they didn't all already know that?

This is nothing new, my darling, any of it.

Not even what must have happened to you.

"Worshippers" begin to arrive around twilight.

"I was picnicking here, with my kids," one woman, call her "Susan", explains. "And I thought I heard this sort of a...voice in my head, and I just suddenly felt...thankful. Like giving back, you know? And now every time I do something, every time I add to my Shrine, I get that feeling again."

She kneels in the dirt, using glow-in-the-dark paint to add curlicues and runic patterns to her Shrine's walls. Concluding: "It just felt so... good. And where else do you get a feeling like that, usually, outside of a bar? Like, ever?"

Though Shrine-building looks more like a hobby to non-believers, for many, it can be a full-time job. One person, who asked not to be identified even by pseudonym, must travel two hours either way in order to maintain the Shrine they've constructed. Is it worth it, we ask?

"Oh, yes. Oh, yes."

For others, the inspiration to make their Shrine—while similarly rewarding—seems to have been considerably more direct.

Says "Keith": "It was like a name kind of came into my mind while I was standing here one day, looking out over the lake, so I wrote it down, in there." *He indicates his Shrine's interior, packed tight with multicolored wool and rags.* "Something started telling me what to do, after that. No—I can't try to say the name, so don't ask me. Hell, I won't even try to read what I wrote; why do you think I did this? So I wouldn't be tempted."

Why not?

"Because. It's not for *us.*"

Then who is it for?

He looks away, as though embarrassed. Doesn't answer.

Dear Darrow: Don't think I don't know exactly what it is you resent most about me, these days—the fact that I can still remember when you were soft, and small, and lovely, and loving. That when I love you it's the same way I did when you were still that child, and that I'll never stop. Never.

No matter how hard you try to make me want to.

Only now, however...now that I've spent such a lot of time thinking about it...does it occur to me that what you insisted on telling poor Gran and Granddad, your idea of God as a prayer-eating spider growing fat off the world's misery—cliché as it seems—was far more prescient than even you could know.

If the Shrines' example teaches us anything, it's that one person's god may be another person's something else. A shadow glimpsed behind a screen, blurred out of all proportion; something removed from context, laid horribly open to misinterpretation.

Make your own god: Press here. Tab "A" into slot "B". A Shrine to nothing? Is nothing sacred?

Even unaddressed, your prayers *do* go somewhere, probably. Just—

—not where you think.

Looking out onto the lake, now, I too think I hear a voice in my head—whispery, repetitive, like the lapping waves. It does not seem to speak to me, at least not directly; is the voice yours? Or is it meant *for* you, somehow...part of your memories, your dreams? The ones you didn't bother to write down?

You called, I came. Do you have work for me? If not, you've wasted your time—and mine.

And there will be a price to pay, for that.

Because maybe, just maybe, there is something—not *God*, but *a* god? Something local, something petty. A place-linked god who hovers around the Spit, that artificial between-place, and grazes on prayer, on hope, on awe, the same way bees do on pollen. That milks us like aphids of our small ecstasies, our tiny moments of grace. That doesn't like its herd being messed with. And though one might think even you would understand the dangerous illogic of getting between something unnameable and its food-supply, which—it seems—is exactly what you did. You shat where it ate.

Dear Darrow: I imagine you mid-frenzy, laying waste to everything you can reach—kicking one Shrine down, taking the Blue Jays bat your father gave you for your eleventh birthday to the rest. Grabbing treasures up at random from the dust, the grit, and slamming them back together, a haphazard cairn. Pausing, breathing hard, to admire your handiwork, before spitting on it.

In tragedy's wake, you wanted answers. You wanted life to be explicable, which is...completely understandable, but unlikely. So terribly, terribly so.

Whereas, for me, the very idea of something keeping score—up there, down here, wherever—has always been frankly horrifying.

Rules and regulations, unwritten, inviolable. Making what you did here, at the Shrines—*with* the Shrines—like a prank call, sent collect. Like ringing the doorbell and running away. Like when you knock on the green, weed-hidden door of a fairy hill, but you're not the right person, or it's not the right day, or you didn't have anything to give in exchange, and didn't do it for the right reasons. And so...

You're forfeit. Something takes you, somewhere.

And you don't come back, ever.

How I wish I could have told you this, any of it. But it probably wouldn't have mattered, anyhow; you'd have done what you wanted in the end. Like always.

I never could tell your father anything, either.

These days, "hating" Toronto is so fashionable it's become cliché. Polls prove it. All across the rest of Canada, people universally seem to think we're rich, arrogant, cold, rude, smug; unfeeling, unsmiling, unfriendly; self-congratulatory, self-absorbed, self-centred, self-obsessed, self-satisfied, spiritless...

As Lip *magazine columnist Allin Koss, well-known for his weekly commentary on Megacity ecology, recently wrote: "The Toronto I grew up in might have been on its way to becoming something, but went off the rails a while back. Now here we are, still blithely driving at full speed without a road-map down the proverbial highway to Hell. Take a look: The signs are everywhere. Crumbling roads, bursting water mains, a decaying transit system, trash-covered streets, rampant homelessness, weekend murder sprees, traffic gridlock, smog warnings, contaminated beaches, a sewer system designed to overflow into the lake, a decrepit industrial wasteland waterfront choked with Soviet-style residential towers. If this is progress, I'd love to see what city council considers outright failure."*

The funniest thing about anti-Toronto sentiment, however— whether it comes from outside or in—is that ours is a city populated by people from elsewhere. Survey a room of Torontonians and you'll find recent immigrants from Iraq to Newfoundland, some Anglo transplants from Montreal, a few who came from the Prairies looking to make it big, plus one or two Vancouverites who can't shut up about how much they miss the B.C. bud. In business and the arts, the best and brightest from all corners of the country come here to meet up and make their mark (excepting perhaps, francophone Quebecers, who migrate to Montreal).

But what do they find, when they do? In a place of infinite pos-sibility, it's hard to connect, on any level. Though distractions are everywhere, loneliness runs rampant—and religion, organized or not, just doesn't seem to help. It's all too easy for that innate human impulse towards the mystic to turn into disappointment with every "offered alternative"—live-for-the-moment hedonism, woo-woo paganism, Gnostic secret cultism and proselytizing atheism, alike.

This place, however—the Leslie St. Shrines—is different. Something's happening here—something new. Or maybe very old.

Check it out.

Dear Darrow: It's beautiful up here, surprisingly so. Smell of lake, of turned-up earth, of new grass. The trees are putting forth furled leaves, like popped and shredded cocoons.

It's also cold, though, right now—as I stand out on the very edge of what used to be a loading dock just past the old sugar factory's hulk, with black water roiling around me everywhere I turn to look.

In front of me, the lake; behind me, the Shrines. This clean, forgetful city of mine: Toronto, two cupped hands set shoreward on a lake of muck and tears. Toronto tipping sidelong, a slowly poured-out bowl of pain. Toronto, under the gathering storm.

This world is a pit lined with wounds, always fresh, always green. Much as we may strive to, can we ever possibly deny it? Should we even try?

Misery of miseries. The type of misery that longs for transfig-uration: I don't care what happens, where I end up, what or who

I become, as long as it's not what and who I am right now—no longer here, no longer me, no longer *this*.

Like dogs to stink, like flies to blood, so these hovering invisible presences are drawn to misery. And Toronto "the Good" has always had a slice of pure, cold misery for its beating heart—that same endless reserve of negative energy you identified with religion, denounced wherever you found it as bullshit, a con, a vicious shell-game. The spiritual equivalent of necrotizing fasciitis.

Which means these things will come to us, always. Always. Whether or not we ask them to.

Particularly if we keep on making the mistake of doing them worship.

Photo: The same Shrine as before, at sunset. Around its "neck", a long silk scarf—bright saffron, crowded with indelible penmanship, so cramped as to be almost unreadable—flutters upwards, caught by the wind. A prayer in motion.

Dear Darrow: I know you won't read this—that you can't. So I offer it up instead, as evidence, to anything else which might be listening. As sacrifice.

I come to the Shrines, almost every day. I make that pilgrimage. I think I may have defused your construction, to the best of my ability—re-sanctified it, or perhaps de-sanctified it. I make my offerings, write down my dreams. Wait, uncomplaining, for any sign of a sign—of expiation, of relent. Any sign of forgiveness.

Doing penance *for* you, even though I know that's impossible—and hoping, against hope, to one day see you again.

Dear Darrow, second-generation apostate—believing nothing, knowing nothing. Fearing nothing. I let you do what you wanted, believe—or not believe—what you wanted. I should have tried harder.

I let you down.

Oh, dear Darrow. Oh, my poor little boy.

How I do love you so.

Your mother.

DEAD

Claude Lalumière

My dead brother insists that we stop using his alive name. His mommy asks, "What should we call you, then?"

He smiles, his mouth open wide, the gap in his teeth looking too adorable. Last week, he lost his first baby tooth. I want to rush over and hug him so I can absorb all that cuteness. And I want to smell him, because he still has a trace of baby smell, even at five years old. "I'm dead. Call me *Dead*."

But he isn't. Not yet. It takes seven years to be declared dead, and he's only been missing for a few days. We humour him, though.

The mommies and daddies let me sit in when the police explain what happened on my brother's first day in kindergarten. I can tell the detectives expect me to be sent out of the room.

First they ask who everyone is. Daddy Kent says, "We share the house. We're like one big family." That's not a lie. They make it look like Mommy Jenny is with Daddy Kent, and Mommy Tara with Daddy Neal. They call it fudging the truth. Sometimes it's simpler that way.

Less than an hour after class started, the police tell us, the teacher discovered a heap of clothes. There was a bit of blood on the shirt. She did a quick headcount and realized she was one child short. She took attendance, and of course my brother was the missing one.

The other kids told the police that my brother had lost a tooth, and that explained the blood.

Ms. Collingswood hadn't noticed, but there were so many kids to pay attention to.

Neither the teacher nor any of the children remembered anyone being in the classroom besides themselves. Neither the teacher nor any of the children noticed how or when my brother disappeared.

One of the detectives says, "Did you get a ransom note?"

The other one asks, "Is there anyone you know who would have any reason to take him?"

"Are you pressing charges for negligence against the school and the teacher?"

No to all of the above.

They ask to see his room. They look around, but there's nothing to find.

"If you hear anything, call us."

"We'll do everything we can to return your son to you."

Finally, they leave.

Dead has already told us a different story.

Curled up on Mommy Jenny's pillow, Dead is taking an afternoon nap. He looks so tiny nestled in the mommies and daddies' big bed, as if he were still a little baby. The rest of us are standing in the doorway, admiring him. He's so peaceful. So beautiful. So fragile.

Mommy Jenny whispers, "Nothing must ever hurt him again."

Even as a baby, when he was still alive, my brother was so sensitive to everything. If someone lashed out in anger—at anyone—he would either cry uncontrollably or withdraw completely, his eyes wide with shock and fear. We had to learn never to have temper tantrums and never to scream at each other. We learned to really communicate. We did it for him, but it was a good thing. My brother taught us to be better people.

He taught me to be a better person.

Once, when I was little, I was furious at the mommies and daddies because they didn't get me this stupid toy, and I got so mad. I was so stupid. I made everyone angry, and it all turned into a big fight with lots of yelling. And then we heard a loud, horrible scream—only a short burst, but it was the most terrifying noise I'd ever heard. The sound of a baby being tortured. That's the image that flashed into my mind. We stopped fighting and rushed to the crib. My baby brother's face was rigid with

fear. He breathed in short bursts, like a broken piston. Mommy
Jenny barely touched him, and he screamed again.

The mommies and daddies murmured tensely to each other.

I was so scared. I hated myself for what I'd done to my
brother. I filled my heart with my love for him, and I singsonged
his name.

The mommies and daddies stopped talking. They listened to
me and watched the baby.

After a few minutes, he made a little baby noise. A normal
noise. I continued my song, and his face relaxed. He drooled. His
eyes closed. He drooled some more, and his breathing calmed as
he slept.

The mommies and daddies each kissed me on the head
as they left the room. I sang to my brother the whole time he
napped. When he woke up, he smiled at me. I climbed into the
crib, squeezed in next to him, and hugged him. There were tears
in my eyes as I whispered, "I'll never hurt you again. Ever."

It's time to renew my vow. I say, "I promise never to hurt my
brother."

The mommies and the daddies stare at me forever, then they
nod to each other, and then turn to look at Dead sleeping on
their bed.

Mommy Tara says, "I promise never to hurt Dead."

Daddy Neal says, "I promise never to hurt Dead."

Daddy Kent says, "I promise never to hurt Dead."

Mommy Jenny sheds a tear. "I promise never to hurt my son."

Gently, I climb on the bed. I'm too old for afternoon naps. I
cuddle Dead. I close my eyes.

Everyone is dressed in black. The two daddies. The two mommies. Me. Except Dead. Dead isn't wearing any clothes at all.

Dead pees in a plant pot. A big cactus. His little wee-wee is
funny-looking. Dead reminds me of those water fountains with
statues of pissing cherubs. His pee is colorless, almost odorless,
just like water.

We all laugh.

The doorbell rings. Dead is done peeing, so he disappears.

We all remove the smiles from our faces. We try to look sad.
It's been three months since my brother vanished. My mommy
opens the door. Seeing everyone's grim expressions, I start gig-
gling. Daddy Kent glares at me, and I bury my face in my hands.

Uncle Jerry walks in. His big SUV can seat everyone, so he's
driving us. The five of us (Dead isn't coming) could have fit into

our own car, but Uncle Jerry insisted: "You shouldn't have to drive to the ceremony." The mommies and daddies said, "Okay," because it's best not to make a fuss.

Uncle Jerry kneels down next to me. "Oh, Lilly!" He takes me in his arms and hugs me. "You loved him so much, eh? It's okay to cry."

I peek at the mommies and daddies, and they all look relieved. Daddy Neal winks at me.

Daddy Neal sits up front; Uncle Jerry's his brother. The two mommies climb in the middle seat, with Daddy Kent squeezed between them, holding hands with both of them. I sit alone in the back seat. Actually, I lie down. I take up the whole seat. I close my eyes and pretend that we're flying, that the car is a private luxury jet. The steady rumble of the SUV becomes the hum of the plane. I'm flying. Flying! Flying to a heaven made to order for my brother. Dead's perfect world. I want to be there with him, in that place where no-one is ever mean.

Someone grabs my hand. Immediately, I know it's Dead. Those tiny hands, spongy like marshmallows. Still naked, Dead climbs on top of me and rests his head on my chest. I wrap him in my arms. His soft hair tickles my chin.

Dead's mommy turns to see what's going on in the back seat. Dead isn't supposed to be here. But she chuckles. What all of us want is to make Dead happy. Daddy Kent turns, too. And then my mommy. They nod to each other. Mommy mouths to me, "I love you."

Uncle Jerry says, "Is Lilly alright? What's going on back there?"

Daddy Kent says, "Nothing. Nothing at all." Meanwhile, Dead's mommy stretches her arm and rests her fingertips on Dead's hair.

Later, Daddy Kent says in a voice that's a bit too loud, "We're almost there."

I nudge Dead, and he slides off me. He slips under the seat, out of sight.

By now, Dead is presumed dead, even though legally he's still only a missing person. Today, the entire extended family is commemorating him. For closure, they say. It wasn't our idea. But it was simpler to go along and get it over with. At the ceremony, the aunts and uncles and grandparents all want me to say a few words.

I'm nine years old, but today they all try so hard to treat me like an adult. Why now? The aunts and uncles and grandparents never treat me like a real person. Why isn't a child a real person? The mommies and the daddies don't think like that. They've always treated me and my brother like real people. Today, though, I wish they'd all treat me like a kid, not like a real person. A real person is listened to, and I have nothing to say to these people. They've never listened before; why should I suddenly want to speak to them today?

I don't want to be here with all these people who pretend to know him but don't. I want to be home and play with Dead.

Dead should be in Uncle Jerry's car. Dead should have stayed home. He doesn't even like these people.

Instead, he's under the table, naked, hidden by the thick white cloth. No-one noticed him sneaking into the reception hall. His head is nestled on my feet. I don't want to move and disturb him.

Grandma Diane, whose cheeks are purple with makeup, is the most insistent. "Say something, Lilly. It's okay if you cry. Say something in his honour."

I give my mommy a pleading glare, and she steps in.

"Lilly was closer to him than anyone. Please let her deal with his passing in her own way."

I reach over and squeeze her hand. I'm glad Mommy Tara is my mother.

Before his death, my brother never wanted to go to family events, or parties, or anything like that. But the mommies and daddies didn't want to leave him alone back then, and they made him come along with us. The grandparents and aunts and uncles and cousins would see him arrive, but then he'd disappear. They wouldn't even notice. For most adults, kids are almost invisible anyway—unless they make trouble.

Sometimes, though, my brother would slip out of his clothes. We were always on the lookout for that, so we'd find them first and hide them. We didn't always succeed. So Aunt Carla or Uncle Rob or Grandpa Paul or Grandma Iris would stumble upon the heap of discarded clothes and get worried. The mommies and daddies would try to reassure them. "It's a game he plays." We'd have to search everywhere until we found him, because the aunts and uncles and grandparents would go crazy with worry. "He's run away!" "He's been kidnapped!" They didn't know my brother. Once he'd made it all the way back home; Daddy Kent thought to check and then smuggled him back to the party, and we pretended that he'd been there all along.

Now that he's Dead, they leave him at home. Sometimes he comes anyway. I think that's what grownups call *perverse*. Last week, I asked Mrs. Lincoln at school what *perverse* meant, and her face went all red. She muttered and stuttered, and then the bell rang, so I never found out. I should ask my mommy.

No-one but us ever sees him at those parties. We never know he's coming along until he surprises us in the car on the way. He enjoys it more now because no-one expects to see him, no-one looks for him, no-one talks to him. He can hide and watch. He can play secret games with me without anyone ever noticing.

When he was alive, my brother didn't play with the other kids in the neighborhood. Most people, kids and adults both, have a mean streak, and my brother had no defences against that. The slightest unkind word would shatter him. Once, that jerk Wally Robertson, who's my age and has been in my class every grade, made fun of my brother's ears; because of that he refused to come out of the house for a whole month. My brother was only two and half when it happened. He started wearing a hat—a thick woollen tuque with one of those long tassels—and he wouldn't remove it. Ever. He slept with it on. He took his baths with it.

On his third birthday, he took a deep breath and yanked it off with one pull. He looked in the mirror. "My ears are better now," he said.

I hugged him and kissed his ears. "You have the best ears."

The mommies and daddies cheered, and everyone ate cake. Vanilla cake with lime-poppy frosting. It's been his favorite ever since.

I was four years old when Mommy Jenny gave birth to Dead. Only he wasn't called *Dead* then.

It was Daddy Kent's turn to be named father. Mommy Tara had flipped a coin when she learned she was pregnant, and Daddy Neal got to be my official father. At home, for real, both the daddies are equally my daddies, and Dead's daddies.

The mommies and daddies say that the two mommies are equally mommies to both of us, but that isn't true. Even though they don't mean to, the birth mommies are more attached to the child they carried. Like that time I cut the back of my head on the edge of a dresser because I'd been jumping up and down on the mommies and daddies' bed and there was lots of blood every-where. Mommy Tara held my hand all the way to the hospital.

She held it so tight, as if she wanted her skin to meld with mine, the bones of our hands to mesh together, her life to become my life. No-one had ever held my hand like that.

My brother never hurt himself. At least, not physically. When he was three years old, he jumped off the roof and landed on that bush with the pink flowers. The mommies and daddies were furious. They were so scared that they forgot not to get angry like that, especially not at him. They shrieked and screamed and yelled and blamed each other for not keeping a better eye on him. But he didn't even have a scratch.

The mommies and daddies wanted to bring him to the hospital, in case he'd broken some bones or had some other internal injuries, but he wouldn't go. He didn't want doctors and nurses prodding him. He didn't want to be in that big place full of people he didn't know and who didn't care about him. Already, all these tense emotions were too much for him.

"Stop it," I said, as gently as I could, tugging at their clothes. "You're hurting him."

But it was too late. He ran into the house and disappeared. That was the first time. We didn't see him for a whole week. He'd snatch food without anyone seeing him do it. In the yard, there'd be these spots where the earth had been upturned and then neatly patted down. Daddy Neal dug them up, and, sure enough, there would be my brother's stinky little turds.

One morning everyone came down to breakfast, and there was my brother, waiting to be served. Mommy Jenny, his mommy, celebrated his return by making blueberry pancakes. We never found out where he'd been hiding. We never asked. We didn't want him to disappear again.

But my brother never slept in his bed again. He'd discovered that he liked disappearing. He'd hang out with us during the day, but most times we would have no idea where he spent his nights. After that first week, he always showed up for breakfast, so the mommies and daddies stopped worrying.

Sometimes, at least once a week, he would crawl under my sheets and fall asleep with his head pressed against my stomach. Sometimes we wouldn't sleep, and we'd talk all night. We'd destroy the world and build it back up again, but better. There would be no guns. No animal laboratories. Children could be mayor. Instead of driving cars people would walk everywhere and talk to the animals. There would be no asphalt or concrete on the ground, only earth and grass and sand and rocks, and we could go barefoot everywhere. There would be no police, but lions and elephants would keep everyone safe. Instead of planes, dragons flew in the sky. We wouldn't have to go to school and we'd never grow up and we'd be ourselves for our whole lives and we'd live forever and no-one would ever say or do anything mean.

Now that he's Dead my brother still sleeps with me occasionally, but we don't talk like that anymore. He says, "I live there now." I want to say, *But you're right here.* He's not really, though. Even when he looks right at me, his eyes focus beyond me, at a place only he can see. A better world.

The mommies and daddies don't want to have pets. We love them anyway, but we resent it. When I grow up, I'll have a house of my own and Dead will stay with me and we'll have lots and lots of animals—dogs and cats and birds and hamsters and turtles. There will be no cages, and everyone will get along and have fun and play, and no-one will ever hurt anyone.

Especially Dead. No-one will ever hurt Dead again.

It's Dead's fifth deathday. Only two years to go, and Dead will be officially dead! His skin is ghostly white now, from lack of sun.

After his death, we stopped celebrating his birthday. It's what he wanted: "The important day will be my deathday," he'd said five years ago. The new tradition is that Mommy Jenny makes his favorite cake, and Dead wears a party hat, with an elastic string under the chin to hold it tight and a propeller on top. The hat is blue with big red stars and yellow swirls. It's always the same hat.

That's all he wears. Since his death, he's given up on clothes. Even when he was alive, my brother had trouble keeping his clothes on.

People remember the date. Some years, there's even a little item about it on the news or in the papers, with a picture of my brother. It's such a tragedy, they say. Nobody bothers us or calls or anything on Dead's deathday itself. There are reporters who call or ring the doorbell, but they always do it a few days in advance. On that date, friends and family respect our grief and privacy. So we don't have to pretend to be unhappy or anything. We can party with Dead and have all the fun we want.

The five candles on the cake are lit. We cheer, urging Dead to blow out the candles and make a wish.

Dead takes a deep breath and holds it in, grinning, his cheeks all puffed up. Deathday is always his happiest day. His eyes are wide open, and he looks at everyone around the dining room. Just when I think he'll blow all that air on the little flickering flames on top of the candles, his chin drops on his chest, and he lets all that air fizzle out.

He gets up and leaves the room.

Daddy Neal says, "Hey, where's Jenny?"

We all follow Dead. He walks up the stairs. The door to his bedroom is open. No-one ever goes there anymore.

Mommy Jenny is sitting on the bed, crying. Dead stands next to her, wearing only his party hat with the propeller.

She hugs him and smushes her face on his chest. Her tears get smeared all over Dead.

I'm angry at Mommy Jenny for ruining Dead's deathday. I wanted to have fun with my brother on his most special day of the year. I want to be the one hugging him. Only I wouldn't be crying, I'd be laughing and Dead would laugh along with me and we'd eat cake and we'd lick the frosting off each other's fingers and everything would be okay.

I'm making sandwiches with Mommy Jenny. We each make one. She makes a tomato sandwich with lettuce and mayonnaise. I make a peanut butter and strawberry jam sandwich. I slice a banana into circles, which I put in the middle of the sandwich. There's too much banana to fit in there, so I eat the rest.

We leave the sandwiches on the counter, and then we each go off to bed. "Don't forget to brush your teeth," says Mommy Jenny.

In bed, I wait for Dead. But he doesn't come. I wish he visited me more often. Once or twice a week isn't enough. I sleep better if he's there with me. When I do fall asleep, I dream of Dead's perfect world. In the perfect world, Dead is outside playing with me and a whole family of dogs.

The next morning, Dead doesn't join us for breakfast. But the sandwiches are gone. He doesn't eat with us every day anymore. Even when he does, he's silent. He's always smiling, but I'm not sure if he really sees us. It's been months since he last spoke to me. Sometimes I forget the sound of his voice, and that makes me sad.

Mommy Jenny is yelling at Mommy Tara and the two daddies. "How could we do this to him?" She shouldn't be yelling like that. She swore never to hurt Dead.

Mommy Tara says, "It's too late to go back and change it. It's what he wanted. It's what he needs. We promised."

Mommy Jenny: "No! He's still young. He can have a whole life. A normal life. He's getting worse! When's the last time he even spoke to anyone? He used to spend time with us, but for the past year—it can't go on like this. I won't let it."

Daddy Kent: "He's getting older. It's a phase. All kids do that. Carve out their independence."

Mommy Jenny: "I can't believe...When did you become such an idiot? He should see someone. Hell, we all need to be in therapy. We're crazy! All of us!"

Daddy Neal says, "Calm down."

Mommy Jenny says, "Don't patronize me! He was only five years old! It was a game, a whim. He didn't know what he was doing! We were stupid! How could we let a little boy talk us into this? This crazy, stupid idea. I can't let him ruin his whole life. He's my son."

The mommies and daddies don't know that I'm listening. They think I'm in bed, sleeping. Instead, I'm lying on my stomach on the floor in the hall upstairs. They're in the kitchen, with the door closed, but they're louder than they realize.

I feel a weight on my back. Dead is here. He rests his head between my shoulder blades. His fingers squeeze my arms.

Daddy Kent says, "We're all his parents. All of us. Not just you."

"Fuck that. He's my son. My son!"

There's a loud crash.

"Don't touch me!"

There's another crash.

"I'm leaving. I'm through with this family. You're insane, all of you, and I'm not going to let you destroy my son's future!"

Mommy Jenny erupts from the kitchen and stomps up the stairs. I barely have time to rush back to my room and close the door.

Where's Dead?

The police come with a warrant. Mommy Jenny is with them. I haven't seen her in five weeks.

Since she moved out, I haven't seen Dead either. No-one has. At first we feared she'd taken him, but he's still eating the sandwiches I prepare for him every night.

Once, I made the sandwiches and stayed up all night. At dawn, I had to pee. When I came back the sandwiches were gone.

The police tear the house apart. They look everywhere. We all keep silent, glaring at Mommy Jenny.

But the police don't find anything. They don't find Dead.

Mommy Jenny yells, "What have you done to my son?"

Daddy Kent says, calmly, firmly, "Our" (he puts a lot of emphasis on that word) "son died years ago."

The detective apologizes. "We had no choice. In a case like this we have to follow up on any lead." He leans in close to Daddy Kent, slips a card into his hand, and whispers, "If you need to press charges against her, or file a restraining order, call this number."

In a loud voice, Daddy Kent answers, "That won't be necessary. This is an ordeal for all of us. There's no need to make it even worse."

There's hatred in Mommy Jenny's eyes.

Daddy Kent and I make the cake together. He makes the cake itself, I prepare the frosting. Vanilla cake with lime-poppy frosting. Dead's favorite.

It's Dead's sixth deathday. We haven't seen him for months, not since Mommy Jenny left, but we know he's still here.

He never misses his deathday. We really want him to come out. We're not sure if we should call his name or just wait silently. We compromise and whisper *Dead* occasionally.

We even invited Mommy Jenny. His mother. Everyone would forgive her if she came back. She doesn't show up, though.

Neither does Dead.

We wait up till midnight, then we all go to bed. No-one has eaten any cake.

I cry myself to sleep.

In the morning, there are only a few crumbs left on the table.

Dead didn't want to go to kindergarten. But the mommies and daddies forced him to.

This is what Dead told us the day he died: he lost a tooth, and he bled, and the other kids made fun of him; the teacher saw the kids make fun of him, and she didn't do anything to stop it.

That's it. That's all that happened. It sounds so innocent, only it's not.

Even before, my brother couldn't play with other kids. Not without getting hurt.

Already, my brother feared to be with anyone but us.

Already, my brother had begun withdrawing from the world.

Always, other people hurt him. They weren't especially cruel, but my brother was especially sensitive. How could you warn the whole world about that? Why would they care?

We cared. The two mommies. The two daddies. Me.

"Don't make me go back. It's too hard. The outside world is too hard. I want to be dead," my brother said. "Dead to the world. Let me be dead."

He explained what it would mean, him being dead: dead, but still with us.

The mommies and the daddies listened to my brother's every word, because to them he was a real person. They knew that the world wasn't right for everyone, or that some people weren't made for this world. They were different, too.

"Please," he said. He didn't cry. He was strong. He didn't try to blackmail the mommies and daddies into agreeing. "Please help me be dead. It'll be our secret. Our secret game, and nobody else will ever know."

No-one had spotted him coming back home after he disappeared from school. At five years old, he'd already been training for this for most of his life. He was so good at it. It could work.

I ring the doorbell. The door opens, and there's Mommy Jenny.

I'm prepared for her hatred. Instead, she looks sad. She steps back and motions me inside. Her apartment is small. It's just one room. Everything is neat and tidy. Too much so — like nobody real lives here.

"Do you want some juice?"

"How about tea?"

"Sure." She pours water into the kettle and puts it on to boil. "Look at you. You're a young woman."

"Sixteen."

"When I saw you every day, I didn't really notice you growing up. What I saw was the little girl in my mind."

We wait for the water to boil. Mommy Jenny pours the tea.

Finally I say, "You have to come back."

"I can't. I won't."

"You're being selfish, Mommy Jenny."

"You don't know what it's—"

"Dead hides all the time now. He needs you."

"I don't think so. I don't think he needs anyone."

"Well, I need him, and because you left him he won't come out anymore. We promised none of us would ever hurt him. Ever."

"Promises aren't always forever."

"That's something adults say when they give up. When they don't want to be bothered by their responsibilities anymore. When they're selfish. I never want to be like that. Dead needs all of us to be better than that."

"I'm sorry about the police. I won't do anything like that again."

"That's not enough. It's his seventh deathday next week. Monday. He'll be declared dead. Finally. This should be his best party ever. Don't ruin it. Not again. Come back. Please come back. Make the family whole again. I'm angry at you, but I still love you."

Shit. I'm crying.

I yell at her, "Don't you have anything to say?"

She looks away. She keeps her head turned away from me.

Eventually I leave.

For Dead's seventh deathday, I want to make the cake all by myself. Daddy Kent hugs me and holds me for a long time. "Of course," he says.

So I take out the recipe and mix the ingredients and do everything the book says. Meanwhile, I talk to Dead like he's right here with me in the kitchen. I tell him about school. I tell him about how silly the boys are around me now. I tell him about this girl I like, Indiana, but that I'm afraid to tell her because, what if she doesn't like me back? Nobody knows this.

When it's done baking, I take out the cake and wait for it to cool. Not too long, though; I want it to stay extra moist—the way Dead likes it. Then I spread the frosting all over it. I put on lots. When I'm done, I clean the bowl with my finger and lick the leftover frosting. It's so good.

I bring the cake to the dining-room table, where Mommy Tara and the two daddies are waiting. I take seven candles and carefully arrange them on the cake. I turn off all the lights, and then I sit down. I strike a match and light the candles.

We join hands.

"Everyone close your eyes and clear your thoughts." I say that. The seance was my idea. "O Dead, we call upon you to visit the living. Those who love you wish to celebrate your death with you." I repeat those two sentences three times.

"Dead," I say softly. Again and again, until it slides into a chant. The adults join me. It becomes a round, with that one syllable overlapping with itself, every voice at a different rhythm, in its own pitch. Some of us sing the word in a light staccato; others stretch out the vowels, the bookend Ds subtly punctuating the ethereal flow. No two singers are quite in synch. Yet...It's lovely, as if we'd practiced for months. But we're improvising this part. That one syllable, taking on infinite resonances.

We keep singing, and together our voices grow more and more beautiful.

THE WEIGHT OF STONES

Tia V. Travis

At dawn, on April 29, 1903, a huge rock mass, nearly half a mile square and probably 400 to 500 feet thick in places, suddenly broke loose from the east face of Turtle mountain and precipitated itself with terrific violence into the valley beneath, overwhelming everything in its course....

Nineteen men were working in the mine at the time of the slide. Of these seventeen escaped and two, who are supposed to have been at or outside the mouth of the tunnel, perished.

—McConnell & Brock, *Report on the Great Landslide at Frank, Alta., 1903*

The loss of life has been appalling as nearly one sixth of our people have without a moment's warning passed into that great beyond and been ushered before the judgement seat.

—Frank *Sentinel*, May 2, 1903

The worst mining accident occurred in 1914, when Canada's deadliest mine disaster horrified the Pass and the world. The Hillcrest mine had an enviable reputation as a safe, well-run mine.

Idle for two days because of over-production, the mine opened as usual on June 19, 1914.

Of the 370 or so men who reported for work, 235
headed underground.
Only 46 of them would ever see daylight again.
—*Crowsnest: An Illustrated History & Guide to
the Crowsnest Pass*, J. Bryan Dawson

She sleeps beneath ninety million tons of limestone.

A sigh that might be the wind siphons through the Pass.
Gustiest corridor in the territory, a convergence of plates where
mountains break loose from the sky, where violence is measured
both in moments and eras, where sunlight splinters through
crevices and flowers live and die in darkness. If you listen, you
might hear a grain of sand sift through the labyrinth of boulders.

If you listen, you might hear her breathing.

I hold my own breath and map the movements of her heart...
the rise and fall of her lungs. I held that last breath for her until I
passed beyond the need for it. The desire for it.

Lie still. I will find you.

The river tumbles in its channel. Her voice rises above a ridge
of pressure. Thirty feet below, where the rescue party almost lost
hope, lays the trail she and I walked so many decades ago. I've
counted the lives this mountain has devoured down to the last
ulna and scapula. Crumbled heaps like the rocks themselves,
crushed beneath boots calcified with dust and lamp-oil. Boots
battered down to mule-hide, a century's stink of creosote, blast-
ing-powder, and coke oven—all the detritus of the building of
the Canadian West, above and below. There is not one stone I
have not turned. I searched for her on hand and knee until I bled
to the bone.

Now, I stand with my back to the mountain and form a circle
with my hands—like a surveyor's compass or the mouth of a
tunnel. When I squint through those hands in the sunlight I
almost convince myself I can pulverize those locomotive-sized
boulders with nothing more than the flex of my fingers...the
dynamics of muscle and will.

The strength of my regrets.

At moments like this, these rare moments of absolute clarity when I remember who I am, and who I was, and where she
is—the world has no more substance than that circle of hands.
Wind whistles through on its way to somewhere else as though
she and I were never here at all.

SUMMER, 1922

"Did you hear, that man came by asking again. He knew we dug up the Clarks' cottage."

Will Evans leans on his shovel handle. Turtle Mountain is indistinguishable from the dynamited rock on either side of the road.

"You know who he is, Will?" The kid from New Brunswick has hired on for twenty cents a day and the privilege of bunking under a canvas tent-flap.

Will uncaps his canteen. Drinks.

"He asked whether we'd found anything else."

"We did." A third workman, stripped to the waist, jams boot to shovel. "About ninety tons of limestone." He wipes his forehead with the shirt he's slung over a jack pine stump. "Tell him to come back tomorrow. I'll have more rocks for him." He hacks and spits. Plunges the blade back into dusty gravel.

Bars of perspiration dampen Will's shirt where his suspenders have steam-ironed the cotton. Beyond the boulders on the northern slopes, forest breaks the achingly grey valley.

Will drinks in the green with his eyes as a thirsty man drinks water.

Nineteen years since the Slide buried the town. Sixteen since improvements were made to the hardpan road by the Old Man River. Backbreaking labour through hundreds of feet of boulders, some the size of houses. The limestone is veined with rusty lichen, crusted like blood. First time in twenty years some of these shattered blocks have been exposed to sunlight.

"Too bloody hot for this." The British Columbian runs a hand through a shock of hair matted with dust and sweat. "Not a bloody breath of air all morning."

The New Brunswick boy surveys the cracks in Turtle Mountain's peaks. "What was it like cutting through this the first time?"

"They used more dynamite blasting down to the old wagon trail than they did the first two years running the mine." The British Columbian's back is burnished brown as deer-hide, deepening to Indian red across his shoulders.

"Five minutes 'til quitting time." The foreman, an older man with arms like steel pipe, is accustomed to loading twelve tons of bitumen a day. "You boys best get back to it now."

Will turns his back on the mountain. Eighteen years old, he has lived in the Pass since he was born, long before the Hillcrest explosion of 1914 that killed his father. Long before the Great War that claimed his brother three years later at Vimy Ridge. *First Division, 10ᵗʰ Battalion under Commander Currie.* They'd buried Laurier Evans and his blown-off legs in a rainy cemetery in Villers aux Bois with the other Canadians who died on that muddy scarp.

You come from a long line of phantom limbs, Will Evans.

Missing pieces.

Will touches the sun-warmed miner's tag he's worn around his neck since he was nine. The brass is warped from the blast, notched where the check struck a track. He remembers the stink of singed hair and scorched bone. Burnt strawberry pie, Papa's favorite. The oven smoke was hardly noticeable for the black billows rolling from Hillcrest.

The foreman calls lunch. Twenty shovel blades hit dirt. Men brush limestone powder from blistered hands wrapped in rag. Boys sag cross-legged near road-clearing equipment or atop boulders and swig bottles of ginger-beer. The bulldozer, parked on chunked earth and stone, radiates heat in waves. Workmen swap sandwiches and cigarettes.

"Heard they're gonna build a highway north of the railway line."

The British Columbian huffs. "Not in this lifetime they won't."

"Have you seen him, Will?" It's the New Brunswick boy.

Will knows who he means.

"I've seen him," he answers at last. "On the rocks. Near the old mine entrance. At twilight, when I'm out walking. He keeps to himself."

The foreman reaches for a long-necked bottle. "Owen Lawson used to be an engineer at Hillcrest eight years ago. Chief at Bellevue, now. One of the first rescuers back in the mines after the explosion. They tried to hold him back because of the blackdamp. Bad bit of business, that.... You boys is too young to remember much. The rest of you likely knows from the newspapers but you wasn't there."

Idle talk to pass the time but Will doesn't mind. Too many years have passed. The realization saddens him.

"Why would anyone keep these mines running after so many died?" The New Brunswick boy is all of sixteen. Alone out here. Searching.

The foreman grunts. Unwraps a sandwich of cold tongue. "When I think of the men crushed when the roof caved...boys killed in the chutes. Then Henry Frank losing his mind in that sanatorium with the weight of the Slide on his conscience. Shutting her down was the best thing they ever done. This valley is just one big burial ground."

The British Columbian opens his lunch-pail. "Wasn't men getting themselves killed that closed Frank. It was money. It's always money. Strikes and wages. Lockouts. No market in Europe for our coke and the rails switching to diesel."

"Remember the fire?" The foreman taps open his tobacco can. "Burned inside that mountain for years. No one could put it out. The Frank Mine was bad luck from the start."

The British Columbian shrugs. "No more'n any other. Helluva lot more men died in the War as ever died in the Frank Mine. In any mine. Ask young Evans there. He knows."

But Will isn't listening. He stares over the blasted rock at Turtle Mountain. The sun glitters high above the ridge. Boulders close in on all sides.

The foreman lowers his voice but his words ride the noon heat, suspended on limestone dust. "Will there lost his brother in France but he lost his Papa at home. War's war. You expect to eat a bullet. But Hillcrest had one of the safest operating records in the country. Can't say I heard the same about the frontlines at—"

VIMY, 1917

Will Evans's brother had been named after the man who'd been in office when these boulders careened down the mountainside in 1903. *Canada will fill the twentieth century!* the Prime Minister had promised. But Laurier Evans died thousands of miles from home in the cold mud of an April morning, just like the ones lost beneath these stones.

Cold mud of April.

Stone to mark where you fell.

All around the hospital tent where Laurier Evans died from shock and loss of blood, Canadians cheered the greatest victory in the history of British arms, even as shells still rained on the field. The sergeant sent Laurier's kit home from the Front. It contained little more than blood-spattered spectacles and a bottle of Harlene Hair-Drill, a lucky penny and a letter in Laurier's angular hand describing blinding snow and Sunday services and a French girl he'd met at a farmhouse near La Chaudière... most of all, his amazement at seeing two rabbits dart across the exploding battlefield.

The rabbits, Laurier noted, miraculously escaped both enemy artillery and Canadian pot-shots. *Easter bunnies! Tell Willie when I see him I*

It was the last line he'd penned before hurrying off to battle.

Will still dreamed of his brother's unfinished sentence. His brother's face, his father's face.

And writing-paper white as limestone.

APRIL 29, 1903

Ulla Lawson lies in bed and listens for her husband's footfalls on Dominion Avenue.

The night crew drops off one by one, picks balanced on shoulders hunched like Turtle Mountain. Owen's breath steams his upturned collar. He raises a hand to shield his eyes from the early-morning light slanting through the pines. Perspiration freezes to his body like a sheen of ice on the river.

One hard crack to the surface of that ice, Ulla knows, and the momentum of that constrained river water will break through like a bursting dam. She envisions Owen pausing at the boarding-house steps. Shaking coal-mud loose from his boots. *Have to replace the angle beam in that shaft tonight.* Through the entrance, up the backstairs towards the servants' quarters. *Need to reinforce that bar and bracing or the roof in twenty-six'll never hold. Better talk to Chapman about getting a mason in there to shore up the arching.*

Owen closes the door to their room with a hushed click. It wasn't until six a.m. that he'd crunched down the frosty grade from the tipple and crossed the bridge to the town. Distracted, he hadn't stopped to clean up at the pump but had come directly down from the tipple. His face is streaked black, teeth rimed with the same grit that is so hard to scrub from the sheets. But Ulla is used to the miners' flight patterns: like flocks of dirty geese navigating down endless corridors, beating their frustrations against the coal.

She lies motionless while Owen shrugs off his coat. Too preoccupied to notice her awareness, he sets down his toolkit with a quiet clank. Like a plum-bob, his toolkit has become an extension of his obligations in the mine. Ulla knows he's running a checklist through his shift: calculating where the next crossbeam or cap-piece should be eased into place, determining the ratio of weight, pressure and angle sufficient to maintain the physical integrity of the overlying geological structure and prevent Turtle Mountain from crashing down on their damned fool heads. *And*

if the coal releases from the sides? No amount of timbering will hold it.
It will plunge directly below and crush the main entry.

Outside the window the mountain is a violet-grey haze.
Owen stands before the chest of drawers in their rented room,
hands clenched on either side. *He's holding it like a crossbeam,*
Ulla notices, *like he's still in the mine.* His neck is cordwood tight.
Tension tremors the floorboards, vibrates the bedstead. It's like a
train accelerating through the Pass—Ulla senses it coming when
it's still miles from the siding. Chutes open and close inside her
husband, darkness trapped inside.

"Owen?"

He gazes at her in the mirror above the chest of drawers.
Finally his eyes break from hers in the glass. He blows on hands
that look like chunks of ice. "You should be asleep."

"I was waiting for you."

"There was no need." He hangs his cap and coat on the nail.
Bends over the basin. Cold water and coal dust stream down
with his sweat: ashes and grease. It's like trying to scour a sheet-
iron stove or clean an oiled harness in the galvanized tubs Ulla
uses for the hotel sheets.

"There's buttermilk in the tin."

Owen nods. Unfastens his suspenders.

"And a plate of Lillian's biscuits on the chair for you."

"That was kind of her."

"I saw Mrs. Graham today. They're going to buy another cow
and calf this week."

"Are they." Owen removes his blackened shirt. His bare arms
are charcoal-grey in the morning light. He hardly sees the sun
anymore.

"She invited us for supper sometime. It's a fine farm, every-
one says. Near the river. With John and Joseph back from the
Boer War and the Johnson boys to help, there's plenty of hands.
I wrote Papa that in the fall we might—"

"Ulla...."

He climbs into bed, muscles knotted from replacing beams in
the mine. *How many tonight?* Ulla wonders. The mountain chews
timbers and men and spits them out. She imagines a logjam of
bodies and splintered wood, snagging rocks in the Old Man
River.

The weight of her husband's back presses against her stomach, her thighs. His breathing deepens. Slows. Hitches and stalls.
She jars his arm until he breathes again...steering him up from
the depths, to the air.

And if the mountain should fall, if he were buried alive, his heart trapped inside the mine while his blood runs black as coal? How many rocks will he knuckle to the bone before his strength runs out, trickling between the ruins of hands he'd wanted to save for something better than this.

Lunch over, the crew dozes beneath blazing jack pines. Caps slide low on peeling red foreheads. Will Evans moves towards Turtle Mountain. Listens to the hiss of grasses swallowing his body, the slow lull of river. Farther up on the slopes at the northern limits of the Slide, saplings have begun filling in the bald spots. But nothing grows on the scar where half a mountain fell.

Last week the crew uncovered the remains of the Clark cottage. A family of eight swept away in an icy choke of mud, tree trunks shooting like projectiles across the valley. All lost but the eldest daughter Lillian who'd spent her first night away from home, a last-minute decision that saved her from extinction. Now water seeps into the cracks between the boulders. One day these boulders, too, will dissolve: grain by grain, until no one knows this place or what happened here, or how many souls lie beneath it.

The British Columbian had discovered a slender femur as pitted as limestone. Bleached wood that might have splintered from a river-smoothed branch but upon closer examination proved to be window-casing shaped by a carpenter's lathe.

Timber and more timber. Entire beams heaved aside.

Then a shard of cloudy glass lodged between cleaved stone.

Tattered curtain, ruined wardrobe, twisted iron bedstead wedged deep in the boulders.

Will remembers the foreman's sombre expression.

Another man's dusty cough in the silence.

The shadow of a bird winging high overhead.

They must have thought the world was ending.

All that freezing mud and water from the displaced river. Uprooted tree trunks and crashing stone sparking like lightning and the thundering speed of it, faster than any locomotive the C.P.R. could build, hurtling more than a mile across the sleeping valley in less than two minutes, consuming everything in its path.

Will had gouged himself on a corroded nail when he pried loose a split board. Dropped his shovel. Scraped handfuls of dirt aside—

careful, careful
Powder sifted through his fingers.
He remembers the stillness of the world in that moment of recognition.
Crushing sadness. Mute despair.
A stifling wind rose from the boulders and dried the sweat on the back of his neck. He knelt on what had once been the floor of a room, now nothing more than open space and rotting boards. He could not yet bring himself to tell the others about the tiny bones inside the cradle.
And then the shadow appeared, hovering over him.
At first he thought a cloud had passed over the sun. Then he thought the mountain itself had darkened his vision. When he raised his head his eyes travelled over dusty boots and faded trousers the color of earth until, finally, he met a gaze deep and green as the distant trees.

Owen Lawson opens his eyes to a rectangle of light on the wall.
Hours before, he'd listened to bedsprings creak as Ulla's feet hit cold floorboard. He heard water swish, buttons fastened, hair brushed and pinned, and he fell into the dream of her cool white body curving to his own. When he woke again the room was empty, door closed.
The room is papered in dull mauve like the shadows under Owen's eyes. The square footage allows no more necessaries than the iron bedstead, chest of drawers, pitcher and basin and mirror, wooden chair with his second pair of trousers and shirt and suspenders. Stockings and boots aligned by the bed. After he shaves he washes his hair and face and hands. Scrubs more grit from beneath his fingernails.
He sits down and pulls on his boots. The leather has deepened in hue over time to a rich patina, the clammy sides of a coal car or a shovel handle that's never seen the light of day but has lain underground all its useful life. When he settles his feet into them they're the cold moulded clay of a cave through which water runs.
It must discourage her—the black creases in his clothes, his graphite outline on the sheets. But the sheets are white as air when he returns each morning to find her sleeping between them. Her skin is white as that, too, though her eyes are the depths of a cobalt lake. The mountain's shadow never penetrates her as it does him. In the mine, her body would emit light like

a prism of sunlit glass or all the lanterns in the world pooled together.

You live too much in the mountain, Owen.

She's opened the tall window on the south wall. In the court-yard below, he watches her balance a basket of wet linen between hand and hip. Ulla's shadow moves fleetly as she hangs sopping sheets she's laundered in steam and soap and bluing. From this perspective only the top of her head is visible, hair twisted up in back. Owen knows he would always be able to recognise her from a height by the patterns in her hair, individual as river currents. Wind curls the sheets, a lover's hands yearning for contact, not wanting to release her, seeking magnetic North.

Owen has always envied the simple physical closeness of the sheets Ulla washes each morning, the perfect attention she pays them. She spends so much more time in their company than he himself does: working all night, dreaming darkness half the day. He thinks of her burnt hands submerged in scalding tubs of lye soap, water turning black then grey then clear as she scrubs sheets for miners who lie alone in their single beds at the hotel, still staring at the ceiling after the sun has climbed high above the mountain.

He watches these men enter and exit the mine entrance with dust-speckled horses—Welshmen whose ancestors toiled in the pits; Scottish-brogued Cape Bretoners in search of better-paying work in the West; swarthy Galicians whom some complain stink of garlic and petty conspiracy; French-Canadians with their foreign tongue and dark complexions. Men he knows as well as any miner knows another man, acquaintances he's passed silently in black rooms. This morning all are waking from a dream of someone like his Ulla. Their bodies weight the bedstead like coal on the scale, leaving imprints of their lives on the sheets his wife has washed for them. Will wash again tomorrow.

Jealousy stabs him.

One more year. A year at most.

Even from the upper-storey window there's no mistaking the raw hands she tries to hide from the world. Especially in winter, when the sheets are frozen boards Owen could crack over his knee, splinters flying like shards of ice straight into his heart. Watching her, an overpowering desire wells up in him to take his wife's scarlet fingers into his mouth. Kiss them whole. His bleeding dove.

He remembers the first time she chided him. His irritation rose swiftly only to descend into helpless bewilderment when he sensed uncertainty behind the judgement in her eyes. How can he tell her what it's like inside the earth, how when he leaves her alone in their moonlit bed he enters a realm of darkness and flowing water, directionless wind and ancient ferns whose outlines he sees in the coal when he holds the lantern close?

In your world, Ulla, you never have to worry about the sky falling. There is no weight to the heavens. The blue goes on forever. In the mine...when you look up, all you see is the roof, moonless and starless, a lamp for your sun. There are limits to this world. The sky has weight. When you press it, it presses back.

In my world? Ulla's jaw quivered. *Owen, have you forgotten this is* your *world as well?*

His eyes trace the smooth muscles of his wife's back as she dances with ghosts in the sheets, her hands crimson flames. She glances up at the boarding house.

Before Owen realizes it he's stepped back from the window. Fear courses through his network of veins and all the dark places they lead and he realizes he's trembling. *Maybe she is right. Maybe you've forgotten to which world you belong.*

Turtle Mountain pierces the sky like bone through linen. The sun moves behind a streak of cloud and the temperature drops, no longer spring but a continuation of winter.

It's this mountain.

It absorbs the light, throws the slopes in shadow until the river that runs beneath it gleams like coal or the mine itself, tunnelling through stone, so dark he could follow it for miles and never find his way to the surface.

Owen presses his hand to the windowpane. But Ulla is no longer there. The yard is empty except for the sheets, snapping on the line, angry at their loss.

Papa waved from the garden gate on the last morning of his life.

Cheerio, Willie-o!

Only Alec Evans's lower leg had been recovered, identified by a particular shade of pokeberry-dyed yarn his wife used to knit the heavy woollen stockings Alec wore to the mine.

In the weeks that followed the Hillcrest explosion, nine-year-old Will lived on the boundaries of a world glimpsed from behind partially closed doors. Reflections obscured by mirrors draped in mourning velvet. He devoured, secretly and with morbid fascination, the particulars of the disaster in the Calgary newspapers his aunt and uncle brought with them when they arrived for the funerals.

The leg Edie Evans sewed into a table-linen shroud and buried with ceremony in the mass grave seemed removed not only bodily but conceptually from Will's image of the man who waved to him every morning and swung him high in coal-blackened arms every evening. The hours between were a dark mystery. Missing pieces.

Will scrutinized grainy newsprint, memorised casualty lists.

Evans, A.

That is Papa. As if forming the syllables with his own lips would somehow articulate the unfathomable.

The entire country had learned of Hillcrest and was enthralled in a sensationalistic sort of way, just as they'd been when Turtle Mountain fell a decade earlier. The Prime Minister rushed trainloads of doctors and nurses, relief workers, reporters...all too late.

Send us undertakers instead, one hundred and thirty widows wired back. *Send us coffins.*

The North West Mounted Police pieced together charred bodies in the wash-house. Photographers draped hoods over tripods while grim rescue workers posed with the new pulmotor resuscitation equipment. The town was cloaked in black crêpe and white fog that crept across the valley floor. Snow flecked the funeral cortege, endless lines of carriages, carts and democrats. Horses in black plumes stamped in the cold beside caskets stacked like fruit crates on frozen Main Street, by Miner's Hall, by Cruickshank's store. A team bolted en route to the cemetery and tumbled a wagonload of pine boxes onto the roadside. Numb townspeople gathered up the contents, closed the lids.

One hundred and eighty-nine dead. One hundred and fifty interred over the course of the day. Catholic and Anglican services beginning at ten a.m. on the wintry morning of June 21st did not conclude until nightfall. The women and children who'd lost husbands, fathers, sons, brothers, waited by the mouths of three mass graves lined with shovels.

Will shivered between his brother Laurier and his mother's sister. His aunt's hand encased his own like a glove of ice. Edie Evans held the neatly wrapped parcel of her husband's leg, patting it now and then as if to reassure it.

Soon, Alec. Soon.

Owen Lawson's first thought when the timbers began to groan, then to shudder and crack, was: *How proud you've been.*
The lantern struck stone and went out in a crash of glass.
How proud.
How wrong.

On the morning the road crew uncovered the Clarks' cottage the Hillcrest engineer appeared from nowhere. Formed from wind, dust. The stones themselves.

Will Evans knelt on shattered floorboards while sweat slicked his shirt to his back like greased butcher paper. The cottage ceiling was compressed to within a foot of the floor.

What difference between his own bones, his father's, his brother's? This man, this woman, this child...eight in one family. *We are cast from the same mould,* Father Beaton reminded mourners at the miners' funeral. Calcium and clay. A handful of minerals. *We are not so far removed from them.*

"Who have you found, son?" There was reverence in Owen Lawson's tone. Restraint. But beneath it lay a resolved will of disconcerting intensity.

And weariness, Will realized. An almost insupportable weariness.

A prepossessing man in his forties, the engineer had the look of one who spent life below ground. His eyes were hollow as the depths of the mine entrance no one remembered. As if he slept with darkness and welcomed darkness and built pillars and stalls for it in his heart.

"William?"

Will trembled as if a train were approaching, vibrations in his bones indicating distance, origin. The past that connected him to Owen Lawson, however tenuously, unsettled the young man while inspiring in him a deep and powerless empathy. He pictured Owen Lawson reassembling limbs in the Hillcrest wash-house. Arm with arm. Leg with leg.

"Who lived here, son?"

Will drew a breath. "The Clarks. Everyone thinks it's the Clarks' cottage."

"You found no one else?" As if the Slide swept his life away last night, not twenty years past.

"No, sir. No one else."

"I thought, perhaps...." The engineer sighed, a quiet release that might have been a breeze rustling the saplings. "My wife worked with their daughter Lillian. Strange...that we should all meet again in this way. You are still wearing your father's check," he added, so softly Will barely registered the words.

He found himself thinking not about the Clarks, who'd died before he'd been born, but about the stockings his mother knitted for Papa each birthday: colour all but obliterated by blood congealed in the yarns. *There's a bit of the worsted showing through.* Will's mother pointed this out to her sister as if discussing a dropped stitch to be done over. *It must be his. Yes, I'm sure it is his.*

Edie Evans always believed her husband would die from the violet-sweet gases that collected in the mines. *Like falling asleep in a bed of flowers,* she told Will when Papa was late, as if this were a comfort. A desired end. The explosion—with all its carnage and accompanying chaos—had thrown her expectations into disorder.

The shadow above Will Evans had lifted. The sun, more distant now, had lowered behind the mountain peak.

The shifting light revealed the contour of bones laid side by side on the cottage floor. There was a symmetry to their shining lengths, to the curve of the infant's spinal column balanced in Will's hands.

On the morning of June 19, 1914, Owen Lawson, exhausted from the rescue efforts at Hillcrest Mine, his face unrecognizable from smoke, stood at the threshold of the Evans cottage and presented Alec Evan's wife with her husband's severed leg.

I'll bring him home, he'd volunteered. There was no one else. He felt like a butcher dropping by with a choice leg of mutton.

Evans's nine-year-old son peered behind his mother. The boy could not stop staring at his father's blackened shinbone, cartilage gleaming white.

That's his. Edie Evans examined the red stains soaking the borrowed pillowcase. *That's Alec's stocking. Washed them yesterday morning.*

Owen smelled wind and sunlight and blood in the matted worsted fibres. He saw his wife's hands alongside Edie Evans's in the washtub. He thought of the heavy weight of wool in water, and stocking toes still damp when Alec Evans drew them on in the darkness.

Without glancing up Will Evans knew the engineer had gone, just as he knew the bones he'd discovered would be returned to the darkness of earth. But all he wanted in the world at that moment was to gather them up, every last one. Carry them to the river as his mother carried his father's leg in her best linen table-cloth. Set the bones adrift alongside the cradle and the remains of its tiny passenger...the last letter his brother ever wrote.

Then he would step back on the riverbank and trace their progress down the channel through a chronology of water and time.

And all those lives, half-submerged in the gleaming current, would glide past the face of the mountain and the shadow of the mountain, and drift far from the valley, and fleeing rabbits, and the weight of stones.

Soon, he tells them. He sends them on their journey. *Soon you will be home.*

On Armistice Day, 1967, I turned ninety-two.

All through the morning and afternoon the valley was shrouded in an ice fog that drifted along the river folks call Crowsnest, but in 1903 was simply another bend in the Old Man's elbow. At the eleventh minute of the eleventh hour of the eleventh day, the people who live in this Pass suspended their breaths in remembrance of Flanders Fields and mustard gas...the boys they'd lost in coils of razor wire.

Services concluded, I laid my scarlet poppy on the frozen grave of Lieutenant William Evans of the RAF Bomber Command, shot down in the Second World War and buried alongside his brother Laurier. Fine grey rain began to fall as I returned to Turtle Mountain like a migrating bird.

Most of the mines have been shut down; only four remain in operation. The Pass is settling down to a quiet death. Snow covers the limestone boulders, though it has melted in parts where rain has seeped to the hollows. The grey-white peaks of the mountain are inseparable from the sky. So much has been broken and lost, washed away by torrents of icy mud and rock. Everywhere you walk in this Pass, even in the places where the green has come creeping back—moss between stones embedded in a garden path, grass growing between rails of the whitewashed fences, curtains of trees smelling of wind and water—everywhere you walk you feel stone crumbling beneath your feet, submerging and resurfacing with each step, the landscape itself as transitory as the turning of seasons.

Turtle Mountain takes care of her own. For all my manoeuv-ring she protected me, guarded over me in darkness, kept me from harm's way. It was in the sleeping town that lives ended and irreparable damage was done.

I stand now at the bridge by the Old Man River, arthritic fingers clamped to the frozen rail. My spine is as twisted as a discarded pick. Once I set timbers with nothing but a straight back and my own two hands, bracing myself easily in a shaft pitched at forty-five degrees. Now it is an effort to shuffle across level sidewalks, wheezing the last reserves of air from the black sediment in my lungs. I wonder if she would know me in this body: strong arms she used to admire, now frayed ropes in an old man's coat sleeves.

I find myself envying Will Evans's heroic death at thirty-seven, spiralling through the blue yonder in a blaze of glory. And I wonder whether those who die earlier in life are possessed of a greater sense of spiritual destiny awaiting them in the hereafter or on the pages of history, whether their lives have to be lived more intensely, their essences necessarily concentrated, so that every drop is distilled into a pure, crystalline experience.

There are things that happen to a man that are worse than death. There is life. Decades of life ahead, each year empty as the sky that opens in place of a mountain, closing again with a brutal and incalculable swiftness. Ulla lived to be twenty-seven. I, too, was twenty-seven when she departed this earth six decades ago. I am the only one who remembers her: the swirls of pinned up hair, the cobalt eyes that saw right through me. And when I have gone—

But hadn't I forfeited my own life long ago?

Sometimes I hear my name plainly, as if it were spoken aloud in the next room. Other times it's a nothing more than a sigh, like the wind rushing through drenched boughs on a gusty night.

Across the bridge, the mountain is a heap of shadows; setting sunlight glitters on mounds of boulders. My feet have grown numb in my ice-slicked miner's boots. I return to the empty room I expected never to see again to find that my solitary plate and glass have dried on the drain board, just as I had left them.

CONTRIBUTORS

Leah Bobet

Leah Bobet lives and works in Toronto. Her fiction has appeared in *Realms of Fantasy, On Spec: The Canadian Magazine of the Fantastic, Interzone,* and *Strange Horizons,* and has been reprinted in *The Year's Best Science Fiction and Fantasy for Teens, Science Fiction: the Best of the Year 2006, Best New Fantasy 2,* and *The Mammoth Book of Extreme Fantasy.*

Suzanne Church

Suzanne Church juggles her time between throwing her characters to the lions, teaching her sons how to define infinity, and working in direct sales. When cornered she becomes fiercely Canadian. Her short fiction has appeared in *Cicada* and *On Spec,* and in several anthologies including *Tesseracts 13.* On LiveJournal she scribbles as canadiansuzanne. Suzanne resides in Kitchener, Ontario.

Michael Colangelo

Michael R. Colangelo is a writer from Toronto. He has published numerous short stories in both online and print venues, including *Chizine,* the *Tesseracts 14* anthology, and the *Apparitions* anthology from Undertow Books . He is a former member of SF Canada, the present Membership Chair of the Horror Writer's Association, the former fiction editor for online horror/fantasy journal *The Harrow,* presently an editor for online webzine *Ideomancer* and a former columnist for horror web site *FearZone.* Last year, his short story *Bat Story* received an honourable mention in the 2010 Vaike and Erich Rannu Fund for Writers of Speculative Literature contest. And he is pretty handy with a knife.

Gemma Files

Gemma Files is the author of *A Book of Tongues*: Volume One of the Hexslinger Series, as well as two collections of short fiction (*Kissing Carrion* and *The Worm in Every Heart*), and two chapbooks of poetry. Her short story "The Jacaranda Smile" was nominated for a 2010 Shirley Jackson Award, as was her novella "each thing I show you is a piece of my death", which was co-written with her husband, Stephen J. Barringer.

Richard Gavin

Richard Gavin is one of Canada's most acclaimed authors of macabre and occult fiction. His tales have sold to *The Magazine of Fantasy & Science Fiction, Dark Discoveries,* and *Horrors Beyond,* and have been collected in the books *Charnel Wine, Omens,* and *The Darkly Splendid Realm.* Richard lives in Ontario, Canada, where he is at work on a supernatural novella and a fourth collection of weird tales.

Brent Hayward

Brent's short fiction has appeared in several publications. He is a graduate of the Clarion SF Workshop, at Michigan State, and is the author of the novels *Filaria,* published in 2008, and *The Fecund's Melancholy Daughter,* forthcoming. UK born, raised in Montreal, he is a recently returned expatriate. Currently, he lives in Toronto with his family.

Sandra Kasturi

Sandra Kasturi is a writer, editor, book reviewer and publisher. In 2005 she won *ARC* magazine's annual Poem of the Year award. Her work has appeared in numerous magazines and anthologies, and she managed to snag an introduction from Neil Gaiman for her first full-length poetry collection, *The Animal Bridegroom.* She is currently working on another poetry collection, *Come Late to the Love of Birds,* and two novels: a mythological noir and a steampunk epic involving the British East India Company, the Pinkerton Agency, Harry Houdini and zombies. She lives in Toronto with her husband, co-publisher/writer Brett Alexander Savory.

Michael Kelly

Michael was born in Charlottetown, Prince Edward Island. He is the author of two short story collections, *Scratching the Surface*, and *Undertow and Other Laments*, and co-author of the novel *Ouroboros*. His fiction has appeared in *Best New Horror 21*, the *Hint Fiction Anthology*, *PostScripts*, *Supernatural Tales*, *Tesseracts 13*, and others. He is a Shirley Jackson Award-nominated editor. He currently resides in Pickering, Ontario, with his wife, two kids, a cat, three guitars, and numerous books.

Nancy Kilpatrick

Award-winning author Nancy Kilpatrick has published 18 novels, around 200 short stories, 1 non-fiction book (*The goth Bible*) and has edited 10 anthologies. She writes mainly horror, dark fantasy, mysteries and erotica and is currently working on two new novels. Some of her recent short fiction appears in: *Blood Lite 2* (Pocket Books); *Hellbound Hearts*; *The Bleeding Edge*; *The Living Dead*; *Don Juan and Men*; *Vampires: Dracula and the Undead Legions* (Moonstone Books); *By Blood We Live*; *The Bitten Word*; *Campus Chills*; and *Darkness on the Edge*. Recently she co-edited with David Morrell the horror/dark fantasy anthology *Tesseracts Thirteen*. She is the editor of *Evolve: Vampire Stories of the New Undead*. Her graphic novel *Nancy Kilpatrick's Vampire Theatre* was released in August 2010, and a collector's edition of the seven-book erotic horror series *The Darker Passions* began December 2010. Currently she is editing a new anthology.

Claude Lalumière

Claude Lalumière is the author of the collection *Objects of Worship* and the novella *The Door to Lost Pages*. He has edited eight anthologies, the latest of which was *Tesseracts Twelve: New Novellas of Canadian Fantastic Fiction*. With Rupert Bottenberg, he's the co-creator of lostmyths.net.

Christopher K. Miller

Born in Switzerland on the cusp of the first hydrogen bomb's test detonation. His legitimate professions, in no particular order, include stock boy, paper boy, pot washer, geriatric orderly, union rep, subcontract painter, farmer, technical writer, cookie factory worker, software developer, line cook, dish washer and restaurateur. His father is a semi-renowned theologian. His mother composes logic puzzles for Penny Press. He has two sons, and one granddaughter who wants to be a writer too.

Chris's fiction has appeared in *COSMOS, The Barcelona Review, Hopewell Publishing's Best New Writing 2010* anthology, *Libbon, Battered Suitcase, Nossa Morte, Redstone Science Fiction* and others.

David Nickle

David Nickle's stories have appeared in *Northern Frights, Tesseracts, Queer Fear* and *The Year's Best Fantasy and Horror. Monstrous Affections* is his collection of stories. His novel *Eutopia* will be released in the Spring of 2011.

Jason S. Ridler

Jason S. Ridler's fiction has appeared in such magazines as *Not One of Us, Nossa Morte, Big Pulp, Crossed Genres, Flashquake, New Myths, Necrotic Tissue, Andromeda Spaceways Inflight Magazine,* as well as several anthologies. His popular non-fiction has appeared in *Clarkesworld, Dark Scribe,* and the *Internet Review of Science Fiction.* A former punk rock musician and cemetery groundskeeper, Mr. Ridler holds a Ph.D. in War Studies from the Royal Military College of Canada.

Barbara Roden

Barbara Roden is a World Fantasy Award-winning editor and publisher, whose short stories have appeared in numerous publications, including *Year's Best Fantasy and Horror: Nineteenth Annual Collection, Horror: Best of the Year 2005, Bound for Evil, Strange Tales 2, Gaslight Grimoire* and *Gaslight Grotesque, Poe* (Solaris), *Best New Horror 21,* and *Best Dark Fantasy and Horror 2009* Her first collection, *Northwest Passages,* was published in October 2009.

Ian Rogers

Ian Rogers is a writer, artist, and photographer. His short fiction has been published or is forthcoming in *Cemetery Dance, Supernatural Tales, All Hallows,* and *On Spec.* He is also the author of the Felix Renn series of supernatural-noir stories, including "Temporary Monsters" and "The Ash Angels". Ian lives with his wife in Peterborough, Ontario.

Brett Alexander Savory

Brett Alexander Savory is the Bram Stoker Award-winning co-publisher of ChiZine Publications, has had nearly 50 short stories published, and has written two novels. His horror-comedy novel, *The Distance Travelled*, was released in 2006, followed by *In and Down* in 2007. His first short story collection, *No Further Messages*, was released in November 2007. He co-edited *Tesseracts Fourteen: Strange Canadian Stories* with John Robert Colombo and is now at work on his third novel, *Lake of Spaces, Wood of Nothing*. He lives in Toronto with his wife, writer/editor Sandra Kasturi.

Simon Strantzas

Simon Strantzas is the author of the critically-acclaimed *Cold to the Touch*, a collection of thirteen tales of the strange and supernatural. His first collection, *Beneath the Surface*, was recently reprinted, and has been called "one of the most important debut short story collections in the genre". Strantzas's tales have appeared in *The Mammoth Book of Best New Horror*, *Cemetery Dance*, *PostScripts*, and have been nominated for the British Fantasy Award. He currently lives in Toronto, Ontario, with his wife and a dark storm cloud that follows him wherever he goes.

Tia V. Travis

Tia V. Travis's novella, "Down Here in the Garden," was a finalist for the World Fantasy Award and the International Horror Guild Award. Her stories have been reprinted in *The Year's Best Fantasy and Horror* and have appeared in such publications as *Poe's Children: The New Horror*, *Exotic Gothic 2*, *Subterranean Online*, and *Wild Things Live There: The Best of Northern Frights*. Travis was born in rural Manitoba where her father was a farmer and a miner with the Hudson's Bay Company. She spent most of her life in and around Calgary, Alberta, before relocating to Northern California. She now lives in the San Francisco Bay Area with her husband, author Norman Partridge, and their baby daughter, Neve Rose.

Robert J. Wiersema

Writer and bookseller Robert J. Wiersema is the author of the national bestseller *Before I Wake*, and the Aurora-nominated novella "The World More Full of Weeping." His most recent novel is *Bedtime Story*. He lives in Victoria with his family.

Our titles are available at major book stores
and local independent resellers who support
Science Fiction and Fantasy readers like you.

EDGE Science Fiction
and Fantasy Publishing

Tesseract Books

www.edgewebsite.com

Our titles are available at major book stores and local independent resellers who support Science Fiction and Fantasy readers like you.

Alphanauts by J. Brian Clarke (tp) - ISBN: 978-1-894063-14-2
Apparition Trail, The by Lisa Smedman (tp) - ISBN: 978-1-894063-22-7
As Fate Decrees by Denysé Bridger (tp) - ISBN: 978-1-894063-41-8
Avim's Oath (Part Six of the Okal Rel Saga) by Lynda Williams (pb) - ISBN: 978-1-894063-35-7

Black Chalice, The by Marie Jakober (hb) - ISBN: 978-1-894063-00-7
Blue Apes by Phyllis Gotlieb (pb) - ISBN: 978-1-895836-13-4
Blue Apes by Phyllis Gotlieb (hb) - ISBN: 978-1-895836-14-1

Captives by Barbara Galler-Smith and Josh Langston (pb) - ISBN: 978-1-894063-53-1
Children of Atwar, The by Heather Spears (pb) - ISBN: 978-0-88878-335-6
Chilling Tales: Evil Did I Dwell - Lewd I Did Live dited by Michael Kelly (pb) - ISBN: 978-1-894063-52-4
Cinco de Mayo by Michael J. Martineck (pb) - ISBN: 978-1-894063-39-5
Cinkarion - The Heart of Fire (Part Two of The Chronicles of the Karionin) by J. A. Cullum - (tp) - ISBN: 978-1-894063-21-0
Clan of the Dung-Sniffers by Lee Danielle Hubbard (pb) - ISBN: 978-1-894063-05-0
Claus Effect, The by David Nickle & Karl Schroeder (pb) - ISBN: 978-1-895836-34-9
Claus Effect, The by David Nickle & Karl Schroeder (hb) - ISBN: 978-1-895836-35-6
Courtesan Prince, The (Part One of the Okal Rel Saga) by Lynda Williams (tp) - ISBN: 978-1-894063-28-9

Dark Earth Dreams by Candas Dorsey & Roger Deegan (comes with a CD) - ISBN: 978-1-895836-05-9
Darkness of the God (Children of the Panther Part Two) by Amber Hayward (tp) - ISBN: 978-1-894063-44-9
Demon Left Behind, The by Marie Jakober (pb) - ISBN: 978-1-894063-49-4
Distant Signals by Andrew Weiner (tp) - ISBN: 978-0-88878-284-7
Dreams of an Unseen Planet by Teresa Plowright (tp) - ISBN: 978-0-88878-282-3
Dreams of the Sea (Part 1 of Tyranaël) by Élisabeth Vonarburg (tp) - ISBN: 978-1-895836-96-7
Dreams of the Sea (Part 1 of Tyranaël) by Élisabeth Vonarburg (hb) - ISBN: 978-1-895836-98-1
Druids by Barbara Galler-Smith and Josh Langston (tp) - ISBN: 978-1-894063-29-6

Eclipse by K. A. Bedford (tp) - ISBN: 978-1-894063-30-2
Even The Stones by Marie Jakober (tp) - ISBN: 978-1-894063-18-0
Evolve: Vampire Stories of the New Undead edited by Nancy Kilpatrick (tp) - ISBN: 978-1-894063-33-3

Far Arena (Part Five of the Okal Rel Saga) by Lynda Williams (tp) - ISBN: 978-1-894063-45-6
Fires of the Kindred by Robin Skelton (tp) - ISBN: 978-0-88878-271-7
Forbidden Cargo by Rebecca Rowe (tp) - ISBN: 978-1-894063-16-6

Game of Perfection, A (Part 2 of Tyranaël) by Élisabeth Vonarburg (tp)
- ISBN: 978-1-894063-32-6
Gaslight Grimoire: Fantastic Tales of Sherlock Holmes
edited by Jeff Campbell & Charles Prepolec (pb)
- ISBN: 978-1-8964063-17-3
Gaslight Grotesque: Nightmare Tales of Sherlock Holmes
edited by Jeff Campbell & Charles Prepolec (pb)
- ISBN: 978-1-8964063-31-9
Green Music by Ursula Pflug (tp) - ISBN: 978-1-895836-75-2
Green Music by Ursula Pflug (hb) - ISBN: 978-1-895836-77-6

Healer, The (Children of the Panther Part One) by Amber Hayward (tp)
- ISBN: 978-1-895836-89-9
Healer, The (Children of the Panther Part One) by Amber Hayward (hb)
- ISBN: 978-1-895836-91-2
Hell Can Wait by Theodore Judson (tp) - ISBN: 978-1-978-1-894063-23-4
Hounds of Ash and other tales of Fool Wolf, The by Greg Keyes (pb)
- ISBN: 978-1-894063-09-8
Hydrogen Steel by K. A. Bedford (tp) - ISBN: 978-1-894063-20-3

i-ROBOT Poetry by Jason Christie (tp) - ISBN: 978-1-894063-24-1
Immortal Quest by Alexandra MacKenzie (pb) - ISBN: 978-1-894063-46-3

Jackal Bird by Michael Barley (pb) - ISBN: 978-1-895836-07-3
Jackal Bird by Michael Barley (hb) - ISBN: 978-1-895836-11-0
JEMMA7729 by Phoebe Wray (tp) - ISBN: 978-1-894063-40-1

Keaen by Till Noever (tp) - ISBN: 978-1-894063-08-1
Keeper's Child by Leslie Davis (tp) - ISBN: 978-1-894063-01-2

Land/Space edited by Candas Jane Dorsey and Judy McCrosky (tp)
- ISBN: 978-1-895836-90-5
Land/Space edited by Candas Jane Dorsey and Judy McCrosky (hb)
- ISBN: 978-1-895836-92-9
Lyskarion: The Song of the Wind (Part One of The Chronicles of the Karionin)
by J.A. Cullum (tp) - ISBN: 978-1-894063-02-9

Machine Sex and other stories by Candas Jane Dorsey (tp)
- ISBN: 978-0-88878-278-6
Maërlande Chronicles, The by Élisabeth Vonarburg (pb)
- ISBN: 978-0-88878-294-6
Moonfall by Heather Spears (pb) - ISBN: 978-0-88878-306-6

Of Wind and Sand by Sylvie Bérard (translated by Sheryl Curtis) (pb)
- ISBN: 978-1-894063-19-7
On Spec: The First Five Years edited by On Spec (pb)
- ISBN: 978-1-895836-08-0
On Spec: The First Five Years edited by On Spec (hb)
- ISBN: 978-1-895836-12-7
Orbital Burn by K. A. Bedford (tp) - ISBN: 978-1-894063-10-4
Orbital Burn by K. A. Bedford (hb) - ISBN: 978-1-894063-12-8

Pallahaxi Tide by Michael Coney (pb) - ISBN: 978-0-88878-293-9
Passion Play by Sean Stewart (pb) - ISBN: 978-0-88878-314-1

Petrified World (Determine Your Destiny #1) by Piotr Brynczka (pb)
  - ISBN: 978-1-894063-11-1
Plague Saint by Rita Donovan, The (tp) - ISBN: 978-1-895836-28-8
Plague Saint by Rita Donovan, The (hb) - ISBN: 978-1-895836-29-5
Pock's World by Dave Duncan (tp) - ISBN: 978-1-894063-47-0
Pretenders (Part Three of the Okal Rel Saga) by Lynda Williams (pb)
  - ISBN: 978-1-894063-13-5

Reluctant Voyagers by Élisabeth Vonarburg (pb) - ISBN: 978-1-895836-09-7
Reluctant Voyagers by Élisabeth Vonarburg (hb) - ISBN: 978-1-895836-15-8
Resisting Adonis by Timothy J. Anderson (tp) - ISBN: 978-1-895836-84-4
Resisting Adonis by Timothy J. Anderson (hb) - ISBN: 978-1-895836-83-7
Righteous Anger (Part Two of the Okal Rel Saga) by Lynda Williams (tp)
  - ISBN: 897-1-894063-38-8

Silent City, The by Élisabeth Vonarburg (tp) - ISBN: 978-1-894063-07-4
Slow Engines of Time, The by Élisabeth Vonarburg (tp)
  - ISBN: 978-1-895836-30-1
Slow Engines of Time, The by Élisabeth Vonarburg (hb)
  - ISBN: 978-1-895836-31-8
Stealing Magic by Tanya Huff (tp) - ISBN: 978-1-894063-34-0
Strange Attractors by Tom Henighan (pb) - ISBN: 978-0-88878-312-7

Taming, The by Heather Spears (pb) - ISBN: 978-1-895836-23-3
Taming, The by Heather Spears (hb) - ISBN: 978-1-895836-24-0
Ten Monkeys, Ten Minutes by Peter Watts (tp) - ISBN: 978-1-895836-74-5
Ten Monkeys, Ten Minutes by Peter Watts (hb) - ISBN: 978-1-895836-76-9
Tesseracts 1 edited by Judith Merril (pb) - ISBN: 978-0-88878-279-3
Tesseracts 2 edited by Phyllis Gotlieb & Douglas Barbour (pb)
  - ISBN: 978-0-88878-270-0
Tesseracts 3 edited by Candas Jane Dorsey & Gerry Truscott (pb)
  - ISBN: 978-0-88878-290-8
Tesseracts 4 edited by Lorna Toolis & Michael Skeet (pb)
  - ISBN: 978-0-88878-322-6
Tesseracts 5 edited by Robert Runté & Yves Maynard (pb)
  - ISBN: 978-1-895836-25-7
Tesseracts 5 edited by Robert Runté & Yves Maynard (hb)
  - ISBN: 978-1-895836-26-4
Tesseracts 6 edited by Robert J. Sawyer & Carolyn Clink (pb)
  - ISBN: 978-1-895836-32-5
Tesseracts 6 edited by Robert J. Sawyer & Carolyn Clink (hb)
  - ISBN: 978-1-895836-33-2
Tesseracts 7 edited by Paula Johanson & Jean-Louis Trudel (tp)
  - ISBN: 978-1-895836-58-5
Tesseracts 7 edited by Paula Johanson & Jean-Louis Trudel (hb)
  - ISBN: 978-1-895836-59-2
Tesseracts 8 edited by John Clute & Candas Jane Dorsey (tp)
  - ISBN: 978-1-895836-61-5
Tesseracts 8 edited by John Clute & Candas Jane Dorsey (hb)
  - ISBN: 978-1-895836-62-2
Tesseracts Nine edited by Nalo Hopkinson and Geoff Ryman (tp)
  - ISBN: 978-1-894063-26-5
Tesseracts Ten: A Celebration of New Canadian Specuative Fiction
  edited by Robert Charles Wilson and Edo van Belkom (tp)
  - ISBN: 978-1-894063-36-4

Tesseracts Eleven: Amazing Canadian Speulative Fiction
    edited by Cory Doctorow and Holly Phillips (tp)
    - ISBN: 978-1-894063-03-6
Tesseracts Twelve: New Novellas of Canadian Fantastic Fiction
    edited by Claude Lalumière (pb)
    - ISBN: 978-1-894063-15-9
Tesseracts Thirteen: Chilling Tales from the Great White North
    edited by Nancy Kilpatrick and David Morrell (tp)
    - ISBN: 978-1-894063-25-8
Tesseracts 14: Strange Canadian Stories
    edited by John Robert Colombo and Brett Alexander Savory (tp)
    - ISBN: 978-1-894063-37-1
Tesseracts Q edited by Élisabeth Vonarburg & Jane Brierley (pb)
    - ISBN: 978-1-895836-21-9
Tesseracts Q edited by Élisabeth Vonarburg & Jane Brierley (hb)
    - ISBN: 978-1-895836-22-6
Those Who Fight Monsters: Tales of Occult Detectives
    edited by Justin Gustainis (pb) - ISBN: 978-1-894063-48-7
Throne Price by Lynda Williams and Alison Sinclair (tp)
    - ISBN: 978-1-894063-06-7
Time Machines Repaired Whie-U-Wait by K. A. Bedford (tp)
    - ISBN: 978-1-894063-42-5